A Poisonous Echo

Joyce is angry that her boss won't leave his wife, so his wife will have to be removed... one way or another!

A poisoning is planned and Joyce sets out to leave a lasting impression... then Joyce goes missing... A malevolent ghost and psychic detectives form the core of this enjoyable stand-alone sequel to Mai Griffin's *Ghostly Echoes*.

~~A Poisonous Shade of Grey~~

Originally published as *A Poisonous Shade of Grey*, the second of the ORIGINAL *Shades of Grey* series – long before any of a number of other *Shades of Grey* were published by other people, this book is a Ghost Story – with little or no sadomasochism in its content! Well, to be precise, it hasn't any! We, the publishers and the Author, give up. Our books came first – our titles were out first – our books are beautifully written and crafted – and we are fed-up with the assumption that this series is in some way a spinoff from any other when, in fact – we repeat – it was written and published FIRST!

In whatever order you read her books, Mai Griffin's series of supernatural thrillers, *Ghostly Echoes*, will grip you.

Published in Great Britain in 2017 by
U P Publications
St George's House,
George Street,
Huntingdon,
Cambridgeshire,
PE29 3GH. UK

A CIP Catalogue record of this book is available from the British Library

Originally released as A Poisonous Shade of Grey under

ISBN 978-1908135-18-6

This is the Third Edition (the First as A Poisonous Echo)

ISBN 978-1-9081357-7-3

9 7 4 8 5 6

Published by U P Publications

www.uppbooks.com
www.maiwriting.com

A Poisonous Echo

Mai Griffin

U P Publications
2008, 2017

In Life and Death there is no Black and White,
No core construct that always must be right,
No path or light that clearly shows the way
But filters through a Deadly Shade of Grey.

When some can hear and others single sight
How can they find a soul to lead them to the light?
Ghostly Echoes make confusion and tend to disarray,
So pander to the madness of what the seers say

In Death's dark realm, where none of us may stray,
The light glints through a Poisonous Shade of Grey.
A Glimmer glimpsed, beyond a heart's endeavour,
Where lost souls wander in their dark forever.

A soul that's lost in Death's last cunning sway
Can still fright the living from the depths of their decay.
A Poisonous Echo sent by the unforgiving,
Reaches out, with hate, to scar and maim the living.

Anon

With grateful thanks to
my daughter for being my biggest fan

All characters are fictitious
... although the creation of Sarah and Stephen Grey
was inspired by my late parents to whom
the series is dedicated.
Mai Griffin 2008

1 – Monday 20th May

He had wiped her out with the 'fast erase'. He couldn't believe he had been so stupid...

Swearing furiously under his breath, he pressed a few more switches: nothing! Perhaps there had been nothing to wipe. No way! Although she might not have rung, there were other people in his world! There were usually a few callers over weekends. His anger with himself, the wretched answering machine and most of all with Joyce – who had no right to treat him like this – boiled over. He grabbed the 'phone violently from its cradle and dialled, hoping she was still at home.

She had been in a strange mood when they left the office together on Saturday. She had cornered him... forcing him to admit that there was no way he'd ever leave his wife or risk losing the children. He could have gone further. He could have admitted that he never had considered such drastic action. Showing compassion, however, he spared her the truth. He would definitely let things cool between them from now on, but dared not risk allowing the liaison to end with an all-out fight; she had the power to wreck his life! He would persuade her that what they had was worth hanging on to, and then gradually ease away from her clutches. They might eventually be able to remain good friends.

He felt aggrieved, it wasn't as if he'd set out to cheat on his marriage but, once started, the affair drifted on casually for years, until he'd come to accept Joyce as a permanent, undemanding feature. Her flat being only a few miles from the office often enabled them to enjoy long lunch hours – she was a good cook – and they took in a show sometimes when he 'worked late'! He had kidded himself that he was being good to Joyce rather than perfidious to the family that he would certainly lose if the silly bitch carried on in this way! All that inane rubbish about 'setting him free'; what in Heaven's name had she been babbling about as she dashed off? He had tried to catch her, but she took an unusually convenient taxi, which accelerated away and melted into the throng of lunch-hour traffic.

Going immediately to her apartment, he had waited ages before giving up and going home. In the evening, and again on Sunday morning, he had tried ringing her from the village pub, without success. Later the problem seemed less pressing, it was difficult to keep finding excuses to leave the house to try again without arousing comment. He had been convinced he would be able to sort things out this morning – now the dumb bitch hadn't come to work!

He was unaccustomed to dealing personally with office gadgets and in a careless second, because his mind had been on her and her parting threats, he had erased God only knew how many important calls. Still rattled, he misdialled... then, drawing a deep breath, he realised that ringing her was the worst thing he could do. It would increase her advantage.

She must have been serious about absenting herself for a few days, giving him a taste of life without her, stupidly imagining that it would be enough to convince him and he would give in! If she really thought he'd choose her in preference to his wife and family, she was crazy. He felt ill as he wondered just how crazy! Joyce had threatened to confront his wife, with or without him – she didn't care – to tell her he wanted a divorce! Surely, Joyce had said it only to goad him. Would she really carry out her threat?

He knew very well that if his wife heard what he'd done he would be out on his ear! If only he hadn't been so weak... If only!

It had started more by accident than any real desire to seduce Joyce or stray from the fold. After a staff dance, deciding he was too drunk to drive to his hotel, Joyce had given him a lift – back to her own bed! The first thing he'd been aware of the following morning was the moist warmth of naked flesh pressed against his, and the weight of an arm over his stomach. He was comfortable and naturally assumed he was at home, although he did wonder vaguely how he came to be there. Then, unfamiliar traffic sounds had penetrated his dimly throbbing senses.

Joyce had stirred and murmured as he turned in alarm, making his senses swim and he had felt so rotten, having lifted his head, that it was easier to accept the situation rather than fight it. He had dozed off and came round again to find her standing above him, her shining red-gold hair tumbling over her bare shoulders: deliciously alluring, charmingly shy, holding a breakfast tray.

"Don't be alarmed," she said, "it's only coffee and toast – perhaps you'll be able to face something more substantial later." Then she'd whispered, as their eyes met, "In fact my darling, you can have anything you like – after last night."

He groaned aloud at the memory of the moment when, groaning inwardly, he had realised that despite having no recollection of the previous night, things had gone far enough for him to be completely compromised. Had he left immediately, the situation might have been retrieved – after all, it had been his wife who insisted he should stay and enjoy the annual 'do'. She had been heavily pregnant and unenthusiastic about going with him, insisting that it would do him good to unwind at a party instead of spending a dull evening, at home, with her and the television... there were friends close by, if she went into labour, she had reminded him.

She had teased his horrified reaction – they had three more boring weeks to wait before he really needed to worry about her! She had even insisted he should stay in town rather than drive home afterwards, so that she could enjoy an early night... if she woke in the early hours, she wouldn't have to worry about his possible non-appearance.

He stared at the telephone, remembering how sweet his wife had been when he eventually spoke to her. Knowing how much he had enjoyed the New Year celebrations the previous year, when she had been the designated driver, she'd been amazed that he was up before midday! If only she'd been present to look after him again! He had tried to tell her what had happened several times during the following week; it wasn't his fault; his lapse into promiscuity hadn't been intentional – but how could he risk upsetting her in her condition? The words had choked him, unsayable.

At the office, his secretary had adopted a conspiratorial self-satisfied air that he was sure had not gone unobserved by the gossipmongers! In private, she had seemed to regard it as the beginning of a grand passion, saying she had always known, from the way he looked at her, that they were 'destined to mean so much to each other'! All those years ago he had thought naively that, if he kept coolly aloof, Joyce would get the message, but she had thought he was merely being discreet. Two weeks later, to his great relief, she seemed more normal and he felt safe reverting to his earlier, easy manner when, as a raw eighteen-year-old, she was first assigned to him. His previous secretary, starchy, in late middle age, had made him feel like a wayward boy in need of a keeper! The freshness of pretty little Joyce and her wide-eyed need for his approval had been flattering. Privately, he admitted to being attracted to her sexually, but he would never have acted on it if she hadn't forced the issue.

One evening, when his barely remembered one night stand was a month old, his last meeting of the day had badly over-run. Wearily pushing his papers into his briefcase, at the end of the session, he had checked his watch, the weather and the timetable and realised that he had three hours to wait for the next train. His wife always worried when he used the car in icy road conditions; so that morning, with great reluctance, not wanting to add to her post-natal depression, whatever that was, he'd agreed not to drive in, so with no car available he had no choice but to wait. One of the typists was sitting on the outer office desk... he could see her long slim legs swinging as she waited for someone out of his line of vision to finish a telephone call. Walking past, on his way out, he realised that it was Joyce trilling away to whomsoever was on the line, "Nothing elaborate – just a re-heat in the microwave" and then, covering the mouthpiece, she had smiled at him. "As my place is so near I'm making eats for a few weary souls. Would you like to join in? You could probably use a drink." He had hesitated, eyeing the other girl who, taking advantage of the interruption, eased herself off the desk.

"See you," she said, waving to Joyce as she departed.

He had naively assumed that she was one of the other guests and had accepted the invitation; anything was better than a long wait at the railway station.

Later, sitting in her otherwise empty apartment, he asked with surprise where everyone else was. The invitation he had obviously been meant to hear had certainly not been for that night ... except for him alone! They must have been seen leaving together an hour earlier so he was already guilty in the eyes of the world and after all, he was only human. Now look where his feeble-mindedness had landed him!

Rather than a torrid romance, it had been a spasmodic affair that drifted on for three years before Joyce began to press for more of his time, then marriage. Her first hints had come almost jokingly and he'd ignored them – fool that he was! He had come to regard her as a modern, independent woman using him no less than he was using her. Even had he been free to do so, he would never marry anyone so brittle ... but there was no way anyone would understand how their association had survived without his wanting it!

His wife certainly would never appreciate how, once established, Joyce's hold had been difficult to break. He really had tried to shake the girl off at first but had, understandably, relaxed when he seemed to be getting away with the deception; the belief that he was keeping two women happy with such little difficulty boosted his ego!

Now, he faced the fact that he had been a fool, expecting it to last forever. Yet, even so, he still felt more persecuted than culpable. He reflected that his wife was actually more at fault than himself for making him go to that wretched party without her, and felt a momentary surge of resentment towards her, too. Then he shrugged and tried to pull himself together. He must think clearly if he were to come out of this unscathed.

If Joyce really did intend to keep away for a few days she would have had to inform somebody so, at last, common sense took over; he contacted the personnel department. The assistant was amazed he didn't know; Miss Hamilton had booked leave for a week, to attend a wedding in Oxford. She asked, "Has your temp not arrived then sir?" ...and at that moment, there was a timid knock on his open door.

2 – Farlow Hollow

Farlow Hollow station was almost deserted when the train pulled in, making the half-dozen people who descended from it seem like a crowd, as they surged through the barrier to the road outside. One or two strolled to parked cars, jingling keys; a young couple with backpacks started walking briskly towards the village. A shabby, stooped figure in a raincoat – waterproof hat pulled down, almost hiding her steel rimmed glasses – went unhesitatingly through a field gate opposite. It swung back easily with only a slight creak and the woman hurried away keeping close to the hedge.

Although taking advantage of its shelter she didn't really care if anyone noticed her. She had gone to the trouble of 'borrowing' her outer coverings from the apartment Janitor's broom closet; his wife was away and wouldn't miss them for a few days. The overshoes were uncomfortably large but she didn't have far to walk. It was worth suffering a bit, but she wished she had left off the black woollen stockings. They made her skin itch even through her nylon tights and the elastic bands holding them above her knees were painfully tight.

At the opposite corner of the second field, she paused to get her bearing. She had followed him by car one night to find out where he lived and had seen him turn into his home lane. She had then explored the quiet village roads, planning what she was now actually doing, so knew exactly where to go. She felt exhilarated. The road to Farlow was on her left and Old Farm Lane, signposted, wound away to her right, on the other side of the bushes that skirted a dry ditch. Her timing was perfect. She even glimpsed him driving off to work.

Careful to avoid being seen, she waited for a cyclist to whirr past before picking her way quietly along the crumbling edge of the ditch to find the house. The hedge wasn't too dense for her to see that the lane was empty and she hurried as her excitement mounted. Everything was going perfectly to plan. Soon she sighted a wide driveway; the gates stood open. A low wall, on which she could read the house name, edged a grove of tall trees on the right. Under her breath she cursed quietly as she saw a car at the front door and someone waiting on the porch steps. It was far too early for a coffee party – she could only hope the woman wouldn't stay long. A glance around reassured her that no one else was in sight, but she decided not to remove her rough outer clothing yet; it would protect her, as she crouched, hidden in the ditch.

To occupy her mind she checked over her strategy for possible flaws. She had left her apartment that morning much earlier than she would have departed to go to the office. It had crossed her mind to ring and leave a message on the answer-phone for him but, deciding he would worry more if she didn't, had rejected the idea. Anyway, she couldn't afford to be distracted, she needed to concentrate; an oversight could prove catastrophic.

It had been essential for the porter to see her leave so she'd been irritated when she'd walked from the lift to find his door and reception window shut. Dismissing the possibility that he might not even be up, she was aggravated – he was the nosy sort, likely to poke his head out at any time, day or night. He never seemed to sleep! Today of all days, where the hell was he?

She walked quietly back to the lift and clanged the door several times before crossing the hall again. This time the window was open, the porter sitting in place as if he had been there all night! He smiled, lowering his morning paper, "Forgot something did you, Miss Hamilton?" So, he had heard her after all!

"Oh, no... I thought so, but suddenly remembered it's in my weekend bag," she laughed. "It would never do to go to a wedding and forget the gift would it." Ned eyed her up and down appreciatively.

"You certainly look smashing miss if you'll excuse the liberty saying so. A wedding is it? Bit early though! You got far to travel?"

It was just what she wanted – the opportunity to tell him her plans: how she would catch up on her beauty sleep on the train to Oxford. Nobody would expect her to do what she really intended, take the inter-city express to Reading with a ticket already tucked safely in her wallet... later, after her mission was completed, she would go on to Oxford. Ned called a taxi for her with more flattering asides about putting the bride's nose out of joint and she was at last on her way – no turning back, nor indeed any desire to do so. Elation was her only emotion.

Oblivious to the heavier traffic as they neared the centre of town and the streets that would soon be jammed with shoppers, commuters and tourists, Joyce day-dreamed ...envisioning herself – sophisticated, noticeable – making conversation with the ticket-office clerk so that he would be sure to remember her, the vision in blue, travelling to Oxford.

She then visualised herself, as she would emerge from the cloakroom fifteen minutes later! She planned to be in there, out of sight, when the attendants changed shift; it was the first critical stage. The drab, unremarkable figure hurrying to catch a train was unlikely to be remembered by anyone. It didn't matter a jot if she wasn't seen on the Oxford route; thousands of passengers travelled anonymously so why should anyone be asked about her anyway?

At the cloakroom, all went according to plan. She had stayed out of sight, her blue leather grip hidden inside a huge plastic bag found in a car park. She had known immediately that it was perfect for her needs: having no idea herself where the advertised shop was, the staff would certainly not know her! Ten minutes dragged by slowly – then, at last, she heard the cheery exchange of greetings between the two attendants. The one who had seen her looking normal informed the newcomer,

"All okay luv, only one, in number four! 'Bye, see yer..."

After the footsteps receded she had emerged slowly, differently garbed, with old cloth gloves concealing her varnished nails. Clutching her shopper and the strap of an old shoulder bag with one hand, she dropped a coin onto the strategically placed saucer with the other and made her way out to the platform. She giggled aloud, delighting in her own cleverness. Anyone could look different by resorting to a wig and thick make up, but facial expression was far more important. Sponge inside her cheeks, lipstick cleaned off, steel-rimmed glasses, and a rain hat pulled over her hair had transformed her, yet it would be easy to restore her appearance to normal before she went to the house. Joyce wanted his vapid wife to see her at her best. It was the moment she anticipated with the most pleasure.

As she reviewed the last few hours she hugged herself with glee... Surely nothing could go wrong now. Resting in the shallow ditch, she trembled with excitement.

Seeking reassurance that it was still there, she felt the small packet of powder through the fabric pocket of her suit and smiled smugly, reflecting that all those years ago, after discovering how effective it was, she had been shrewd enough go back to the shed later, to check the label on that rusty tin...... Sodium Fluoroacetate. She had later looked it up in the library: water soluble, tasteless, colourless and fast acting.

Joyce had lived with foster parents until old enough to work and take rooms of her own. They hadn't invited her to stay on with them – not that she wanted to anyway. They were a plain, quiet couple, dull and unremarkable; she could hardly recall their faces.

She remembered the cat however – sleek and fat, always eating or sleeping, usually on someone's lap! They pampered it sickeningly, talked to it in 'baby talk' and were even annoyed with her when she wouldn't adore it with them! How she hated stroking it and shuddered even now at the memory of her foster-father's harsh grip on her wrist as he forced her hand to slide down the warm, silk, animal back.

She had been six when she went to them and nine when the cat died; she felt virtuous, having put up with the thing for so long.

The solution to her dilemma had presented itself when a friend took her to their garden shed where they sat in the shade eating bruised plums, scraping out wasp-holes with a piece of stick to be sure that no drowsy wasps still lurked.

When her eyes grew used to the dimness and she saw an old tin bearing a red skull and crossbones, the plan came instantly to mind: no tedious thinking: a sure mark of genius. Quickly snatching the last plum, she pushed her companion out of the hut with instructions to shake the trees for more.

Tipping the remaining crisps out of the packet – she hadn't intended to share them but it was an emergency – she filled the bag with powder from the tin, concealed it in her schoolbag and later transferred it to a small screw-top jar, innocently labelled 'CHALK'.

She had been too excited to stay for the rest of the feast and glad she hadn't when her friend was off school next day with severe stomach cramps caused, her mother said, by eating too much over-ripe fruit.

Without the faintest stab of guilt, Joyce remembered using the wasp-stick to lever off the lid of the tin and scoop out some of the contents. She experienced only smug satisfaction... the stuff was definitely poisonous!

During the ensuing weeks, the cat had several bouts of sickness, which worried and puzzled Joyce's foster mother who alternately blamed the animal's natural greed and the hot weather. Judging the time right for the final touch, Joyce mixed a whole spoonful of the powder in the animal's dish with a spot of water and watched it disappear as it melted. Just before leaving the house the old lady emptied a tin of nutritious cat-food into it, and became instrumental in poisoning her own pet! The cat pounced on the meal immediately and within minutes of licking its dish clean, the creature went berserk.

Unaware of the drama unfolding below Joyce sprawled on her bed reading a comic until she heard the frantic meowing and crashing. She rushed down but was too late to enjoy the death throes. The black body was stretched rigid: eyes staring: mouth agape, tongue thrust out.

It was definitely dead.

Joyce recalled with satisfaction that even at that age she'd been sensible enough to wash the dish and retrieve the meat tin smearing some liquid from it into the clean bowl. She then tried to make the cat look less gruesome, by re-shaping the limbs, and threw it out near the dustbin. They all mourned the sad demise. Her foster-parents, touched by Joyce's tears, thought she had, after all, been quite fond of poor puss! It had been so easy that she afterwards whiled away many a happy hour planning to use the same stuff again one day... maybe on them!

Her thoughts were suddenly jolted back to the present when the car started up and she risked a quick peep as it emerged into the lane. Crouching flat on the dry earth she didn't move until it drove down the road out of sight. She was relieved. Only the driver had been in it. Her quarry was still inside the house... alone.

3 - Jenny

Jenny had been gone only minutes – there had barely been time to walk upstairs let alone start sorting the laundry – when the front bell rang. She must have forgotten something thought Ann indulgently, opening the door but, to her astonishment, a complete stranger stood there: young and elegant: returning her instantly frozen smile with narrowed eyes. The woman stepped inside quickly without waiting to be invited and closed the door softly behind her.

"I saw you had a visitor," she said, "so I waited until we could have complete privacy."

"I don't understand," Ann gasped, stepping back in alarm. "Who are you? What do you want?"

"There'll be plenty of time to talk now," the woman re-joined, walking past Ann into the sitting room and dropping calmly into an easy chair. "First, we'll make ourselves comfortable and," her eyes flicked to the coffee pot and tray, "enjoy a cup of coffee." She removed her soft leather gloves, leaned forward, and touched the pot lightly with the inside of her bare wrist. "Not quite drinkable I think. Why not bring out some fresh and then we can settle down to a nice cosy chat?"

In abject confusion, Ann took the tray to the kitchen, replenished the milk jug and actually re-started the percolator before anger took over from her instinctive good manners. Who was this insolent creature? Perhaps she had devised this as a gimmicky way of selling something expensive... and useless! Well, she had wormed her way in now, so she could have her coffee and then go. Ann's curiosity was sufficiently aroused to indulge her that far, but she had better talk fast or out she'd go anyway! It was a heavy washday. She had no time to waste on a long sales pitch!

When Ann returned, the woman was standing near the window holding a photograph of Cathy and Chris that had been on the sill.

"So, these are the babes," she said pleasantly, "Quite alike, as I had expected: very pretty too."

Putting down the tray, Ann relaxed slightly, then immediately stiffened again, with foreboding. Who was this person to have expected anything, or even known about the children at all? Perhaps research into the background of potential customers was essential in her line of work! She turned to find her unwelcome guest seated again, still holding the treasured picture in a strangely possessive way, which annoyed Ann intensely. She retrieved the photograph and replaced it in the window. Sitting again on the settee, she demanded an explanation.

"Coffee first," was the girl's response, "you'll probably need it!"   Shaking a little, nervously aware of the implied threat, Ann filled the cups with steaming black coffee and noticed that a slight soapy scum had risen on one; in her understandable haste, she must have been careless, rinsing it under the tap. Never mind, it was hers – the cup in front of her visitor looked alright and Ann couldn't have felt less like a sociable drink anyway. She sat on the edge of her seat warily.

"You had better tell me immediately what business you have here, with me," demanded Ann, "or you'll have to leave," she added, standing to make her point.

Completely unmoved, the woman settled back and patted her hair with a confident gesture. It was impossible not to notice her well-kept, smooth hands and beautifully manicured nails... Instinctively Ann tried to conceal her own. With a disdainful shrug, the beautiful intruder indicated that she should resume her seat and Ann's rising anger changed first to incredulity, then sick fright as the words she was hearing began to sink in. She collapsed and sat numbly as the stranger, with pretended delicacy – belied by the malicious gleam in her eyes – tore her world to shreds.

"I'm Joyce Hamilton your husband's secretary," she announced. Noting the bemused expression on Ann's face, she smirked and continued. "No doubt you've heard of me. I have actually been much more to him than that for several years now, but I assume from your glazed expression that you never guessed... For goodness sake have a drink," she added urgently, rising to put Ann's cup into her shaking hands. Forgetting that it was unclean, Ann lifted it to her lips and was startled out of her daze by the excited dart of triumph in those suddenly narrowed eyes as the stranger relaxed.

Sipping her own coffee daintily, Joyce observed Ann's hesitation and leaned towards her urging her keenly to drink, as it would make her feel better.

More in control, aware of every nuance, Ann raised the coffee slowly to her mouth. There was no mistaking the way the girl was holding her breath... poised in anticipation: but anticipation of what? Why should this husband-stealer want her to feel better? More likely, she wished her harm. Good God thought Ann – has she put something in my drink! Surely not! How? When she replaced the photograph in the window; it could have been then. There had probably been at least twenty seconds to do whatever she had done – if indeed she'd done anything at all. In her confusion and fright, Ann was ready to believe the worst and she forced herself to think clearly.

Assuming she was right, it explained the strange white

scum and she was obviously dealing with a maniac intent on harming her. Ann's mind shied away from the bizarre possibility that an attempt was being made to murder her: that only happened in books! It must be intended to put her to sleep – leaving this madwoman free to nose about the house. For what purpose Ann could not even conjecture: it was hardly likely to be theft and would surely be an outrageous way of satisfying curiosity! She decided she must pretend to drink and gradually appear to fall asleep. She would then see what happened next. Experimentally Ann raised the cup, hesitated, and lowered it again to the saucer.

There was no mistaking the anxiety in those glittering green eyes, which never left hers. Next time she put the cup to her mouth – without allowing the liquid to pass her tightly pressed lips – she tipped it as though drinking long and with pleasure. Witnessing this, Joyce relaxed and sat back contentedly, closing her eyes for a moment, which gave Ann a chance to push the still-full cup out of sight, behind the pot.

Joyce's emerald green eyes opened lazily and gazed at her speculatively for what seemed an age, before her full red lips parted with a sigh and she spoke again.

"Actually, I'm trying to persuade him to live with me in town – my flat is spacious enough and so handy for the office. We won't give it up as I intend to go on working with him. He hasn't agreed yet. He seems to like it here in the wilds. I suppose this place would be adequate for weekends: for a while, anyway." After staring long and hard at the stunned and silent Ann, she leaned forward and with fierce intensity hissed, "He keeps putting off asking for a divorce but I know it's the children he doesn't want to lose, not his dowdy wife! With you out of the way, we can be together. I will make him really happy."

Ann answered shakily, forcing herself to stay calm, faking drowsiness. "What in God's name makes you think

I would go away to leave you a clear field?" It seemed imperative to keep the girl talking and in the almost euphoric mood she had been in since assuming that Ann had swallowed her coffee. Unfortunately, she became restless and stood up. Ann was terrified in case she noticed the full cup but she sauntered away from the table. With a flamboyant flourish, Joyce commented on the 'tasteless' furnishings but she approved of the size of the room. At the window, she fingered the curtains critically.

While Joyce was looking the other way, Ann reached tentatively for the scummy drink... seizing the opportunity to return the coffee to the pot, covering the clatter with pretence of rising to remove the tray. The girl spun irritably to face her. "Sit down," she commanded, returning to her chair, once again holding the children's photograph. "Tell me about them – their likes and dislikes – I need to know everything. Anyway, sit down, don't take the tray away I want more coffee. My throat is quite dry with all this talking."

Ann was thunderstruck. She declared that it was too cold but her protestations were of no avail; the girl said it didn't in the least matter. Trying to distract her with questions also failed.

"For goodness sake, never mind, I'll pour it myself," said Joyce, pushing Ann away. Her long lean fingers bit into Ann's arm and her red talons felt like knife tips through the thin nylon overall. Her grip was so tight that the pain blinded Ann to all else and she recovered too late to prevent Joyce drinking. She wondered why she had tried to stop her anyway – hopefully, the coffee really was drugged! If the girl passed out soon it would give Ann a distinct advantage. It would then be possible to ring the police to have her removed and locked up – preferably in a padded cell!

Ann shrank back into the deep cushioned seat and tried to appear calm; through half-closed lids, she eyed

Joyce warily. Whatever had been added to the coffee, if indeed anything had, it certainly did not appear to be having an immediate effect. Her uninvited guest chattered on with great animation, revealing her plans as if she truly believed Ann would hand over to her – not just Eddie, but the children too. More convinced than ever that she was dealing with a sick mind and sure too, that her imagination had been running wild when she'd thought herself physically threatened, Ann wondered how she could either leave the house to get help, or use the telephone in the kitchen, unobserved.

While her mind raced, the shrill voice trilled on excitedly and she was appalled by what she was hearing... "You need have no worries about the family. I'm a very good cook as your husband has often said. He loves my food. He always says it's a welcome change to have interesting meals! These curtains aren't at all bad but the loose covers are insipid – quite the wrong shade of beige – they'll have to go."

Every few minutes she paused to peer closely at Ann, although she didn't seem to be waiting for comment. Ann just crouched, tight-mouthed, numb, praying that the ordeal would soon end and that the girl would just go; she was obviously mentally deranged. Should she tackle Eddie about this odious woman's visit? On the other hand, would it be better to pretend it never happened. Joyce was unlikely to tell him herself and as long as he believed Ann to be ignorant of his real relationship with the girl – he had after all refused to leave his home and family for her – perhaps, in time, everything would be right again. If only she had thrown the girl out before hearing of Eddie's infidelity! She was a weak fool, a fool with an over-active imagination and muddled brain. There had been no drug; Joyce was as wide-awake as ever!

Ann ceased wallowing in self-recrimination abruptly.

The dreadful monologue stopped in mid-sentence and

the even timbre of the throaty voice rose to an eardrum-shattering shriek! On the brink of recovering a vestige of composure, Ann was launched violently into a scene of nightmarish horror. The honeyed tones choked to a stop; the glittering eyes grew wide with disbelief. The luscious lips parted and brown foam began to bubble from Joyce's gaping mouth. She clutched her throat, as if attempting to silence the revolting gurgle; the other hand clawed the air wildly, reaching for Ann, who shrank away... but she should have used the moment to run out of range. She was trapped in the low depths of the sofa as the writhing body rose and jerked towards her. Terrified, her own screams deafened her... and as the woman's full weight bore down on her, Ann mercifully lost consciousness.

4 – Second Thoughts

He felt thoroughly exhausted as he packed up to go home. The day had not gone at all well. Half-expecting Joyce to relent and ring up, he leapt to answer every time the damn telephone shrilled. It was, he knew, a leap of dread as much as hope. He desperately wanted things cleared up between them, cleared up and back to normal, not confused with promises or threats he could only half believe.

He knew he had been feeble to let things drift on, but Joyce had seemed happy enough to continue their haphazard relationship until now... What had changed? He had never for a moment let her think he would consider a divorce.

With a rush of inspiration, he made up his mind to promise her a holiday – a whole week together – a business trip: out of the question for his wife to go. It should be possible ...he knew of a couple of seminars which were to be held shortly. Away from the office, he might be able to talk some sense into her: cool her down a bit. He might even be able to introduce Joyce to some other unsuspecting bloke... There were always plenty on the lookout for a girl with her talents!

He found an Oxford contact number by searching Joyce's desk and hoped it was perhaps the girl who was getting married. All day he had fought the urge to use it, but now he could excuse himself – persuaded that he had a good reason. He would tell her about the seminars. The promise of a few trips together should calm Joyce down.

She had been in an exceptionally bizarre mood when they parted on Friday! Merely the thought of her confronting his wife put him in a state of panic... He couldn't stand another night of uncertainty. He first dialled the number of her apartment in case her earlier absence had been only for shopping; she might not be going until tomorrow. He allowed it to ring several times, and then tried the porter's room. Ned recognised his voice. He seemed surprised that her boss had to ask, but yes, Miss Hamilton had taken an early train to Oxford this morning... "No problem sir, no trouble at all," Ned informed him. Considerably relieved, he called the Oxford number. Almost immediately, a woman's voice answered breathlessly,

"Joyce, is that you? ...For goodness sake, where are you? I met the four-thirty as you said, and hung about for the next train – then thought I'd better come home in case you rang... Joyce? Who is that? Who ..."

He replaced the receiver with a sinking sensation in his stomach. If Joyce had caught the early train, why had she not expected to arrive before late afternoon? What had she been up to all day? Where was she now? Endless questions teemed in his tired brain. Frantic, he dialled his home number then changed his mind immediately, unable to credit that Joyce really had confronted his wife without first discovering if he had already buckled under her ultimatum and confessed to their dalliance himself. It would be more like her to work on him further, forcing him to do the dirty work – being instrumental in shattering his own life. There are, after all, other possibilities. She might easily have had other friends to visit. She might even have done some shopping in town before catching the train. He must get a firmer grip on himself before he reached home.

Threading through the heavy traffic was worse than usual. He was not concentrating wholly and it took a great deal of effort to control his wild imaginings. He endeavoured to appear normal ... to put Joyce out of mind. He would deal with the situation as it developed: keep his head. Turning into the lane he suddenly felt quite calm. This was the real world – the other, a fantasy.

5 – The Bride

Sleep eluded Elaine Davies that night. Dan, her husband-to-be, snored heavily in the next room. Her friend Joyce should have occupied the other twin bed, but it stood, counterpane gleaming coldly in the half-light, a silent reminder that she had failed to come and take possession.

Apart from her natural concern about the girl's whereabouts, Elaine was extremely disappointed. She had been looking forward to going over all her wedding plans with a new audience – there were so many things they hadn't been able to talk about over the telephone. Where could she be? Elaine also wanted to be sure that Joyce understood why she had not been invited to be a bridesmaid. Was that it? Had she really felt slighted and decided against attending the wedding as just another guest?

When Elaine asked if she would be upset not to 'stand' for her, Joyce had laughingly protested, agreeing it would not be a good idea. Not only was Joyce the taller of the two friends, she was the same height as Dan when she wore heels. She said the disparity would ruin the group photographs! Although Elaine privately agreed, she tactfully refrained from saying so. No, she averred, she was obliged to have Dan's young sister and nieces as bridesmaids and his nephew as a pageboy – the entourage was already bigger than she'd really wanted – it would have been lovely if it could have been just the two of them without the kids – but! You know...

Of course Joyce knew. Elaine felt transparent – as she

always had since they were children. Joyce always seemed able to read her mind, contriving to be several jumps ahead, making hard reality of schemes only nursed, half-formed in her own head. Joyce was invariably the ringleader of their mischief so it was also galling that Elaine had usually been the one to suffer the consequences. She even recalled being ill for a week after a shared fruit-eating binge when Joyce had not even had a mild twinge of indigestion! Joyce had always had a glib tongue too. She could talk her way out of anything with a serenely innocent air that completely disarmed authority. Elaine, if guilty, always looked it! However, she never begrudged Joyce her ability to escape punishment and was careful to avoid involving her in any confessions.

If the truth were known, she was afraid of bringing Joyce's wrath down on her own head. Her unpredictability had always fascinated Elaine but this most recent example of Joyce's capriciousness was not in the least endearing. This week – the most important of her life – was being disrupted. She would never speak to Joyce again if she were deliberately ruining it!

Whatever could have befallen her! Elaine kept wondering, making up new and increasingly unlikely scenarios as the small hours wore on drearily. Dan theorised that she had simply changed her mind about coming by train and her car had broken down. When she asserted that, were it so, Joyce would have telephoned, he pointed out that Elaine had in fact been out all day. He was right, of course. She'd caught an early bus to Oxford and, after shopping, lunched with Dan. Then she'd had her hair done. From the salon, she went straight to the railway station to meet Joyce. Back to square one ... No Joyce! She thought about the funny 'phone call. Someone was on the line, but had hung up without saying anything! Dan was dismissive of the non-call...

"It happens all the time: wrong number."

He then insisted that they go to bed. If Joyce hadn't either arrived or contacted them before nine-thirty in the morning, she could start to panic with his blessing! Her bedside clock glowingly informed her that it was three-o-clock and she had never felt farther from sleep... six and a half hours to go! The faint light of the dial made the shadowed corners of the room deeper: more impenetrable. Elaine, who had never been frightened of the dark, became slowly more aware of the gloom around her. As tiredness undermined her judgement and sapped her strength, she felt threatened, imagining that something – somebody – some entity hovered...! An uncontrollable shudder shook her as she chided herself and turned over. With a supreme effort of will, she concentrated on the small clock-face until sleep came, but the wrathful presence haunted her dreams.

6 – Tuesday 21st...

"When would you like your lamb delivered Mrs Tiller?"

The surge of horror that leapt to her face as Ann stared at the butcher, tongue-tied was, fortunately, interpreted by him as lack of comprehension. "The whole lamb you ordered. It's ready." He repeated himself patiently.

She had a sudden vision of the body that, since yesterday, had half-filled her freezer, shrouded in black plastic under a layer of frozen food. She had not yet fully recovered from the shock of her husband's parting shot as he left the house earlier...

"I'm glad you topped up the freezer," he had shouted from the garage. "It's much more economical to run when it's full"... My God, thought Ann, I wonder how glad he would be if he knew that most of what filled it was his girlfriend!

"Mrs Tiller – the lamb – when would you like me to deliver it?" The butcher's small round eyes stared over a pair of half-circle spectacles as he lowered his head and tucked his double chin into the top of his blue-striped apron.

"I'm terribly sorry," said Ann, swallowing her panic, "There has been so much extra stuff to freeze – vegetables from the garden... I just haven't room for it after all. Can you hold it for me please, just for a week or so?"

On Thursday, Eddie would be taking the children to his parents for one of their long weekend visits. They went two or three times a year; she never accompanied them. It was supposed to be 'a real rest for mummy', according to their Grandma, but what she really meant was that she could have her son all to herself again!

They were not really on bad terms, she and her mother-in-law, but they had a fragile relationship that they both knew would stay cordial only if not tested by close proximity! Cathy and Christopher adored their grandparents and were so excited by the coming trip they didn't appear to be aware of anything strange in her behaviour, not that they were likely to do so at seven and five years old. Eddie too, was preoccupied with his job and plans for the weekend, but perhaps, reflected Ann sadly, he no longer loved her... was not concerned enough to sense her deep distress.

She was suddenly mindful again of her surroundings. Mrs Hoskins, the Butcher's bustling, kindly wife, stood transfixed behind the counter and was staring at her, openly concerned. In the dimness of the small village shop, with its crowded, tin-heavy shelves, Ann nervously swept back a wayward strand of fine hair from her eyes and tried in vain to tuck it behind her ear. She suddenly felt overwhelmed. The air was thick with vegetable odours rising from the wire trays, carelessly stacked, which tripped feet and snagged tights. Like an automaton, Ann took what was being pushed at her and heard the woman say,

"This will really do that cold of yours some good, you poor thing, your nose is quite red!" It was a packet of lozenges... "And here, have a tissue for your eyes – streaming they are!" Mr Hoskins was retreating to his lair at the rear of the premises. Ann wondered what he had replied to her request. He was probably annoyed. To hide her confusion, she was glad to admit to a cold and added the cure to her basket. She mopped her face and threw the tissue in the bin as she went out into the street. She must get a grip on herself and not give anyone else reason to remember her behaviour as odd. She couldn't afford to draw attention to herself in this way: not before she had got rid of the body.

At home, after putting away all the groceries, Ann sat in the spare bedroom gazing at the girl's clothes. She would have to dispose of them – but how?

It was odd that she had never considered Joyce a threat to her marriage but, from the way Eddie always spoke of her, how could she possibly have guessed? It was shocking to discover that "Good Old Jo," his secretary, had the looks of a fashion model, assured and beautifully groomed. Inevitably, her mind again retraced the events of the past twenty-four hours.

Yesterday had begun normally enough. Her neighbour Jenny came in early for Ann's shopping list, as she did every Monday. On Fridays, Ann did the same for Jenny. It suited them both to cut down on trips to Reading. It saved petrol and more importantly, if delays occurred because of heavy traffic, at least one of them was still at home to take care of the four children after school. Their two houses shared the narrow lane to the road and they joked that if only one at a time was driving out and about, the other would not have to reverse a mile to allow free passage!

As always, they had coffee as they went over the required items. Many things were cheaper in town than in the village shop but as far as was reasonable they liked to support the local traders, so things were added or crossed off and new lists made. Their two families shared a comfortable relationship altogether. Jenny's twins were only five, but they got on well with Cathy and Chris who assumed the role of 'boss' unopposed! It was a pleasant association without being too intimate. Too much lack of privacy would have been unwise for people living in such close proximity but the four adults were also good friends. Ann's whole life was comfortable and well-ordered or so she had thought, until now! She was utterly devastated by the appalling revelations and subsequent events, after Jenny drove away.

As she sat on the bed contemplating Joyce's beautiful clothes, her senses reeled again, as sickeningly as they had when she came round, after fainting the day before, crushed under the weight of the girl's body. She would never forget those wide, mad eyes staring through her, into death.

The once beautiful face, inches from her own, was distorted – smeared with vile coffee-coloured froth. The shining, scarlet lips were curled back over pale gums in an agonised fixed snarl. The girl was unmistakably dead!

Screaming uncontrollably, Ann had pushed herself free and fled blindly to the bathroom where she was violently sick. She had no concept of time as she cleaned herself up and showered, her mind mercifully blanked out what had just happened – unable to cope with the revulsion.

When she emerged, in a state of trance-like calm, Ann was almost convinced she'd had a terrible nightmare; she would find everything normal again. The scene of devastation and the corpse in the sitting room brought her speedily to her senses. Staring at the twisted figure on the floor Ann groaned aloud, despairingly. What could she have done? She had not been certain that anything was wrong with the coffee. God only knew what poisonous substance had been intended for her, but it had caused the girl's gruesome death. She was not hypocritical enough at that juncture to feel sorrow at her rival's fate – it served her right; justice had triumphed, the biter bit! Good grief: was she losing her mind? She should be working out a plan of action not spouting clichés!

Her first instinct, and firm intention, had been to ring the police. She actually got as far as dialling but realisation slowly dawned that her husband's sordid affair would become known; and for goodness sake, it must have been a miserably cheap affair! She always did the household accounts and Eddie kept little money for himself – just cigarette money, as he put it. Joyce, judging by what she said, had obviously seduced him with little private suppers. No, not suppers, they would have been lunches; Eddie was hardly ever late home in the evenings.

Something else the girl said came back to her: she had waited for her visitor to go, so that they could be alone. She must actually have been hiding when Jenny left! It was now patently obvious. She had come to commit murder! She was sure to have provided herself with an alibi and must also have been careful not to be seen in the immediate vicinity, so she wouldn't have come by car, thereby attracting attention in a small village. She had been barking mad but not necessarily stupid! The more Ann considered all the angles, the more the conviction grew that she was right – nobody else on earth knew that Joyce had been here. It followed therefore, that the best way of dealing with the ghastly situation was to keep it quiet.

Because Ann felt no responsibility for the woman's demise – and hoped, by concealing it, to keep her marriage and home intact – she had set about her task with determination and efficiency. A glance at the clock told her that time was on her side; could it be merely two hours since Jenny left? No one was due back for lunch and casual callers were few; the long stony road put people off. Ann suspected that even the postman waited until he had enough mail to make the trip worthwhile! So, she could count on being undisturbed until the children or Jenny returned after four-o-clock.

First, she had dragged the dead girl to the cloakroom and thrown after her, all her belongings; handbag, gloves, a shoe that had fallen off in the hall as a leg caught in the doorway and an embroidered lace handkerchief which had fallen near the window and was almost hidden under a chair. She left the body on the tiled floor then, while worrying what to do with it, she tackled the sitting room. The tray had been overturned leaving a mess of milk, sugar and coffee that looked daunting but, fortunately, none of the crockery was broken. Ann was amazed to realise how childishly pleased she was that it had survived intact: already, more mundane things were taking precedence over the unreal disclosures and events of the last few hours, from which she felt curiously detached.

On her knees, as she scrubbed the carpet, odd things Joyce had said floated through her mind: how could she accept that he had been thinking of leaving her? Eddie was so considerate ...and they had always talked easily to each other. She wouldn't believe it. Joyce had obviously schemed to take Eddie away and when she failed, this had been her last resort – murder! The contemptible creature had been insane. She had wanted Eddie at all costs but Ann could understand why, and was equally willing to go to any lengths to keep him. If she had known of the affair, might she even have contemplated drastic action herself...? Even murder? She shuddered; she could not answer honestly.

What of the future? With Joyce out of his life, Eddie was sure to forget her in time... Ann would win him back. Was she really dowdy? Had Eddie implied that she was, or even told his secretary that he had an unattractive wife? Such a betrayal seemed completely out of character, but she wondered; how well did she really know him after all?

When the room was restored to its usual neatness, Ann had surveyed it with satisfaction. Quite surprisingly, there was no messy evidence of Joyce's death throes: all that bubbling brown mess. Ugh! She shuddered – it had been difficult to focus her attention. Knowing the carpet wouldn't dry for hours, she decided to explain it by saying she had over-watered a pot plant. To support this she had moved one to the coffee table and wet the soil until it could hold no more. Water brimmed to the edge of the container and she reflected that Eddie wouldn't dare to criticise; he often nagged her about forgetting to water the damn things ...then she'd had the presence of mind to water all the others too.

At last, there had been no excuse for putting off what she most dreaded. She forced herself to return to the grim scene in the cloakroom with everything necessary to conceal the body. She could not bury it clothed, it would make it too easy to identify... although, with any luck, it would never be found!

Three hours later, stripped naked, Joyce lay firmly bound in black mulching plastic – bought for the strawberry bed in a moment of enthusiasm, but never used.

The actual stripping was a merciful blank in Ann's memory. Sickened by the horror of it all her mind must have slipped a cog and operated on automatic through most of the ordeal. Her first plan had been to hide the body temporarily under the firewood piled in the garage. The logs wouldn't be needed for months so there was no fear of Eddie moving them, but whichever way she tried, it was impossible to stack them tidily over the oddly shaped bundle. Had she been able to straighten the body out it would have been easier to wrap, but it refused to co-operate and finally it had been simpler to bend it. In retrospect, with a commendable air of detachment, Ann felt that she'd done a good job. It was a smaller parcel than she had dared hope, in spite of the yards of plastic. Had Eddie been in a position to comment, she smiled grimly, he would say it had obviously been wrapped by the owner of a sticky-tape factory with no faith!

When the logs slipped yet again, Ann had to pause to regain her breath. She was badly out of condition for coping with such physical exertion. She was soaking wet with perspiration and had the horrific thought that it would be four or five days before she could dispose of the body properly. Somewhere she had heard that if someone died in what was called 'full flesh' they burst and...! Leaning weakly against the freezer she had also realised that in very little time the body would smell, the garage was always faintly warm – probably because of the freezer – the freezer! The solution to her dilemma: it was certainly big enough and only half full. Stocks had dwindled far too low but a visit to the cash and carry always resulted in parting with more money than they expected so she had been putting off the trip. Before revulsion overcame her, Ann emptied it completely and had heaved the black bundle into the cabinet. There were sufficient packages and boxes to hide it completely, still leaving enough space overhead to replace the wire baskets holding smaller items. Ann had finally closed the lid with relief. All that remained to do was to collect up the clothes, hide them somewhere and clean the cloakroom; no problem, it was fully tiled. A side door gave direct access to the kitchen from the garage and as she hurried through to tackle the distasteful chore, she had noted with satisfaction that she still had a good two hours left to prepare for the return of the family. Satisfied at last that all was sparklingly clean, Ann had packed the clothes into an old suitcase and pushed it under the spare room bed.

With no time to do more than remove all the labels and burn them in the lavatory bowl, Ann regretted having no a furnace or even a fireplace, she could have burned the lot: hat, bag, shoes too! A bonfire was out of the question. Even if she waited until the weekend to light one, she couldn't hope to cover the traces well enough to escape Eddie's eagle eye. Later, standing at the kitchen sink, she turned on the hot tap and washed her hands again ...would they ever feel clean? Looking over the field towards Jenny's house, 'Far Acre', she reflected on their good fortune, being in such a lovely quiet spot – just the two properties, built at the same time by a local speculator. There was no danger of other dwellings springing up. The farmer wouldn't part with more land, which was why it had appealed to them. Country born Eddie enjoyed the decent sized garden and space to breathe fresh air. Standing there alone, the peace was almost tangible and she couldn't bear the thought of losing it all.

Slowly, Ann had discerned something in the garage behind her, moving – scraping... then she distinctly heard a faint cry and three sharp metallic raps! Her raw, already frayed nerves, could take no more: in her imagination, she saw red talons tearing through black plastic to scratch and tap on the icy freezer wall and, with an anguished shriek of terror, she collapsed in a dead faint onto the tiled floor.

7 - Aftermath

Stunned and preoccupied as she still was, with the sheer horror of her situation, heedless of precious time slipping away, Ann fingered the lace cuff of Joyce's midnight blue blouse. It was exquisite ...so delicate; it seemed such a shame to burn it, but she couldn't retain it, even to give away, Eddie might recognise it! She thrust it from her with sudden distaste; the stains had washed out but the girl it had recently adorned and her shattering revelations were still fresh in Ann's mind, preventing her from focusing her thoughts on current problems. Again, they drifted back to yesterday...

...It was half-past-four when Jenny drove up to the porch. Simultaneously, the four children came laughing and shouting to the back door and burst into the kitchen. Ann was still white and shaking a little when she greeted them all. As she went through the ritual of putting the kettle on and preparing to make tea, she felt Jenny studying her closely. "Here, let me help. Is anything wrong?" she asked kindly. "You look shattered. Have you had a bad day?"

They handed out biscuits to the eager whirlwinds pausing briefly to consume drinks of squash... then sent them to play in the garden while they settled down themselves.

"I'll take the tray," Jenny insisted firmly, leading the way to the sitting room.

Ann swallowed her tea with difficulty unable to focus her eyes properly on Jenny sitting opposite, in the chair so recently occupied by another, whose image persisted in looming between them.

Taking a deep breath Ann tried to look at ease. "I really am stupid ...but would you believe – when the man came to read the electric meter he frightened me half out of my wits and I fainted!" She tried to make it sound funny but realised she had failed dismally. "The poor man was terribly upset." Ann tried to make light of it as she repeated his words: *"...'I saw your kitchen door open Ma'am and didn't want to creep up on you, so I knocked on the freezer top to let you know I was here.' ...*Then he went on the defensive... *'You did say it was all right for me to let myself in that way as the meter is in the garage'...'*

His tone had been accusatory, but her collapse had really frightened him, and no wonder! Ann convinced him that it was not entirely his fault and, after taking the meter reading, he had departed happily – probably framing the tale dramatically, as he would tell it to his cronies at the depot. Jenny was not so easily convinced and asked if Ann was dieting and had gone without lunch. Glad to agree that it could indeed be the cause of her faintness, Ann admitted she was anxious to lose weight but would have to be more careful.

"Well it's either that, or you're pregnant!" Jenny rejoined, almost hopefully, and grimaced when she was informed that the Tiller family had been planned and was now complete.

As Jenny chattered on, images of the other woman's final moments continued to distract Ann. She could hardly concentrate on what Jenny was telling her: shopping ...sold out ...prices ...traffic: all such unimportant things when she felt close to bursting with anguish. Nothing could ever be the same again.

Soon afterwards, the twins were carted off home still shouting. Chris and Cathy, also over-excited, refused to have beans on toast or anything else because they were too full of biscuits. It didn't happen often, so Ann was only too pleased to let them calm down in front of the television before their bedtime while she prepared dinner for herself and Eddie. Joyce's remarks about her cooking had stung and she found herself being much more adventurous than usual. She added chopped herbs, a glass of wine and, as an afterthought, a carton of cream. That should enliven things a bit, she decided – then wondered if Eddie would notice!

In the half hour before he came home, questions she needed to ask revolved ceaselessly in her head. Had Joyce told him she would be away? Was she expected in the office tomorrow? Would he miss her terribly when she never, ever, returned? With a stab of apprehension, as she gazed at the expensive clothing spread before her, Ann realised that someone was bound to miss Joyce eventually and would report her absence to the police. One day at a time, she cautioned herself and closed her mind to the future. She refused to consider that she would ever be associated with the girl's disappearance. Her conviction that Joyce would have been extremely efficient at covering her movements gave Ann confidence.

After they had eaten last night and she'd cleared up, Ann took coffee into the sitting room where Eddie was already snoozing in front of the TV. She deliberately made a slight commotion as she poured it out and placed it near him; there were so many things – questions about their whole relationship, which she was bursting to explore. As direct queries were not possible, she was compelled to be devious, using her wits to obtain information without making him suspicious.

Ann felt frustrated to screaming pitch, dreading his dozing all night, but the meal had been a great success and he was obviously well sated. Eddie had noticed the difference in the flavour of the food and had praised her efforts, but this only made her feel worse. He must have thought it insipid before, although he'd never complained! He had even noticed her dab of lipstick and clearly approved, which again made her suspect that he had previously noted her complete lack of make-up, but was not interested enough to comment! Unfortunately, when he woke to have his drink, his favourite program was on and ended any hope of talking. He fought his tiredness to stay awake until it ended, whereupon he went straight up to bed declaring that he was too weary to bother with a nightcap of hot chocolate...

At that point Ann gave up but, aimlessly moving the delicate lingerie from one pile to another, she reflected that it was no wonder sleep had eluded her last night. Whatever she discovered about the past would not change her present predicament. She needed a clear-cut plan for the disposal of the body before Thursday because she would have only a few days to carry it out... If only a high-rise building were being built nearby, with lots of deep holes waiting for concrete to be poured in, as there always seemed to be in gangland thrillers! She smiled grimly. Even then, getting anywhere near it with her black plastic bundle would be next to impossible. A man could probably move around a building site and get away with blue murder! Everyone would remember a female. The local refuse tip was a possibility, but a guard at the gate might recognise the car; Eddie often took garden rubbish there; she had to be more ingenious than that...

Unable to relax, Ann had eased first one way then another but her brain refused to help. It continually dredged up the events and revelations of the morning, churning over the incredible situation she was in until she wept with weariness. If Eddie had wakened then, she would have told him: her resistance to despair completely gone. She longed to be taken into his strong warm embrace and comforted. He always knew best what to do; he could take care of everything, making their world right again. Ann almost lost her head and reached for him to blurt it out, getting it all over and done with, but there arose in her a fear that perhaps, if he really loved Joyce, he would be enraged. He might not hold her responsible for the girl's dying, but if he suffered real grief at her death, Ann did not want to witness it! She must continue to hope the affair had not been important to him. If Eddie were deeply dissatisfied with their marriage, her concealment of Joyce's visit and all she had said would be to no purpose.

Even if he succeeded in solving all her immediate problems, their relationship would be destroyed. Sleep ultimately overwhelmed Ann, but her brain fought against it all the way... If he had stopped loving her, she clung to the hope that it was only temporary; she'd win him back. She had let herself go a bit, but she would adhere to a strict diet, exercise and look after her hands properly, sort out her wardrobe, cook exciting things and be more help to him with the garden. She'd do something about the curtains or the loose covers or ...or anything: anything to make him love her as much as she believed he did until the arrival on her doorstep of his lover – his young undeniably beautiful mistress ...but how could she compete with even his memories of Joyce?

Ann felt utterly empty and hopelessly lost.

8 – The Groom

Before leaving on Tuesday morning at 8.30, remembering his promise, Dan Bailey peered cautiously round Elaine's door and gazed anxiously at his sleeping fiancée. Her short dark hair was a tousled frame around her pale face. She looked comfortable but had probably not enjoyed a good night; otherwise, she would have woken naturally by now. Leaving a note for her, he crept quietly out of the house. She was having a week off – it didn't matter if she slept all morning he reasoned.

He was furious with Joyce for worrying Elaine but not really surprised; he suspected it was calculated deliberately to annoy. He had never liked the girl and was amazed that Elly regarded her as a friend. Joyce had a mealy mouth but in his opinion was jealous of their coming marriage. As a child, Joyce's circumstances were unfortunate and he thought she might always have envied Elaine who had parents and an attractive, comfortable home. He suspected that Joyce was a liar – exaggerating about her affair with the boss too! Even after years of chasing, she still hadn't lured him from his wife! As he started the car in front of the small town house, which they had been renovating for the past two years in readiness for this week, he determined that the scheming, calculating female could not be allowed to disrupt their lives. If they never set eyes on her again, it would be the best wedding present he could wish for.

9 – Rage

How had he survived through last night! The normality of home had suddenly conflicted painfully with the abnormal events disrupting his working life. Damn Joyce to Hell! What was she up to? If she wasn't in Oxford, she might turn up at the office today, full of repentance! He dismissed the luxury of the thought reluctantly, brooding instead on the injustice he was suffering. Other men had a bit on the side: took it for granted as a right: did it all the time with no comebacks. He, who'd had it virtually thrust at him, was put through all this nonsense... it wasn't fair!

The streams of traffic ahead surged away as he stamped on the brake angrily... even the lights were against him! His temporary secretary was driving him mad already – asking for work and completing it so damned fast he had to keep hard at it himself, when he needed breathing space to concentrate on his own problems. Sighing heavily, he put his foot down as he joined the glut of vehicles pouring along the motorway.

10 – Ann

Ann had not expected to sleep at all, but when she came round drowsily on Tuesday morning the few hours she had achieved obscured, briefly, the traumatic events of her private black-Monday. The sun flickered sharply through the curtains as they swayed gently over the open window. She could hear windows downstairs opening too as Eddie made his customary tour of the house to ascertain that all was well. She heard the tap running as he filled the kettle and mentally followed his progress as he came upstairs and woke the children. They were both quite good at getting up and preparing for school. Christopher always took charge, supervising Cathy, making sure every night that she made a neat pile of all the things she needed for school the next morning. He naturally had to show her by his own example! Because he was older and safer on the stairs, Chris took his things to the ground floor cloakroom to wash and dress, leaving the family bathroom to his young sister.

Eddie had their en-suite bathroom to himself so there was never the mad rush there had always been in her own family when she was a child. With two older sisters, their one bathroom was hardly ever free when she needed it. Ann had never felt well prepared when she left for school and was often late; her sisters were always immaculate, which did nothing for her own self-confidence. Enough space for each member of the family to enjoy a measure of privacy had been an important factor in their choice of house. This one was perfect for four and they prided themselves on their foresight and organisation. Everything was perfect; no, everything had been perfect until yesterday!

The utter horror of her situation again sickened her, as she grew more awake. She had tried despairingly to convince herself that it had been a nightmare: hadn't really happened, but knew, fear drying her throat, that her trials were only beginning.

She was brought wholly to earth by the children's happy screams as they chased their father along the landing, begging for one more piggyback and just one more cat-swing... "Come and see, Daddy," pleaded Cathy, "I did tidy away my toys. There really is room to swing now, enough for a really big cat!" Their voices grew fainter as they progressed happily down to the kitchen and she lay quietly with her own dark thoughts.

The only useful thing she could do, before the family went away, was to get rid of those damned clothes. As burning was impossible she'd just have to think of something else. The even more daunting problem – the burial ceremony as she euphemistically thought of it – was far too difficult to plan when her mind was endlessly spinning with a whirl of comparative trivia! Even after they left, she found it impossible to concentrate on her usual chores.

The urge to check again everything she had done the day before was irresistible. First, the dreadful bundle: still there, it had not disappeared miraculously in the night. Next, the carpet: quite dry now, it was not stained. Last of all, the suitcase: it too was as she had left it and she still didn't know what to do about the beautiful things it contained. She decided that the underclothes could safely go in the drawer, hidden under her own. Although more expensive than she was in the habit of buying now, she did own some lovely things she never wore. She'd never wear these either! Later she could give them away: in a year or two. The tailored suit was different. Even hacked up and buried it would give rise to suspicion if it ever surfaced. Maybe she should take it into the woods and burn it? No... the way her luck was going, she would end up by starting a forest fire!

Perhaps it would be better to dump the whole suitcase; it was old and rarely used. She could go to a big railway station and leave it as 'Left Luggage'. Surely though, items were opened if they remained unclaimed over a long period. Would anything in the case arouse suspicion? Yes, she knew it definitely would. She had taken all the labels off everything and she could not leave the handbag inside the case anyway. Until now, she hadn't looked inside it. Opening it felt somehow like prying which, she acknowledged even to herself, was the height of stupidity after the things she had already been forced to do! Apart from credit cards, the wallet contained a small amount of cash – it could go into the charity tin at the post office. There were no keys or train ticket: only a dainty handkerchief. With a deep sigh, she pushed the case back under the bed. It was a woefully inadequate hiding place, but only she ever went into the spare bedroom. It was safe for the time being. When she had finished the ironing and prepared the evening meal she would return to the problem. Perhaps a solution would dawn during the day. Part of her welcomed the challenge; it allayed her concern about an even more dangerous task – the disposal of the body!

While Ann continued her daily round of tidying and dusting, her head ached with the same, nagging problems, but no ready solution dawned. There was still a lot to do if the family were to go away looking respectable. Her mother-in-law would have nothing to criticise if Ann could help it. Actually, Martha, Eddie's mother, had never commented adversely on the children's clothes but, after a previous visit, Ann found a new pair of socks among

Christopher's things when she unpacked. She examined the similar pair he had taken with him and discovered a small hole in one of the heels, which she had completely forgotten to mend it in her haste to pack.

Ann couldn't decide whether she was more annoyed with herself for being sloppy or embarrassed at being found wanting. Would she have felt better if Granny had mended the hole? Probably not! She would have been happier if she had been able to kid herself that it hadn't been noticed at all! She wondered if all wives had the same neurotic defensive streak when dealing with their in-laws and had to admit that hers were extremely pleasant towards her. In future, she vowed, if indeed she had any future – at which thought she began shaking inwardly again – she would try to be less suspicious of Martha's every move.

By the time Ann took a tea tray upstairs and hauled out the suitcase again, to sort it on the spare bed, it was after two – well into the afternoon. Skipping lunch had saved time but, feeling ill, Ann had wasted it lying down, unable to function, until a baby bird fluttered against the bedroom window. Failing to get a foothold, it chirped frantically for a few minutes before giving up and flying back to the cherry tree. The tree was very old and losing its strength. It would have to come down one day but every year the blossom was so heavenly that the dreaded day was postponed. When yet another winter passed and the tree survived both heavy frosts and wild March winds, it was gladly granted a reprieve. The cherries, the handful she managed to net, saving them from the birds, were almost black and absolutely delicious when ripe. Ann morbidly wondered if they would be able to enjoy this year's crop together...

The telephone jangled, snapping her out of her trance and making her spill tea down the front of her overall, which she quickly unzipped to save her dress as she hurried to the main bedroom to take the call, trying to step out of it as she ran. Ann had never been able to ignore a ringing telephone; the strident summons, insisting that all else take second place, always made her rush headlong to answer. She flopped on the bed and kicked her feet free as she gave her number. It was Eddie.

As soon as she heard him mention Jo, her ears went almost deaf with the fierce pounding of her heartbeat. His voice sounded far off and hollow, as if she had a bad head cold, and she knew she needed time to recover. "Oh, would you mind hanging on a minute Eddie, I've left something coming to the boil downstairs – I'll have to take this in the kitchen...!" She dropped the instrument noisily onto the glass top table and sat staring at it. After a few deep breaths, she picked it up and asked him to say whatever it was again, as she had been distracted. It was important, he said, and he hadn't expected to need her to do it because Jo would have done it during her lunch-break under normal circumstances. Ann clutched her throat as the roaring in her ears came back. So! Circumstances were not normal; but how abnormal did he think they were?

"Jo's off – didn't I say? Well anyway darling, will you?"

"I'm sorry, I missed what you want me to do... and I don't think you did tell me about Jo. Where is she?"

He wanted Ann to buy his mother's favourite chocolates and father's tobacco in the village today. If she couldn't, then he would have to make time to shop himself, in town, but she knew how busy he was; it would be a big help. Of course she would; yes, no problem, she could manage it. She had finished work except for cooking dinner! Please, please she thought, tell me about Joyce!

"I thought I mentioned it to you," he was saying. "She needed a week off as she had a personal problem to deal with: very mysterious, wouldn't confide in me. But I have to look for big changes when she comes back! ...When?

Oh, next Tuesday."

A grim smile formed on Ann's face. There had certainly been some un-looked for changes in Joyce! ...Eddie was still talking.

"I'm really sorry to burden you. It slipped my mind that she wouldn't be here, I'm so used to relying on her for small errands."

As Ann backed her old car out of the garage, she eyed the gleaming white freezer balefully. The very idea of Eddie relying on another woman – that woman, for anything, infuriated her! It was past three and she could have done without the shopping trip. Coping with the clothes was postponed yet again!

Although she didn't usually bother, she climbed out of the car and pushed the garage doors together. She wished it were possible to secure them, but the crumbling foundations at one side prevented the lock from ever working again. They were having the builder in to repair the damage, so at the same time the garage was to be extended to take both cars. To preserve hers, the older car, Eddie's sometimes bore the brunt of the weather and stood outside, which was patently ridiculous. She liked her old banger anyway, and the money a later model would cost was better spent improving the house... in fact she felt lucky to have a car of her own at all. Eddie had been keen for her to drive. He said he didn't like to think she was stranded in the middle of nowhere, with no means of escape! He had always been so good to her... it was hard to fight back her tears.

The village was quiet, as always in mid-afternoon. Since being by-passed, having to steer round sleeping dogs and abandoned toys was quite normal. Once away from the house, Ann relaxed and began to feel far removed from all that had befallen her. Small talk with Mrs Hoskins, who ran the grocery side of the thriving business, did not demand much effort. For one who professed never to gossip – insisting that everything confided in her was, *'as safe as a doctor's surgery, my dear'* – she was always brimming with fascinating snippets of information.

Any family within a good ten-mile radius of her shop enjoyed the concerned interest of Mrs H.! Ann usually enjoyed listening, merely making a mental note never to let slip any of her own personal business. Today she was not so easily diverted but in spite of her anxieties, Ann began to take in and be amused by all the latest Farlow happenings.

Mrs Hoskins was always sure things were true.

She heard more with her own ears, and saw more with her own eyes, than anyone else Ann had ever known. "I had it straight from the horse's mouth dear," she affirmed, with a knowing pull-back of her double chin – lips pursed, "out of work again, and with all those children to support. Of course, Social Security supports them doesn't it? If I was that poor woman, I wouldn't boil him another egg! Not 'til he brought home a wage packet! It's you and me love that provides for the likes of him! Things always going up, taxes and all... it's a scandal: just not right if you ask me."

The flow was interrupted when Mr Hoskins came smiling from the rear of the shop. He wiped his hand briskly on his blue-striped butcher apron as he smiled at Ann, wishing her good afternoon. He apologised for butting in and asked her, "When would you like your lamb delivered Mrs Tiller?"

ll - The End of the Day

The case of clothes drew Ann like a magnet. An hour after her return from the village she still sat with it on the bed, helplessly admiring the dead girl's finery, fingering the quality. The girl had certainly known how to dress and, Ann reluctantly admitted, had been extremely attractive but, even so, didn't seem to be Eddie's type at all.

How little Ann really knew him! At least he would be pleased she had done his shopping, which in fact she almost forgot in her haste to leave the shop!

The sound of laughter broke her reverie. School over, the children were running eagerly home to start the most important part of their day!

Hearing the door slam downstairs, Ann replaced everything hurriedly and shoved the case out of sight, yet again.

Rising wearily, she pulled the counterpane straight and re-checked the piles of spotless, beautifully ironed clothes she'd prepared for the coming jaunt. No holes this time she reflected with satisfaction. Gradually, it dawned on her that everything was too quiet.

Hurrying uneasily along the landing, she heard Cathy in the hall. "Mummy, come and look! Mummy, where are you? Why aren't you in the kitchen?" She sang out accusingly as Ann hurried downstairs. "I want to show you something very, very good."

Ann tried to admire Cathy's artwork, at the same time filling the kettle, and attempted to stem the child's excited chatter. "Where is Christopher?" she asked.

"Oh, he's all right, he's home. I did this picture all by myself. I had a star for it," Cathy continued proudly. "Look! This is you mummy and that is daddy and …"

"Cathy! If Christopher is home, where is he?" At that moment, Ann heard the unmistakable creak of the freezer lid and saw that the door into the garage was ajar. Startled, she dropped the kettle heavily onto the draining board and ran into the garage, Cathy's voice trailing after her…

"We tried to find the ice cream you promised we could have after school, but it's all muddled in there and we couldn't find it. My hands got too cold," she complained, "and Christopher won't let me have the big gloves. *Please* look at my star…"

Pushing the door wide, Ann saw Christopher leaning into the open chest and reaching for more of the frozen packages, which he was transferring to a nearby bench. "Stop … Stop it at once, you naughty boy," she shrieked. He was wrenching with every ounce of his strength at a corner of black plastic!

12 – Elaine

Hours earlier, in her sleep, Elaine had stirred when Dan's car revved below her window and drove away but soon settled again and didn't come round properly until ten-thirty. At first, she couldn't believe it was so late or that Dan had gone without waking her, then the memory of Joyce's disappearance flooded back. Grabbing her housecoat, she dashed down to the hall to look for any messages and found only the one Dan had scribbled on his way out.

"No news. Forget her and get on with your own thing, she'll turn up when she feels like it – probably her idea of a joke! Stay cool.

Love D."

Elaine felt almost angry with him for making light of the situation but still, it was the sort of trick Joyce might well be playing to make her look silly for going into a panic. With half an eye on the clock she kept busy, completing household tasks, endless lists and confirming final arrangements, but by teatime could stand it no longer. Elaine first telephoned the porter at the flats who confirmed that Joyce had left yesterday. The company Personnel Department then confirmed that Miss Hamilton had gone on a week's holiday and gave Elaine her own telephone number! After staring numbly at the instrument for several minutes, willing it to ring, she picked it up again and called the police.

13 - Jenny

In Farlow Hollow, as Jenny Dean heard the twins come to the back door she waved her thanks to young Christopher – such a responsible little boy, absolutely reliable. Matthew and Sally had not been going to school for many months so all four children were escorted by a teacher who travelled home this way and parted from them where the dirt track joined the main road. Chris then herded them up Old Farm Lane. He always waited at the gate, until Jenny waved to assure him that she was taking over the twins, before he turned back to go home, glowing with self-importance, leading his little sister by the hand. Only after his duty was done was he free to follow his own pursuits. It didn't seem to dawn on him that the system was as much a safeguard for him as for the others. Jenny, who could just glimpse the back door of the Tillers' through the trees if she went to her dining room window, waited to check that they actually went inside before relaxing with her own two.

They were so lucky, she reflected, to have such super neighbours. Eddie and Ann were roughly the same age as she and Bill and in similar circumstances although Jenny suspected that their own income was much higher. Perhaps Eddie was just careful with his money but he never bought Ann surprise presents or flowers whereas Bill enjoyed buying her expensive gifts. Eddie's idea of a birthday or Christmas offering for his wife was likely to be something for the house rather than a piece of jewellery!

Admittedly, the Tillers also ran two cars, but one was obviously on its last legs and even Eddie's was a middle-aged saloon. Bill had bought a new car for himself when they married seven years ago – and replaced it several times since! The first, because it had only ten thousand miles on the clock, became hers. She didn't use it much – had added only four thousand in the last three years – and feeling a sentimental attachment to it, had declined all Bill's offers of a replacement. Of course, she had never discussed all this with Ann but she knew that they couldn't have much put by, because Ann had mentioned that they needed a second mortgage to have the garage extended. Jenny wondered what Eddie spent his money on; perhaps he was keeping another woman on the side... possibly that extremely attractive redhead he had been with at the Railway Hotel a few months ago!

Jenny had decided one day, on impulse, to go into London to visit the Royal Academy Summer Exhibition. It was nearly over so she couldn't postpone the trip even had she wanted to do so. Because the twins were being collected from school that day to go to a friend's birthday party, she had plenty of time... it was only a twenty-five-minute train journey by Inter-City from Reading and having lunch with Bill was always fun. She hadn't been able to reach him by 'phone to tell him she was on her way, but as he worked near the tube station and always used the same bar for a pre-lunch drink she had no trouble locating him. Eddie also had an office nearby so she was not surprised to see them together. Actually, Bill saw her first as she stood at the entrance searching the crowd for his familiar face and he waved delightedly.

After a quick word with Eddie – it was then that she noticed Eddie's companion – he hurried over and took her arm. "Don't look round at Eddie", he whispered, "pretend you haven't seen him and for God's sake don't breathe a word to Ann about his lunch date!" While they were eating later, Jenny – slightly agog that she had stumbled over a neighbour's indiscretion, questioned Bill about the stunning girl-friend. He assured her that it was nothing serious! Eddie wouldn't be such a fool. It was merely a casual lunch with a colleague. "But you know what wives are," he grinned, digging her in the ribs, "he would be in the dog house for nothing! Just dismiss it from your mind. I promise you, he's not carrying on a lurid affair!"

In spite of his assurance, she secretly felt disloyal to Ann. Travelling home later, she blithely dismissed the notion as absolutely absurd... Eddie, just less than six feet tall with fair, wavy hair, was attractive enough to attract any female on the prowl but was not the type to fall! Jenny sometimes felt that he disapproved of her own natural frivolity. She found herself giving her skirt an extra tug down, if it rose too high in his presence and guarding what she said more than she usually did. He was a bit on the old-fashioned side, but very likeable.

They played Mah Jong regularly once a week, visiting each house alternately, so that providing suppers was also shared. Bill had learned to play in Singapore in his army days and had brought a set back with him. She smiled again as she remembered Eddie's protests at being coerced into learning. He said he'd had better things to do when he was serving his country and didn't like games anyway! Now, she was sure, he looked forward to 'the twittering of the sparrows' as much as everyone else. Like themselves, the Tillers had few other local friends with whom they exchanged dinner parties. Bill worked hard and, even when he was home early, always had files with him to deal with in the peaceful atmosphere of home. He said it was chaos in his office, too many interruptions and no reliable help to cope with minor problems.

Ann often remarked that Eddie's secretary was a fantastic help to him: uncomplaining. When their workload was heavy, she even took work home to type. If only Bill could get someone like that! Perhaps when the twins were older Jenny could go to work as his secretary again – Bill always said he'd been an idiot to marry the best P.A. a man ever had! Jenny knew the mouse he had promoted from the typing pool when she left. The woman, Faith, was apparently no more capable now than she had been then, but Bill was still putting up with her. "She really tries," he sighed when Jenny commiserated, "and how do I know if any of the others would be an improvement? At least she makes a good cup of coffee!"

By the time the train pulled into Farlow station that day, Jenny had made up her mind that Eddie's lunch date was not important enough to mention to Ann; why worry her for nothing! She was personally quite convinced that Eddie was a faithful, even rather dull husband, who wouldn't have the nerve to conduct an extra-marital affair! Since then, she'd had no reason to change her mind. It occurred to her that Ann might not feel up to taking her turn with this Wednesday's get together; as Eddie was taking the children away for the weekend she must be busy. Jenny decided she would volunteer to cope herself instead, but she would ring up to ask rather than drop in … Now, she must hurry to prepare dinner.

Jenny took pride in being an efficient homemaker, just as she had been an efficient secretary in the office. Bill was inclined to be untidy, but she organised him now as she happily had then. He was always teasing her about the way he didn't dare put anything down unless he wanted it washed and pressed and he never let her forget how she actually did that to his wallet when they were first married. "Into the washing machine it went with my trousers! It took her hours to iron out the paper money – all small denomination, naturally! But if you ever want money 'laundered', I recommend my wife without any hesitation! The wallet of course was never the same again, which is why I never let her get her hands on it!"

This always raised a laugh at her expense, but Jenny was tolerant enough not to resent his anecdote. He made a big show of plumping up his own cushion as he stood, to show guests how 'well trained' he was, but when he put his arm round her and gave her a hug to show them that he was a very happy slave, she took it all in good part.

She was naturally proud of her home and equally proud of Bill. He was tall: as darkly handsome now as he was when they first met and still in good physical shape. He didn't show his thirty-five years. Although a little older, Jenny was confident that she still looked good. She wondered if middle age was creeping up on her, noticeable to all but herself! Had any grey hairs mingled yet with her light brown curls?

Sally and Matthew, who had been watching television, came rushing in panic to find her, howling in dismay... it was broken! By going round the house, trying switches, she discovered that it was merely a power failure. Jenny looked towards the village but it was not yet dusk: impossible to tell whether it was a general failure. If it didn't come on again within fifteen minutes she'd ring Ann to ask if her supply had also gone. For now, it was no problem. She didn't need to open the refrigerator and her freezer was full, so it could stand a twelve-hour cut without coming to any harm. Then she remembered that last summer there had been a failure that lasted not a mere twelve hours, but sixteen!

14 – The Office

Wendy, Joyce's stand-in glanced at the digital clock on the opposite wall and confirmed that it was time to take in the boss's refreshment tray. She was proud of the way she was handling things. If she could make a good impression he might recommend her to another executive even if unable to take her on himself. She was sick of the typing pool and was sure she could be a good P.A. Yesterday had been a bit fraught. He seemed irritated whenever she asked for guidance – after all she wasn't psychic, but today she had taken care of several routine letters herself and been complimented on her initiative. When she entered his office, he was staring out of the window and appeared unaware of her presence until she put the tray near his desk.

Swinging in his chair as she turned to go, he unexpectedly stopped her. "Do you know Joyce Hamilton well?" he asked. "I mean – did she mention when she expected to go Oxford. Is she calling anywhere else before going to her friend's wedding?" He hesitated, looking almost embarrassed Wendy thought. She had heard that something was going on between them, but had dismissed the rumours; offices were hotbeds of gossip. Now she sensed that the stories were true... just wait until the girls heard this one! His obvious disappointment when she said she hardly knew his secretary and had no knowledge of her movements was almost pathetic; they must have had a row. She knew he was married with a family too, and any desire she had felt to work for him evaporated. He was despicable and Wendy knew she'd be glad when the week ended.

He left his office that evening before Wendy finished clearing her desk. He'll be home early for a change, she thought wryly! Then, on the point of leaving herself, the telephone rang. It was the internal line from one of her friends in Personnel:

"He's gone has he? Well anyway, it's not up to us to inform him – but I couldn't wait to tell you. Miss Toffee-Nose never got to her friend's! In fact, they don't know where she is! Yes, of course I'm sure. I listened in on the call. The police will be round here next! I knew you were ambitious love, but didn't think you wanted her job that badly! What have you done with her?" Wendy giggled obligingly and passed on her suspicions that there really had been a Big Affair but it was probably over and Joyce would stay in hiding until he apologised or something! They speculated at length about Joyce but it was surprising how little either actually knew about her.

Later, walking to catch her bus, Wendy tried to recall exactly what he had asked her and in what tone of voice. His anxiety may have been overplayed; he might really know where Joyce had gone. Was he worried only in case her movements could be traced by anyone else? Was he indeed anxious to have her found or... or not? And if not... why?

15 – Dan and Elaine

Elaine was not comforted by the conversation she had held with the local police. She could tell they thought her foolish for bothering them when her friend was quite likely to turn up – she had, after all been missing for less than twenty-four hours! They implied that she could hardly be described yet as genuinely 'missing'. The man who took her call passed her on to his sergeant eventually and he, at least, made a note of her telephone number.

Dan was sympathetic, but tired after his day's work. He wasn't at all surprised by the attitude of the police; they had enough real problems without taking on what might prove to be no mystery at all. However, he had a friend on the force and promised to contact him later in the evening if they still had no word from Joyce. There were two 'phone calls as Elaine prepared their meal. Each time, she expected it to be her errant friend and became increasingly agitated when it wasn't so.

Before they ate, Dan rang up his old friend Terry White, a Detective Sergeant in the CID. Terry was based near Reading, Dan's hometown. He couldn't offer help officially. He echoed the advice already given but came up with an interesting idea. He reminded Dan about a kidnapping case in which he had been involved last summer. "Do you remember that three-year-old being snatched – Kate Mead? We had been on the case for a couple of weeks and getting nowhere with it, then the Chief called in this psychic, Sarah Grey, and in no time at all we knew that at least the child was alive!"

Dan not only remembered; he actually knew Mrs Grey. He told Elaine excitedly. "Your young bridal attendants have a grandmother, Gertrude Bailey, who is on the guest list – my Aunt Polly, of course..."

"Just a minute," interrupted Elaine, "why do you call her Polly if her name is Gertrude?" Somewhat impatiently, Dan explained that his aunt had been housekeeper for the Grey family since before he was born. His cousin (the children's mother) was then about three years old. In the morning room, there was a parrot, which Gertrude taught to say "*Hello Polly*," but he only ever said it to her, so they all caught the habit!

"We even came to use it in the family – just an affectionate nickname and she's happy with it – so what the heck!" Dan was eager to proceed. "Aunt Polly still lives with Mrs Grey as a sort of housekeeper companion and there have always been hints that the woman is clairvoyant or something. I thought it was all rubbish personally but the police use her sometimes, so she must be good. It might be worth calling her in to help!" He grabbed the telephone directory and searched through the Greys without success. Although reluctant to involve Jane he was on the point of ringing his cousin for her mother's number when he recalled that both she and Mrs Grey lived with Sarah's daughter who was also widowed... an artist, and as he admired her work he knew her name well: Clarinda Hunter.

Within minutes, he was dialling and asking to speak with his Aunt Polly. The woman who answered had a pleasant, firm speaking voice and informed him that Polly was out. "Did you say you are Dan, the young bridegroom-to-be?" she asked. When he confirmed his identity, the woman said that his aunt was away for a few days – helping to look after her grandchildren because Jane was so busy preparing them for the big day, his wedding on Saturday! She said she was Sarah Grey and asked if he would ring Polly at his cousin's home or leave a message. Deciding to go in at the deep end Dan said he had really hoped to speak with Mrs Grey herself.

From the instant she had picked up the receiver, Sarah found it almost impossible to hear what Dan was saying. She thought at first it was a bad line but then a shrill voice, unmistakably behind her, shouted, *"Can you hear me? ...Can you?"* She was alone in the house, and in spite of her acceptance of the paranormal, Sarah was only human... she spun in alarm. Dan's voice, speaking quietly into the 'phone, was almost drowned out by the repeated, frenetic barrage hurled at her from someone she could hear but not see... *"I know you can hear me... you must be able to see me! I heard them talking about you. Don't you dare ignore me – you have to do something about that woman! ...She murdered me!*

Sarah couched a silent prayer for help and tried to concentrate wholly on Dan's words. She guessed he was the cause of the visitation. After hearing about the disappearance of Elaine's friend she asked him to ring back in an hour – she would give the problem some thought. On returning to the sitting room, Sarah sat down quietly and gave her demented ghostly visitor an opportunity to resume the assault on her senses. Eventually, she heard the voice again; it sounded more controlled but communication was not as easy as usual and, whenever she failed to grasp what the girl was saying, it grew worse. Sarah perceived that the obstacle to clear understanding was the girl's own intense fury.

Anger emanated from her in almost tangible waves and with every puzzled look from Sarah it became raised in scale until rage drove her to screams which ceased abruptly, leaving Sarah alone again in her previous peaceful isolation.

Repeated sessions during the following hour at last grew more coherent and at one point, the demented spirit became calm enough to materialise for a few brief seconds. As Sarah sat waiting for Dan to ring back, she sorted out in her mind what she'd been told and how much of it she would tell him. The spirit of someone named Joyce, who had died violently at the hands of a woman, was haunting her.

The woman was certainly not Elaine, or indeed anyone associated with her. In four days' time she and Dan were to be married; there was nothing either of them could do to help Joyce now. Why say anything to upset them. The telephone rang again and Sarah went to the hall to take Dan's call.

16 – Meanwhile...

After speaking to Sarah, Dan and Elaine talked over what she had said. "Well, she really is amazing," Dan mused, "she actually used Joyce's name several times before it dawned on me that at no time had I given it to her myself, not even when I first rang ...anyway she says we must proceed with the wedding and put Joyce completely out of mind for the time being. We can be absolutely sure she won't come!" He took Elaine's hand. "I told her we were spending Saturday night here and on Sunday going on honeymoon to London. When I said we would be driving through Reading, she invited us to call in. She says the situation is in hand and will give us more information then."

Elaine looked worried in spite of his assurance, pointing out that it sounded ominous – Joyce must be dead! Dan tried to sound confident when he said it wasn't a foregone conclusion; Joyce could be suffering from loss of memory or been involved in a minor accident. Anyway, they had other things to worry about and he was happy to put his trust in Mrs Grey. He ended further discussion by switching on the TV. He still considered it quite likely that Joyce was deliberately staying away to disrupt Elaine's composure. If he proved to be right, their childhood friendship would come to a speedy end – he would make sure of that! He had known as soon as he met her that there was no depth to her; she was no good. He barely took in the information passing before his eyes. Could she really be dead? How and why? Had she had an accident, or been the victim of foul play? No way! Whatever else, Joyce was no victim!

17 – Family Matters

Polly came home soon after Dan's call. As she carried her small suitcase upstairs, Clarrie drove up outside. Sarah, having already prepared the evening meal, was thumbing through a magazine, her smooth, rather square face fixed in a slight frown – but it was not what she read that troubled her; her mind was preoccupied with the missing girl.

Polly was the first to join her and knew immediately that something untoward had happened. Sarah put aside her journal and nodded as she admitted that she did indeed have an interesting story to tell but would wait until Clarinda came down, to describe her extraordinary evening. Sarah could not help a stirring of alarm when she thought of the vengeful spirit of Joyce Hamilton, but knew they would both be supportive. She didn't doubt that she'd need all the support she could get to control the angry ghost.

Polly was naturally eager to talk about her daughter and the wedding – the children were so excited – so it was easy for Sarah to question her about Elaine. It transpired that Polly hadn't yet met Elaine and had no knowledge of her friends or family. She was looking forward to meeting them all on Saturday. "Well," said Sarah with a smile, "You'll have another chance to meet Elaine on Sunday. They are visiting us for tea!" Polly could hardly conceal her impatience when Sarah refused to elaborate until Clarinda came down from her studio. She was putting away her painting gear after her day out and seemed to be taking much longer than usual.

When Clarrie did appear at last, she looked incredibly white and shaken. "What on earth has been happening here tonight?" she asked in a tremulous voice, almost collapsing into her chair. Sarah was naturally shocked and demanded to know what she meant. Her daughter was also psychic but not so accustomed to dealing with the afterlife as she was herself.

Clarrie took a deep breath and explained. "Just as I was about to leave my room, a young woman appeared between me and the door. She was just standing there watching me. I saw her and stopped. We stared straight into each other's eyes and she suddenly went crazy – raving and shouting! I couldn't take it all in; I was rooted to the spot until she faded out but even as I ran downstairs I could still hear her voice." Clarrie's voice faltered as she gazed at her mother. "She screamed something about me being another one and if I was no help to her either, she would kill me and see me in Hell!"

Sarah understood now and was full of compassion. Clarinda was clairaudient but other than in a dream state had only once before seen a ghost close enough to touch – and that had been a gentle soul not a raving lunatic. No wonder she was so shaken!

"I assume the voice eventually rose to such a high pitch that it became inaudible," she commented. When Clarrie nodded, Sarah went on to tell them of her own encounter with the same entity.

Polly was thankful that Sarah had not told the young couple of Joyce's fate but she was agog with anticipation, aware that they were now involved in another mystery. How and where had the woman died? Dan had already given Joyce's home and office address to Sarah; she would enlist the help of her old friend Alec Holmes, a Detective Chief Superintendent in the CID, who would be sure to advise her. He might even start making enquiries himself when he heard the girl had been murdered.

Clarrie's colour returned to normal but she still shook slightly. She stood and paced around the room, continually lifting her long, fair hair away from her neck and shoulders with both hands as though her skin crawled, or the room was too hot. She repeated something specific the girl had said – "*His bitch of a wife won't get away with it*" – which Polly immediately suggested could indicate that she'd been having an affair with a man whose wife had found out and got rid of her, permanently. Sarah, however, pointed out that it could also mean that she'd been left off a dinner party guest list!

Without more information, there was little they could do but Sarah insisted that she and Clarrie should stay together as much as possible. Since Polly moved in, Clarrie's spacious studio had also become her bedroom. She loved the freedom it allowed her, to paint into the night hours if she felt like it, without disturbing anyone! Now Sarah declared, "I shall sleep on your spare couch Clarinda, until this matter is cleared up."

"Surely mother, we don't need to go to such lengths?"

"You forget I met the girl too. If she threatened to kill you, I believe her quite capable of trying!" Sarah was adamant. "I don't often make judgements on such short acquaintance, but if she was half as obnoxious in life as she is in death – I'm not in the least surprised that she was murdered!"

Polly laughed until her ample frame shook and the tension lifted a little but the lights simultaneously flickered and went out. Before their horrified gaze in the firelight, the coffee tray rose from the table, hovered above them and then, with a resounding crash, was thrown by an unseen hand into the grate. Before they recovered from the shock, both Sarah and Clarrie heard a menacing hiss...

"How dare you... nobody laughs at me!"

Clarrie needed no more convincing. She allowed her

mother to move into the studio with her. Polly hadn't heard the voice but she had seen the tray lift through the air. It was the first time she had personally witnessed anything supernatural. She was actually more elated than frightened and to the amazement of the others was not at all put out by having to retire to her room alone. "I'm probably better off on my own," she said, "In all my sixty-odd years, ghosts haven't bothered me. I sit with you two for five minutes and I'm under attack from flying saucers!"

As they lay in the darkness later, Sarah said, "Thank God for Polly. We need her down to earth common sense to keep us from taking ourselves too seriously." Clarrie was well on the way to sleep as she heard her mother remind her, "Never forget, our best defence against evil is prayer – plain old fashioned prayer. Good night dear. We'll triumph in the end. Have faith!"

18 – Problems Mount

The evening had not gone at all smoothly for Ann. For that matter, the afternoon had also been quite traumatic. After the freezer-emptying escapade, she had to explain her apparent over-reaction. Their terrible crime of course, was keeping the freezer open for such a long time. The food could have been ruined, she informed them. It would certainly put an added burden on the electricity bill; they had to be punished. She informed them they would have to contribute to it by handing back a quarter of the week's pocket money! It made sense to them, which was the important thing, and would not really hurt them, as they were sure to have a generous handout from their grandfather at the weekend.

With this knowledge, Ann was able to shrug off any guilt about frightening the poor little things half out of their wits by her fury. They had never seen her so mad; they were dumbstruck and were still subdued.

She had left them eating ice cream at the kitchen table – after all, she believed a promise should be kept – and finding that they were still being allowed the treat revived them slightly. Ann hoped they would have forgotten the episode completely by the time their father came – the less attention drawn to the freezer the better!

After replacing the food even more carefully, completely concealing again the dreadful bundle, Ann shut the lid firmly. This time she locked it. It had occurred to her to do so yesterday, but as she didn't usually bother, she thought it might give rise to comment.

Now, too worried to risk Eddie also searching through it, she turned the key in the lock. She couldn't imagine why he would ...but then she recalled that he had indeed opened it for some reason as he left the house that very morning! He might understandably be curious about what she had, according to appearances, just bought!

Eddie always asked how much the Cash and Carry cheque was made out for; he was sure to ask her this evening, in order to enter the amount into the account book. She would write one out immediately and keep it on one side to spend this weekend. She often did the bookkeeping to save his time but he held the actual reins when it came to spending money. He wasn't mean, or wary of allowing her to handle things entirely alone, but he had a horror of overspending and perhaps going into the 'red' at the end of each month. No amount of persuasion would make him accept that because most people lived happily on borrowed money, it was right for the Tillers!

Mortgages were different of course. Taking one out originally had gone against the grain but he had to agree they were a necessary evil and obtaining a second, for improvements, hadn't been so traumatic. Ann put it down to his strict Northern upbringing... "Never a Borrower or a Lender Be," was one of Martha's most frequently quoted old saws.

She still put weekly sums separately into labelled cups: *Gas – Telephone – Electricity – Insurance.* She felt smugly virtuous when she handed the money to his father on receipt of the bills. If she had not removed it from her housekeeping allowance in the first place thought Ann, it would still have been in the bank, but try telling her that!

Thrift was definitely in Eddie's blood and Ann accepted that it was better than if he'd been like Bill Dean who was always splashing money around on flowers or extravagant hand-made chocolates to bring home to

Jenny. Ann would have worried if Eddie had wasted his hard-earned salary on silly luxuries – after all, he worked for hours in the garden to keep the house filled with blooms most of the year!

Putting the cabinet key safely on a high shelf out of sight, Ann decided, if questioned, to remind Eddie of several recent local thefts from freezers. Until the garage was secure, he would agree that locking it made good sense. They had been waiting weeks for the builder to start on the extension. She was particularly keen to have a proper surface there instead of the compressed earth floor that existed now. The dust, which blew into the kitchen every time the door opened, made a lot of extra work. Ringing the firm to ask when they hoped to come was a regular weekend chore; it was a pity she couldn't risk saying how she really felt about the way they dilly-dallied but if she did, they would never come back at all!

The children were holding an earnest discussion when she re-joined them. They were laboriously writing numbers on her kitchen notepad. There was much sucking of pencils and it transpired that they were trying to divide their pocket money by four. Christopher then persevered in his attempts to multiply it by three (because he was good at multiplication and wanted to show off) but as this did not tally with Cathy's result when she did an ordinary 'take-away' sum, he was getting rattled. Much amused, Ann gave them each fresh paper and, feeling much more sanguine about the whole episode, said that if they each worked out their own and the sums were right, she wouldn't take it from them after all!

Letting off steam, although regrettable, had left her with a feeling of calm resignation. The moment for reporting the arrival and unorthodox departure of her unwelcome visitor was long gone; there was now no alternative but to conceal the consequences. She was therefore able to greet her husband, when he arrived, with her customary normality.

Eddie on the other hand had a distracted air and looked tired. He was much quieter than usual and Ann had to repeat herself continually as she tried to draw him out. Joyce's absence may not have surprised him but he might be missing her company; it could explain his mood, but she would not allow herself to pursue that line of thought!

When he did suddenly speak of his own volition, Eddie broke into a smile. "By the way, the builder called the office this afternoon. He's been trying to ring you; you must have been in the village. Don't hold your breath, but he has promised to come on Saturday and thinks they will be able to tackle the floor early next week. Sorry it will be happening when I'm not here to help, but he says his men will shift the freezer for you. We only need to clear away the rest of the clutter."

In her sudden confusion, Ann could not immediately see the effect of these arrangements on her own dilemma, but at least it sank in that he was not contemplating emptying the cabinet and moving it himself! It was all she needed to know for now! By Saturday, her embarrassing parcel should be a long way away, so she managed a few cries of astonished delight and told him not to worry ...she could manage everything: no problem! At the same time, Ann saw how pleased he was that the project would soon be under way and took it as a clear sign that leaving home had never seriously entered his head. The girl's stupid rambling made no sense! A man bent on absconding with another woman does not commit himself to spending on the family home – the law doesn't allow a wife to be turned out of their joint property.

With fresh heart, Ann persuaded him that she could cope with clearing the garage before Saturday so he could do a bit of work in the garden as planned, until supper was ready. There was at least an hour of daylight left as

Eddie started mowing the lawn.

Watching him work – the weakening sun burnishing his strong, bare arms – she knew that whatever he had done, she loved him. Anything she must endure to keep him would be worthwhile. It then occurred to her that he had gone out there without having a cup of tea. She would make a pot anyway, and take a mug to him. When she went to the kettle it was cold yet she distinctly remembered switching it on as he arrived home. She tried the cooker and light switch. Without a doubt, there was no electricity!

Ann gripped the edge of the table in consternation. How long had it been off? All had been well when she closed the freezer lid; surely, the indicator light had been on when she refilled it ...Oh God! Had it really been on? Could she be sure? No... It was impossible to be certain.

She swallowed hard and shuddered.

Less than half of the contents had been frozen already and might even have begun to soften after lying about in the warm garage. Renewed contact with the unfrozen bulk of the cabinet's content was sure to have raised the temperature of the whole lot. Nothing could be solidly frozen, not sufficiently to withstand a long power cut. If Eddie became aware that the current was off, he would immediately panic about the frozen food. It was always the first thing he worried about when the electricity failed, especially as the freezer contents were not insured, something they were always saying they must do but never actually got round to doing!

Ann tried to assuage her dread by remembering last year. After an exceptionally long power failure, they had dreaded opening up the freezer but the contents were either still frozen or at least so cold that they hadn't suffered. They were amazed to discover that even the ice cream was edible, although such a treat at breakfast was a mixed blessing! However, it had, after all, been during the winter and being in an outbuilding at that time of year undoubtedly helped. Now, having had a day's sunshine on the flat roof, the garage was warmer than the house!

Ann's mind raced to another chilling thought. She recalled a neighbour's offer, if ever it happened again, to take their stock into his own cold store – an offer that Eddie would want to take up rather than run the risk of losing all their stock. She knew he would insist on ringing him immediately rather than disturb their benefactor during the night. He would not delay the transfer until after l0pm and risk adding eight or more hours of deterioration time, should the cut last all night. Almost groaning aloud at this latest setback, Ann stood with both hands on the gleaming surface of the cold kettle. What on earth was she to do?

19 - Sarah

After their alarming introduction to the demented spirit of the departed Joyce, both Sarah and Clarrie, to their surprise, had a quiet night. Immediately after going to bed, lying in the silence, Sarah had mentally remonstrated with the troublesome ghost - promising to help only if she stayed calm and changed her threatening attitude. Sarah didn't delude herself that this was the reason for their undisturbed night but, at the time, getting it off her chest had helped Sarah herself! She worked on the theory that death did not automatically change people but if they had been nasty in life, it usually inspired contrition and a desire to change.

When their immortal soul was threatened, even the most evil began to take an interest! Learning how to improve was as essential in the after-life as it was desirable on earth ... but Joyce was an unknown quantity and, in her present state of mind, totally unpredictable. Sarah desperately wanted to help, but not knowing the object of Joyce's hate, she felt helpless.

Praying for guidance, Sarah at last fell asleep.

20 – Ann

Striving to overcome the waves of nausea churning within her as the sun sank lower, Ann had tried to think positively... If only she could avoid Eddie finding out and getting agitated before they needed to light up, the power might be back by then. She could delay his noticing anything amiss by making a cold meal: ham salad and tinned fruit and a glass of beer as soon as he finished outside. Then she'd keep her fingers crossed that by sunset the crisis would be over.

Christopher interrupted her thoughts with his own urgent problem; was his sum right, or would he lose some of his allowance after all? "I have worked it out lots and lots of times, mummy, and mostly it comes out this way! It's right, isn't it? Cathy gets a different answer with hers every time and wants me to help her, but would it be cheating?" Ann had to smile at his anxious little face.

"You are a good boy darling," she said, "you have done it beautifully – and it's right too. As you have asked me about helping Cathy it won't be cheating, but please don't do all the work for her!" He raced off, gratified, puffed with importance. "Make sure she really understands how to work it out, won't you?" Ann called after him. She was profoundly thankful that they were too occupied to worry about not having a television programme to watch. Ann looked over to the Dean's house where, when it was on, she could usually see the front porch light glinting through the trees. It was often on all day because Jenny was hopeless at remembering to switch it off. Only at dusk, of course, did it become obvious, but she was reasonably sure that it was now off. At least the fault was general.

She went out to talk to Eddie, taking a glass of squash with her. He really did look exhausted, she thought, seeming glad to rest for a moment – he was about halfway through his cutting. Ann searched the recesses of her memory for something to ask him: something ordinary but reasonably intelligent, about the office. Somehow, she had to get him into conversation about that bitch. She needed desperately to know a lot more than he had ever before volunteered. "What's wrong?" she asked as he stretched wearily. "Is your back bad again? Didn't you succeed in replacing the old uncomfortable swivel chair you have to sit on all day?"

This only drew from him a wry shake of his head and a long sigh. After a disconcerting silence, she tried again. "How is Colin er– what's-his-name? – Bates, these days? Has he recovered from his operation?" Eddie looked slightly bemused – possibly by her apparent interest in a man whose name she wasn't even sure of! Anything to make him talk, but it was no use. Something must be bothering him, something he could not discuss with her. Ann gave up. Bitterness welled up inside her. She could only suppose that 'Good Old Jo' was occupying his thoughts, the Jo who had a personal problem to deal with and had needed some time off! How could Eddie suspect that Ann herself was Joyce's problem... or that the change she had promised would be a change in his own circumstances! No longer tied to his 'dowdy wife', he would have been an eligible widower!

At least the change of menu kept her busy and she had only half a mind on her troubles. The friendly splutter of the radio as it came back on went unnoticed and did not immediately convey the message to her brain; the freezer was working again. Eddie came to the kitchen door and kicked his boots off outside as he sat on the step. He was always considerate about such things and he carried them in only after banging off the loose dirt.

"What on earth are you doing, working in the dark you silly goose, you'll chop your fingers off ... then I'll have to cook the vegetables myself as well as grow them!" He clicked the light switch and to Ann's surprised relief it came on, blinding and startling her. She jumped and almost did cut herself! Eddie went into the garage through the connecting door shaking his head as if despairing of her. It was as much as Ann could do to stop herself going after him, but of course he was only going in there to clean his boots. There was no reason why he should try to open the freezer... or was there?

So many unreasonable things had happened in the last thirty-six hours that she felt driven to prepare herself for anything! Her mind constructed a series of scripts as if to ensure that she would have a ready response to any eventuality:

'Hey, Ann, why have you locked the freezer?'

'What were you looking for?'

'That's no answer! Why is it locked?'

'Burglars... we are not insured!'

'I'm not a burglar. Where's the key?'

Then what ...would she give him the key? 'Here's the key – let me get whatever it is.'

'No, you get on with the cooking.'

'I would be quicker – I know where everything is.'

'I want to check if there's space for more frozen beans – what's the matter with you? Are you hiding a body in there?'

...She'd have to confess. 'Oh, God, I hoped you would never find out.'

'Find out what?'

'That I know all about you and Joyce ...and yes, there is a body in there – hers!'

'Darling, what a relief... she is out of my life at last.

I've been wondering how to get rid of her. We can leave her in there forever, nobody will ever know!'...

"Look out! Snap out of your daydream – something's boiling over!" Eddie called as he re-entered the kitchen and startled her out of her crazy fantasy. Perhaps all she had endured really had unhinged her, Ann thought as she turned down the heat and tried to laugh. She had put the soup on and opened a can of new potatoes to brighten up the cold meal while her mind was wandering: running in automatic again!

As soon as Eddie went to shower, Ann had to re-assure herself that the great white monster was still locked It was of course but she was beginning to feel obsessed. Locking the door as she returned she tried to turn a mental lock on her mind to stop it turning in the same useless groove. She then called the children to have their supper. An early night would do them good anyway. If she succeeded in getting them to bed quickly, she could work on Eddie again when he had eaten. He didn't seem as tense as he had been when he first arrived home so she wouldn't give up. The more information she could glean about Joyce, the better equipped she would be to deal with the present situation and with any fond memories Eddie held of the girl, which might still threaten their marriage.

Only a field away, if Ann had but known, another potential threat was taking shape. An eccentric old woman who was virtually ignored by most of the local inhabitants, stood at her broken gate with her back to the setting sun. She contemplated the two house rooftops in the distance. The trees and hedges hid the rest of the buildings frustrating her beyond measure: if only they were not there!

Yesterday, from the same vantage point she'd witnessed something which had perplexed her ever since.

Had she been younger – more agile – she would have hurried over for a closer look. She didn't see many strangers on foot. The first had been of little interest – she could have been a Gypsy. The second, who must have had some connection with her, looked far more out of place. Why was she walking on the rough field path all dolled up in city clothes?

She kept her eyes almost glued on the lower end of the lane for hours afterwards but neither of the women re-appeared and there had been no traffic in or out until that Mrs Dean came back in the afternoon. It was a mystery. She was annoyed with herself... if she had not been too idle to walk over the field straight away she would have seen where they went. She had a feeling that somebody was up to no good and now it was too late for her to discover what it was! She hadn't felt up to it today, but tomorrow she'd go and have a look around ... keep an eye on things for a few days ... perhaps ask in the village, who they were!

She couldn't bear not knowing all there was to know about her neighbours. She had very few other interests in her dull, lonely life.

21 - Eddie

After dinner, Ann and Eddie sat together in front of the television. Having watched the evening news bulletin Eddie leaned back in his chair and became absorbed with the daily paper. His change of mood seemed to stem more from his pleasure in having managed to do his gardening before he went away than from anything else. After commenting favourably on the meal – a new recipe she had tried – he reverted to more mundane matters.

"If it rains before next week," he said, "It doesn't matter now, the grass is cut and most of the weeds have been raked out. I couldn't have expected you to do that as well as all the clearing you will have to do for the builders."

Ann gazed with scant attention at a situation comedy film, noticing only when the audience roared with laughter. She didn't find anything in it sufficiently amusing to raise even half a smile and gloomily wrote all the spectators off as half-witted. She was bursting to talk but couldn't devise a natural way of asking what she most wanted to know.

Even under normal circumstances, they seldom discussed Eddie's work. Ann rarely met and was unlikely ever to become friendly with any of his colleagues because his office was in town. She knew that other husbands – Bill for instance – were full of chat about their working day. They enjoyed re-living moments of triumph or needed sympathy when things didn't go smoothly, but Eddie always said that his home was a place to forget his job. She had respected his wish to escape and relax to such an extent that she had long ago lost all curiosity about his office life. Now she regretted her complacency.

Suddenly, he dropped the newspaper onto his lap and looked over to her brightly. "By the way," he chuckled, "you will never credit where Jo is now." Bereft of speech, Ann stared at him blankly and he looked apologetic. "Oh! Sorry, I didn't mean to interrupt your program. I'll tell you later," he said, going back to his paper.

Recovering her composure rapidly, glad that the light where she sat was not bright enough to show her burning cheeks, Ann said hastily. "Oh I'm not really listening to the TV, I was miles away – thinking of something else – please do go on."

Eddie smiled as he said Jo had been very mysterious about her short holiday, but a temporary typist who knew her well had told him all about Jo's little scheme. "She has booked into one of those health clinics – she went in on Friday evening for a five day 'crash course'. I can't think what she hopes to achieve in five days!" He dropped his paper to describe, with widely waving arms, a Reubenesque figure in the air... "You should see her, she's not just plump she's fat! It would take at least a month of solid dieting to cut her down to size!"

Ann tried to sound amused too as she answered. For some reason, he wanted her to think Jo was unattractive. As she knew that the girl was (or rather had been) the very opposite, she would have to be careful how she handled the conversation so that he didn't change the subject. It seemed, in retrospect, that every time he'd ever mentioned Jo, Eddie always went out of his way to give Ann a mental picture of someone who was ordinary, and no possible threat to her place in his affections. Why, at this moment, did he bring her up again in that vein? She became aware that he was speaking again.

"It must be because of the conference next month... I promised to take her because the hotel business service is always fully booked whenever I want to work. She will be a great help to me but she probably wants to improve her chances with all the young executives!"

So, that was it. How long she wondered, had he been planning to take Joyce away with him! As long as she didn't know what Joyce was really like, she was unlikely to object to their little business trip! What a cunning way to break it to her ... a conference he had to attend ... a secretary without whose help he really couldn't cope; although, of course, she was of no interest to him at all as a female!

Ann shook with anger. Was this really the husband she'd always adored? The man she had regarded as upright and beyond reproach in every way? She choked back her feelings, forcing herself to speak. "Perhaps she has no dress sense. Some fat people contrive to look very attractive ... their size is unimportant." He protested that in Jo's case she dressed quite plainly, but still looked gross!

Ann then pursued another matter that worried her. She wanted to find out if there were relatives who would miss Joyce when she didn't return to London. "Won't her parents mind her going away with the boss?"

"Her parents ...? Oh, I think she lost them years ago. I don't know much about her background." Eddie hesitated – he hadn't expected to be quizzed – then he continued, "but I think a year or two ago she took in an old invalid aunt – with a cat: now, apparently, the flat is full of cats! They don't know which are related and which are strays but Jo is too good-natured to upset the old dear by getting rid of them."

Ann managed to ask who was caring for the aunt now, and Eddie smiled. "A friend looks after the menagerie if Jo feels like getting away for a rest, or this time," he grinned, "to take some heavy exercise!" He grinned and went back to his reading.

Having met Jo, Ann was stunned to silence. A woman

like that would find no room in her life for an invalid aunt and her cats! It was such an elaborate lie – devised only to impress her with Jo's lack of desirability. Her eyes stung with suppressed tears. Unable to stay in the room with him any longer Ann rose shakily and hastened to the cloakroom where she could weep freely into the loudly gushing water as it swirled in the hand basin. Bathing her burning eyes with cold water did not entirely restore them to normal so she made a show of sniffling into a paper hanky as she went through to make the bedtime chocolate drinks.

"I think I'm developing a cold," she said placing his cup on the coffee table next to his chair where he had now settled to watch TV again. "If you don't mind I think I'll go to bed." Eddie said he'd be up in a minute but she just didn't care. She hoped that tonight she could lose herself in a deep sleep – God knew she was weary enough to sleep forever.

...Forever! Was this how people felt when they committed suicide: when they gave up? She pushed the thought from her... no way was she giving up! Strangely enough, her sudden decisiveness had a calming effect on her churning thoughts. She slept almost as soon as she lay down, her problems obscured... until tomorrow!

22 – Wednesday 22nd

The old woman picked her way carefully along the edge of the field looking for berries, mushrooms or bits of wood for her fire according to the season. No one ever bothered with her – she was just Little Mary as far as the village folk were concerned: a 'newcomer' who had turned up twenty years ago and never left. She did have another name but nobody remembered it. Only one person in Farlow really talked with her at all. Little Mary, just four and a half feet tall and plump enough to make her appear even shorter, was always sure of a welcome from the accommodating Mrs Todd.

Mary's disgustingly smelly old dog repelled most people, making them cross the road as the drab pair approached, but Alice kept several cats which generated enough odour of their own to make her uncaring of that which emanated from the elderly mongrel. The cats ignored Blacky who was definitely too wobbly and fat to have chased them anyway. He lay contentedly across Mary's feet – presumably, to ensure that she didn't leave without his knowing – and stirred only to eat whatever Mary left on her plate. He eagerly licked it clean when she held it out for him.

Successive cakes and biscuits were all shared in this manner and Alice, for all her personal sloppiness, always remembered to give Mary the cracked plate. Alice proudly regarded this as proof of her fastidiousness and would have mentioned it to any other visitor – as she often did to her husband, if any had actually called, but none ever did.

Alice Todd lived next to Little Mary along the track adjacent to Old Farm Road, just a bit nearer to the main highway than Mary's cottage, and as always on a Wednesday morning, she was having her once weekly stab at cleaning the house. If she cleaned up on Mondays it always needed doing again before the weekend; by confining her efforts to the middle of the week the house achieved an aura of mediocrity most of the time. She used to have the place quite presentable every Saturday, but the sight of her husband messing it all up with beer cans and newspapers as he sprawled in front of the television sport program upset her. Why bother, she decided.

Alice had seen Mary go over the field more than an hour earlier and knew that when the old woman returned she'd have an excuse to stop work. Mary usually shared a pot of tea with her. As she vacantly pushed the vacuum cleaner repeatedly over the same bit of carpet, gazing more at the television than the floor, Alice eventually became aware that it wasn't sucking. "Damn thing's full again!" she muttered. Impatiently, she switched it off with her foot and, as the button jabbed painfully through her worn slipper, she kicked it in disgust and wound up the cord. That would have to do for today – she'd empty it next time, she thought, as she pushed the whole thing into the under-stair cupboard. One of these days, she would have to sort the cupboard out; she could hardly force the stupid contraption into its usual space.

The kids – and her husband too for that matter, piled all their junk in there, out of sight, expecting her to keep it tidy – on top of all the other work she had to do! There was no justice and she shouldn't have to put up with it! Her husband, Elvis, was hardly ever at home – Mary often remarked on the fact, smirking when Alice protested, that he did stay in to watch the television sports, but his job in a garage workshop was stifling... he liked going out to enjoy fresh air.

Mary would have thought he'd be glad to stay in with his feet up but even on Sundays he took the two children out while Alice pottered alone at home in worn-out bedroom slippers and permanently stained aprons. Mary would have gone with them if it had been her husband and said so quite often, but Alice had the video recorder that Elvis bought when the boys were tiny and evenings out were curtailed. Alice's shopping list always had 'films' at the top.

As she limped painfully back to the kitchen, Alice made a half-hearted attempt to tidy up on the way. When the motley pile began to weigh heavily on her arm and she was wondering how best to dispose of it she caught sight of Mary coming. She hastily lifted a chair cushion and bundled everything underneath – newspapers, magazines, a sweater, two odd socks and a half-written letter. They joined all the other forgotten items, to be sorted later! Her duty done, Alice went happily to put the kettle on.

Mary was well aware that people went out of their way to avoid her but didn't care about the villagers... she had Alice. Alice kept her in fits – she always had all the local gossip. Nevertheless, today, Mary was the one with a fascinating story to tell. Mary was rarely able to contribute to their pool of information so today was a red-letter day. She was excited and breathing heavily when she arrived at the Todds' back door.

"Alice! Alice... come here quick and help me up the steps with it," she gasped, catching sight of her friend through the open window, already sitting at the kitchen table with her 'elevenses', the striped tom cat wrapped round her neck. "Look what I've found!"

The large plastic shopping bag soon lay between them on the floor. The name of the market colourfully stamped on its side was unfamiliar to both women: not a local one.

Mary clutched the top to conceal the contents, obviously determined to make the most of her strange tale before revealing the contents.

Her voice sank to a whisper... "I saw this woman, you see, quite early on... no I don't know what time it was, it doesn't matter... well, I think she must 'ave come from the station. The 8-o-clock to Oxford 'ad just pulled out. I never saw 'er before anyway, but I didn't take much interest then."

As Mary paused for breath, Alice pointed out that there was no Oxford train except Mondays and Fridays – not at 8-o-clock anyway ..."Not today! I'm talking about early Monday," Mary said irritably. "That's the point! It was Monday I saw 'er and take a look," she continued, "Look what I've found today."

From the bag, she pulled a raincoat and sou'wester, then a pair of overshoes and some black stockings with the feet cut off. Rolled into the stocking tops were two elastic bands. As Alice gazed, astonished, a pair of steel-rimmed spectacles joined the growing pile. "There," said Mary, "What do you think of that! These are what the woman had on – the first one I saw the other day!" Alice could not even guess at any reasonable explanation, but they were quite tatty old things.

"Where exactly did you find the bag?" she queried, interested in spite of herself... she had a feeling that Mary wasn't telling her everything.

"Under the 'edge near Old Farm Lane, near them two new 'ouses," Mary said... then in answer to Alice's next question, "Yes, I suppose it was quite near the dustbins." It suited Mary to go along with the idea that they had been discarded deliberately even though she had found a crumpled rail ticket in one of the pockets. The coat was far too long for her so she offered it to Alice, but she wanted to keep the hat and especially the shoes. She was secretly aware that there must be more to their abandonment than appeared on the surface, but if she told all she knew, she would get 'involved', and she didn't intend admitting to anything that would make her friend suspicious. Alice might even want her to go to the police!

It was not, she excused herself, that she knew much at all, but she had seen a second woman, all dressed up to the nines, walking away from the bushes where she had found the bag this morning. She was wearing pale blue and had walked up the lane not down to the road, which Mary thought was odd. People wearing such high heels usually went by car in the country; the only vehicle she had heard nearby for ages was that young Mrs Dean's – going out, about five minutes earlier. It was the other thing she'd found in the plastic bag that she was not going to tell anyone about – not even Alice. It was something that no one would ever consider throwing out with the garbage and she had never owned anything so beautiful. The small, blue leather case hidden under the clothes was quite heavy. Mary had peeped into it quickly and seen enough to excite her greed ...she'd definitely lose it if she told anyone of its existence!

She guiltily refused to consider at length the possible reasons why anyone should hide such a bag and not collect it. Common sense told her that only one woman was involved – up to no good; why else would she have arrived in disguise. She must have expected to return for her things within hours – at least on the same day! Even a little rain would have made the ditch soggy – and case might have been ruined. But whatever had happened to stop her, Mary didn't want to know! She was determined to keep that case. She had opened and rummaged in it under cover of the huge plastic bag and seen enough to know it was packed for an overnight stay somewhere; the lace nightie proved that much.

Now it was safely concealed outside under some old sacking – she'd pick it up later on her way home. Only her eyes would enjoy picking over its contents. Mary almost hugged herself with glee, and then became irked when she noticed that Alice, who had been groping in the bottom of the bag, was holding something else in her hand – something that had not been there before ... Damn, she silently cursed her own carelessness, it must have fallen from the case when she groped inside.

"What is it?" she said aloud. "Looks like a wallet."

Mary was furious with herself for not taking everything home to examine first, before showing anything to Alice... if it was stuffed with bank notes Alice would insist on reporting her find.

It was actually a photograph holder with several snaps inside and Mary felt suddenly apprehensive when she saw a young woman's face smiling up at her – she was sure from the red hair it was the girl she had neglected to mention!

"How strange," murmured Alice, "there's no way these could have been meant for the rubbish bin Mary. The cover itself looks like real leather. Perhaps you should take them back to the house and ask?"

Mary peered intently at the man, who appeared in most of the photographs and said with a laugh,

"Not likely! I've seen *him* often enough driving in and out and I know that's not 'is wife 'e's cuddling! That's why they were in the trash I expect – I'm 'aving nothing to do with them."

Alice examined the photographs much more closely, her interest quickening at the sudden revelation that her snooty neighbour's husband was two-timing her!

There were dates on the back of several. Two, which showed the pair hugging each other, were the earliest – taken years ago – they looked like party snaps.

The most recent of those with dates showed them alone together in what was clearly a bedroom. There he was, sprawled in an armchair with a drink, a protesting hand raised and, in another, the practically naked woman was making up her face at a fancy mirror. The armchair where he'd been photographed was reflected at the other side of the unmade bed! It didn't take much imagination to know what that dirty pair had been up to!

For a malicious moment, Alice pictured herself showing that stuck-up cow the sort of husband she had! Still, if his wife wasn't the one who threw the pictures away, why should she be the one to shop him? She knew she would never have the nerve anyway, but next time she saw her in the village she'd view her with different eyes. She would be unable to hide her scorn... fancy not knowing your husband was playing around; and for all her edge, not knowing how to keep her man happy!

On an impulse, feeling smug now in the role of an observer, wondering how long the man could cheat on his stupid wife without being found out, she threw the photographs into the ash bucket. It surprised her that Mary was not only un-protesting but she even looked pleased. The rest of the morning passed quickly as they speculated about the affair obviously going on under their noses and its possible outcome.

What had happened to the shabby woman Mary described, Alice wondered, and why had she carried the photographs with her? Blackmail! That's what! Perhaps she'd been going to blackmail him or just show his wife for spite. The mystery excited Alice but also unsettled her. The woman never returned to pick up her bag! Why?

Mary theorised that she had simply changed her mind – cold feet – and craftily added that she'd seen a similar figure later, returning to the station: hurrying in fact. Perhaps her train was due and there was no time to collect her old mackintosh – it wasn't raining anyway.

Alice felt a stab of disappointment tempered with a sense of relief perceiving the problem solved. She did not have to worry her head and take responsibility for deciding whether they really should report it to somebody after all.

With the fat black dog waddling unsteadily at her heels, Mary left eventually and walked slowly toward her own home until she was out of Alice's sight. She smirked, knowing that Alice was watching with no suspicion that they would soon double back to retrieve the real prize from its hiding place.

After waiting a few minutes, Mary risked going behind the Todds' shed, where she lifted the old tarpaulin and dragged the case out.

She cursed when, because it was heavy, a sharp stick tore the fine leather.

Clutching it, Mary felt no twinges of guilt over misleading her friend by her second 'sighting' of the stranger. If Alice suspected that the stranger might still be around, she would insist on finding her. The woman would then know who had taken her case and want it back! It was Mary's case now.

23 - Elvis

Alice sighed, rising reluctantly from her chair. The washing up bowl being already full she dumped the coffee cups on the draining board. Eyeing the mess balefully, she decided to leave it until later; Elvis wouldn't be home for hours! One of her favourite shows was coming on... she could probably get the kids to clear up anyway by bribing them with extra pocket money!

The children did indeed tidy up the kitchen but because they couldn't lift the heavy ash bucket outside to empty it, the photographs were the first thing Elvis noticed later that evening when he came home and washed his hands at the kitchen sink. He picked them out, dusted them off and looked with amazement at the two faces.

He knew the man. At least, he'd seen him in the local pub often enough - he lived over the field - and the girl was definitely not his wife! Well, well, well - what a turn up! What in hell's name were the snaps doing in his trashcan? How had they come into his house at all - let alone why had they been chucked away!

Tucking them in his hip pocket he strolled casually into the living room to find out, if he could hold Alice's attention away from the TV for long enough!

Alice was annoyed with herself for not having disposed of them properly but finally satisfied him that, even if somewhat bizarre, her explanation for their presence was reasonable.

Elvis asked why she had thrown the snaps away rather than return them and she insisted it was for the best. If the old woman had been trying to blackmail the fellow, she wanted no part of it; it was no skin off her nose if he was cheating on his wife; it was probably her own fault. Alice would not be the one to tell her!

Alice expressed her views so forcefully that Elvis, in consequence, didn't reveal that her feelings on the subject were far removed from his own.

As he slumped into his favourite chair, aware of the hard bulk pressing into his thigh, he tried to work out a way of using this evidence to his own advantage.

24 – Little helpers

Barely a mile away at "Near Acre" the dinner was looking after itself in the oven – a casserole had been the least trouble to prepare today. Ann had just finished ironing the last few shirts – they would be nicely aired ready for packing tomorrow, when she heard Eddie's key in the front door. It was a sound that normally gave her a surge of pleasure, but now her every nerve seemed stretched – dangling her over a cliff edge. What new revelations might be in store?

Could she withstand the urge to confront him with his lies? Would it be wiser? ...No: for three days respite it was not worth jeopardising their future. She had to be strong, even though exhausted – not only from the strain of going over the whole thing interminably in her aching head, but because of the additional physical work!

The children were playing upstairs. It had been raining during the afternoon ... muddy clothes, feet and floors couldn't be tolerated today. Judging by the volume of excited shrieks and the stampede across the landing, they had heard daddy too. "We've been very good daddy," Cathy shouted, almost falling downstairs in her enthusiasm. "Come and see what we've done!"

"Just wait a minute young lady. Give me time to say hello to mummy." He came and pecked Ann's cheek. "How did your day go love? Busy I expect! What are we eating? It certainly smells good!" He hesitated before allowing Cathy to drag him off. "When will it be ready? Have I time to check the car over?" On being assured he could take all the time he needed – nothing would spoil, he went up to change into his old slacks, pulled along by Cathy who had been hopping impatiently from foot to foot, swinging on his arm during the whole exchange.

"You will be really pleased with me and Christopher Daddy. We have been great big helps to mummy." Cathy could scarcely contain her glee. Ann followed with her arms full of laundry, amused but wondering what they had been up to. They'd certainly been quiet for the last hour, she recalled. Then to her consternation, she heard Christopher say,

"We've packed our things for the week-end, Daddy. We couldn't find the new cases so we used the one under the spare bed..."

"It had some things inside it," Cathy butted in, "but we tipped them out!"

Eddie laughed. "I'll bring your suitcases down from the loft before I go out," he promised, striding away along the landing to the spare room, telling the children how sorry he was but they would have to re-pack, or what would Nana say if their luggage was old and tatty – but yes they had been good to try.

Ann could visualise the scene as he walked into the room. Joyce's suit, underclothing, shoes and handbag, all on view! He would surely recognise some of it! Before she could think of any way of intervening, Eddie pushed the door open and stood gazing at the heap on the floor.

Ann gripped the banister rail to steady herself. His face as he turned to her was a picture of astonishment... she felt her face drain of colour. It was the end! She felt sick and avoided him by turning abruptly into the bathroom, locking the door to gain time to gather her wits. She must get the children out of the way if there was going to be a showdown. She could send them next door with a note. Jenny would not mind looking after them for an hour or two.

Five minutes later, all was quiet outside but as she braced herself to emerge, Eddie shouted and banged violently on the door. Ann trembled as she reached for the lock but his voice was surprisingly normal. "Hey come on, how much longer are you going to be in occupation?"

She turned the key and walked out to face him but he moved past her and shut her out, calling through the door, "You said you weren't collecting jumble this year! You grumbled so much last time about the sorting, pricing, fetching and carrying! You're just too soft. Why can't someone else do it for a change?"

Ann could scarcely believe it: a reprieve!

Pausing only to say she was not organising – just helping, she fled immediately to find a plastic dustbin liner to contain the "jumble"! Pushing them inside she viewed the clothes with new eyes. She had just been presented with a solution to the problem they presented.

Ann had completely forgotten the 'Bring and Buy' on Saturday …she'd had other things on her mind! It was to be held in town about ten miles away, in aid of the NSPCC. Dozens of people helped and others even brought things to sell while the sale was actually on, but if she could get there on Friday when the stalls were set up and chaos reigned, it would be even better.

She would take a few bits and pieces of her own to explain her presence and contrive somehow to leave an extra bag on the heap. The women who graded the items, separating jumble from 'Boutique' would not be astonished by the quality of the clothes; some very expensive people donated their off-casts every year. Ann had once bought a lovely dress there herself, which must originally have been sold for over £100 and it had cost her less than a tenth of that! Elated, having come to a decision about at least one thing, Ann put the bag away. Timing the trip could wait for now – it would depend how successful she was with her major disposal project!

25 - Unofficial Enquiries

Sarah and Clarrie, in Mapledurham, formed a plan of action. Alec had returned Sarah's call after only a few hours and been most helpful. Detective Inspector Algy Green was on the trail of information and he had been in touch with the Oxford branch. The constable, who took the original report about the missing girl, although he told Elaine it was far too early to start official inquiries, had in fact made a note of all she told him. When Elaine again rang the station at ten-o-clock he reported her friend's disappearance to his sergeant. The machinery rumbled into motion and soon afterwards, the local police in London contacted Joyce's office.

Algy followed up the lead immediately by ringing the firm's personnel officer. He verified that she had left on Friday for a short vacation and when he rang the porter where Joyce lived, he received confirmation that the man had seen her depart. The locals were trying to trace her movements at the railway station. There was nothing he could usefully do in that direction but, using his initiative, Algy had obtained the name and address of Joyce's boss.

Alec passed the information to Sarah, saying he was sure the man would be interviewed in London rather than at home, so if she wanted to tackle the mystery from the domestic angle she would be treading on nobody's toes!

Polly telephoned Elaine to tell her what was happening. She and Sarah intended going to Farlow tomorrow to make a few discreet inquiries. Clarinda was driving them, as she wanted to paint in the area anyway. A client who lived near Nettlebed had commissioned her to produce three local landscapes of her own choice. Farlow was local enough to fit the bill so she was hoping to find some good views – thus combining business with business!

While Clarrie worked, Sarah and Polly would do a bit of quiet sleuthing and even if it came to nothing they would have had the pleasure of a day out!

Before dinner, Clarrie loaded her stool, sketching easel and paints into her car. Polly had prepared a picnic for her; it could be put in the box tomorrow. She was all set for an early start.

While Polly put the finishing touches to the evening meal Sarah compiled a list of questions they might ask if they actually came across anyone likely to have the answers! Talking to the man's wife would be tricky. According to Joyce, she was her killer! Sarah decided to resort to subterfuge. She and Polly – two harmless sightseers – would knock on the door for information and hope she could pick up some 'vibes'. It was quite likely that Joyce herself would try taking a hand in things! It was a moot point if that would help or hinder!

Investigating a murder was chilling but really rather stimulating! Sarah was actually looking forward to tomorrow ...she prayed that she would be equal to the challenge.

26 – Neighbours

Jenny and Bill who had expected to visit the Tillers to play Mah Jong were instead spending the evening at home. Jenny was disappointed when Ann turned down her offer to play hostess, preferring instead to cancel their engagement for this week; she couldn't help feeling that Ann had more on her mind than merely preparing for the holiday weekend. When Jenny strolled round to talk to Ann during the morning to suggest changing the game's venue, quite amazingly, she found her long-lost scarf pin in the lane near their gate.

She was delighted. It was undamaged too, in spite of all the traffic that had driven in and out since it had fallen there. Jenny told Ann excitedly as soon as she answered the door but Ann hadn't seemed at all interested.

It was a long time since she'd worn it – easily nine months. In fact, she hadn't missed it immediately and never even told Bill it had gone. He might have been upset – it was one of the first gifts he ever gave her. He had given her so many presents of greater value since – she didn't wear it much, but she was pleased to have found it at last.

As Ann was obviously too preoccupied to share her delight she naturally asked if all was well and had been informed that of course it was! Jenny couldn't help wondering again about Eddie and the glamour-puss she had seen with him, but almost immediately dismissed the thought! Eddie was not the type.

Knowing of Ann's embarrassment over the socks last

year Jenny guessed she was on edge about sending the children to her in-laws and privately considered Ann's reaction stupidly defensive – out of all proportion to the cause.

Jenny realised that she was in no position to judge. Bill's mother was an amiable, easy-going woman who only dusted when it was un-avoidable and allowed clothes mending and ironing to mount up until, in her own words, it was worth while getting out the iron or the sewing machine! Jenny was confident that she took care of Bill much better than his own mother ever had.

Ann was still competing with Eddie's!

After ensuring that the roast in the oven was cooking to perfection, Jenny rounded up the twins and sent them upstairs to prepare for bed. They had been looking forward to sleeping-over with Cathy and Christopher so, as consolation, they were given a special treat for tea followed by a longer than usual bedtime story from mummy.

Reminding them which story she would be reading, Jenny gazed lovingly at their eager little faces and again reflected on how much she had to be grateful for. Poor Ann.

27 – Packing up

Wednesday evening at the Tillers' proceeded almost normally on the surface. Eddie had complete confidence that Ann would pack the essentials for his few days away. He selected a few magazines to include for bedtime reading, and then relaxed. After dinner, he sat to enjoy what would probably be his last opportunity to watch TV until his return on Sunday.

Re-packing the children's case under Christopher's critical eye took all the tact Ann could muster. Cathy was playing happily, before going to bed, but her big brother didn't trust their mummy to include everything they wanted and couldn't possibly go without. Ann was extremely patient with him, reminding him that clothes as well as toys would be needed and daddy wouldn't want to take lots of small bags and extra loose items. There was nothing he hated more at the end of a long journey than having to make countless trips to unload the car! At last, by getting him to acquiesce to the removal of Cathy's bulkier treasures, then pointing out to him how unfair it would be if Christopher did not give up some of his own, Ann succeeded in closing the lid. Unconvinced, worried that she might still not be satisfied, Christopher gazed at his mother suspiciously for a few moments, but when she picked up the case and took it downstairs he went happily to undress and brush his teeth.

28 – Art to Heart

After his wife had put the children to bed, he could hear her clattering as she cleared up in the kitchen before coming to join him for one of her favourite weekly comedies. He wondered if she had noticed how he kept staring at her, searching for any change in her demeanour. Surely there would be, if Joyce had spoken to her on the phone or, God forbid, actually visited the house! Sometimes she seemed to be giving him funny looks, but that could be merely a response to his own attitude. He was trying to appear normal and probably failing; if only he could call it a day and go to bed … God, what a day it had been, he sighed. He yearned to be alone to sort out his thoughts. The office had ticked over adequately, Wendy was coping quite well really, but still Joyce had not been in touch. She probably wouldn't now, he decided.

She would keep him on tenterhooks until next week. Bitch!

Now there was even more to worry about. A chap he hardly knew – Elvis Todd, who lived over the field somewhere, had waylaid him in the lane, as he turned off the main road. Without any preamble, Todd produced a batch of photographs, waved them under his nose claiming that a friend of his wife had found them. "She was going to throw them away but I recognised you," he said with a sly wink. "I considered returning them to your wife – pity to lose such good pictures; they cost a bomb these days don't they?"

There was no way he could misinterpret Todd's

sickening leer and the man was right …these particular photographs would certainly cost him a bomb; he was being blackmailed! At first, he had kept his head, maintaining coolly that his wife would not be interested in snaps of an old friend; they had no value to him either so Todd could do what he liked with them, but even as he said it his blood ran cold at the thought that his words might be acted upon. If his wife saw them, she would never understand … the time for forgiving had long passed.

To his surprise, Todd put the pictures back into his pocket and shrugged, "Well, if that's the case and they are part of your past, I might as well do as you say and throw them in the bin! …No sense in ruining the little woman's peace of mind is there?" Turning away, he started walking towards his old station wagon, which was parked, on the grass verge. Then he hesitated and, looking back, added, "By the way, I've heard that you are an art-lover …bit of a collector in fact. Come and look at some of my work, here in the car."

As he gazed at Todd's pictures, his heart sank. They were just daubs. What was he supposed to say? He did not have to wonder for long.

With a sly smirk on his face, Todd was feeding him the lines he expected to hear. "You can only be impressed by them, I'm sure," the wretched man was saying … "a genuine 'Primitive', I think that's what people would call me. I can only let you have these two at the moment, if you actually do want to buy them that is, but I can produce two or three a month. They would be an excellent investment for your future … only a hundred quid each! Cheap at the price, don't you agree?"

He was trapped and they both knew it. With the purchase of the paintings, he couldn't cry 'blackmail' and was confirming that he couldn't risk the photographs being taken to his house in his absence! He tried to put off the purchase by claiming to be out of cash but Todd said that was no barrier to doing business – what impoverished artist would ever turn down the chance to sell a pair of paintings, he laughed, rather than accept a cheque!

As the now not so poor painter drove away with a friendly wave, he flung the canvases into the boot of his own car and threw a travelling rug over them. If he had anything to do with it they would never see the light of day again. If they did he'd have a hard time explaining what merit he had seen in them, and it appeared he would have to buy more of the damned things to preserve his way of life.

What a prize idiot he had been to put at risk all he loved most in the world, for an association he could easily have done without – which hadn't really been that much pleasure, tarnished as it was by secrecy and guilt. He didn't deny being flattered by Joyce's devotion and as she seemed satisfied with the small part of his time he spent with her, he allowed the affair to drift on, in spite of his deep feelings of shame.

Uppermost in his mind now though were the photographs – found in the village presumably. Joyce must have been in Farlow this week after all!

Perhaps she was still around, waiting to pounce! Had she deliberately 'lost' them knowing he would be recognised and his hand forced? He could believe almost anything of her now, but if that was her little scheme, it had come unstuck. She had most likely banked on their being handed to his wife ... when she learned that they were being used to squeeze money out of him she'd be sorry!

Of course, to tell her what he thought of her and her crazy scheme he would first have to find her, which was more or less where his thoughts had been when he left the office! Where the hell was she?

29 – A Sad Affair

When Ann had settled the children and tidied up she took the coffee to the sitting room where much to her annoyance, Eddie had already fallen asleep in front of the television. Perhaps she should bide her time – allowing him to go into his usual cycle of viewing and dozing as his interest waxed and waned – but her crying need to talk about Joyce would not permit her. She sat watching him with mounting frustration. Her vivid imagination ran riot, uncontrolled, placing him with Joyce in the most intimate of situations...

Joyce reclined alluringly on cream satin sheets in a deep blue silk nightgown – which matched the lingerie upstairs! Thrown carelessly on a white fur-topped dressing stool was a matching negligee ... the soft bedside light gleamed on her dainty high heeled, deep blue, silk slippers as she provocatively pushed them off with her slim toes ... A man leaned over her lovingly – hungrily. Eddie! ...

Ann shook her head trying to lose the tormenting images of Eddie and Joyce together, but they persisted in coming between her and the flashing screen, insinuating themselves like a tongue exploring an aching tooth.

Somehow, she had to find a trigger to start him talking: had to convince herself that he really loved her and not his mistress.

The program ended and the contrasting volume of the first advertisement was so loud that Eddie woke up and reached for his coffee. Before the news came on, Ann turned the volume down and tried to open a conversation but could not immediately blurt out the question she'd formed before Eddie forestalled her.

As she was swallowing and clearing her throat, he said, "When are you taking the jumble to the hall?"

"Friday afternoon," she croaked.

"Well, be careful driving. The bank holiday crowds will be setting out, adding to the usual chaos," he advised. By the time the happy thought sank in fully, that he apparently cared about her safety and Ann recovered from her astonishment, the news was on and he pressed his remote control to increase the volume again. While the reader's voice droned on, Ann rehearsed the casual question that she hoped would spark a reaction. No, she corrected herself – she hoped Eddie would not react at all! The seemingly innocent topic had come to her in a flash and she eagerly waited for an interval.

Short film clips replaced the news desk – scenes from all over the world were interspersed by studio interviews... would it never end! Back at the desk, the reader introduced the sporting commentator. Eddie wasn't a fan of any sport in particular but she held her patience ...then, at last, the advertisements came on again and he lowered the sound himself. This was her chance.

Ann said as brightly as she could, "Do you remember asking what I would like for my birthday?"

"Yes of course," Eddie confirmed, looking expectant. "If, for once, you have a clear idea what you want, it will be a weight off my mind... What is it then?"

"I would like something personal – frivolous – a teddy perhaps!" Ann said, taking the plunge. She then added, "Silk ...lace – deep blue!" She searched his face keenly for any change of expression but he merely appeared surprised and remarked in an amused tone,

"Well if that is what you've set your little heart on, fine. I can't imagine why – you have already caught me! Unless you are setting your cap at some other man!" He looked slightly worried and continued. "Can you tell me if you have seen exactly what you are hoping for? Heaven only knows where I'm likely to fill that order. Is the colour really important? I suspect black would be a whole lot easier! Anyway, I'll do my best."

Ann was torn between pleasure, that blue underwear held no significance for him, and annoyance at the prospect of being landed with a present she would be loath to wear – with no-one but herself to blame too! She forced herself to laugh. "Don't worry – I was only joking. I only wondered if perhaps I was becoming a bit dull. I thought you might like a change of image." Eddie rose immediately to put his arms round her.

"Don't you ever dare change," he said quietly, "I love you just as you are. Come on," he smiled, "bed-time. Time to get into your old red flannelette!"

Ann's heart was lighter as she went upstairs. Eddie's words and affectionate teasing calmed her. Whatever she had still to endure, to hold him, was undoubtedly worth it. She was more than ever convinced that whatever Joyce had felt about Eddie – there was no way he could have regarded her in the same light. Poor sick girl – in retrospect Ann almost pitied her.

Lying awake in the darkness, she formed a plan of action for tomorrow. It would go into operation as soon as the family left. No more time would be lost in self-reproach or fretting about the future. She was now committed and completely under control! For the first time since Sunday, she slept soundly through the whole, long night.

30 – Alice

Alice Todd eventually tore herself away from yet another of her daily 'soaps' – it would have been difficult to name anything which she didn't consider worth watching – and went to chase the children to bed. They didn't share their mother's addiction to 'the box'. She supposed, with a deep sigh that, even though it was nearly dark, they were most likely running wild again in the field at the back, kicking a stupid football: getting filthy! Why couldn't she have had girls instead of boys? Alice had to admit they were quite good about helping around the house, even though they were barely nine and seven years old, but she wouldn't have to bribe girls – it would be part of their training!

Elvis had been out of the house for hours; she had imagined he was playing with his sons, re-enacting last Saturday's Match of the Day, but he wasn't with them after all. He probably went off to the village for a drink with his mates! She was puzzled by his absence but didn't have much time to ponder over it – the car suddenly swung under the lean-to shelter at the side of the house. Knowing that if he had been to the pub he would have returned much later, Alice waited before calling the boys, curious to know what he'd been up to. Elvis was annoyed to see her standing there when he came back from what he regarded smugly as his successful mission. He had not expected to be missed and wouldn't have been if he could have joined the boys again before Alice's program ended! Before she could start an interrogation, he waved the cheque at her – taking care that it was not close enough for her to read the amount.

"I've just sold a couple of my old oil paintings," he announced. "Seeing that bloke in the photos reminded me that we got talking in the local a couple of weeks ago ...he was interested in seeing some of my stuff so I decided to strike while the iron was hot." He stuffed the cheque in his wallet and to Alice's astonishment took out four fivers. "Here you are kiddo, buy yourself something," he said. "My new patron wants first chance of everything I paint from now on!"

Alice was beside herself with pride and excitement. She had never taken Elvis's interest in art seriously; in fact, she had never liked anything he produced. Every picture looked messy and she privately thought she had seen better work on the infant school walls! It was ages since he had actually produced anything. When they first came to the village after they were married, he had put two oil paintings into a local exhibition, and even at only £5 each nobody wanted them. Thoroughly deflated, he hadn't painted anything since ...or even mentioned them. They must be the two he had just sold, she realised, obviously for much more than the twenty he had given her! Clutching the notes as she stood gazing after him – he had volunteered to get the boys organised for bed – Alice dreamed of all that this could mean to them. It was only a beginning but perhaps other people would now want paintings by Elvis Todd! Perhaps he would be famous one day and they would be rich... She could hardly wait to tell little Mary.

31 - Oxford

In Oxford, Elaine huddled in an armchair, hugging her slender waist as if her ribs hurt, but it was her head that ached. She was thoroughly upset by the unexplained disappearance of Joyce and worrying about her wedding arrangements. She listened ruefully as Dan tried to convince her that there was nothing else she could do. They had told the police, in fact his friend Terry promised to keep him informed of any progress they made in the search for Joyce.

So far, her movements had been traced to the station where she definitely purchased a ticket and was seen heading for the departure platform about fifteen minutes before the Oxford train left; had she boarded it she should have arrived mid-morning. They figured she either broke her journey somewhere en-route, intending to catch a train later to arrive at the time she had given Elaine, or had other business to conduct in Oxford before meeting her at the station in the afternoon.

Dan looked anxiously into Elaine's wide, blue eyes and her gaze met his steadily. She wanted to believe that there was a simple explanation and could almost convince herself that Joyce was playing some weird practical joke on them. Many times, as they grew up together she had detected a deep, almost spiteful side to the girl's sense of humour but it had never been turned on herself ...she was Joyce's best friend: perhaps her only friend! Anyway, Dan was right. She could do nothing other than give the police a few names and telephone numbers and hope for the best. She owed it to Dan now to devote herself entirely to the wedding and to entertaining their many other friends and family.

Elaine's parents were insisting on being responsible for all the traditional expenses that fell to the Bride's parents although her father had now retired from business and was not wealthy. For their sakes too, she must put Joyce completely from her mind and make their sacrifice worthwhile ...but she couldn't help speculating. Would Joyce make a dramatic entrance at the church, or had she made a permanent exit? If it were a practical joke Elaine vowed never speak to her again! Either way, Joyce was probably part of her past. Elaine studied the guest list, crossing off those to whom she had already written in thanks for the gifts received. Momentarily, her eyes rested on Mrs Gertrude Bailey – Aunt Polly, and she wondered about Polly's friend, Sarah Grey.

Dan really seemed to think the woman could tell them where Joyce was and whether she was alive and well... or not! Personally, she considered talking to the dead not only impossible but indicative of a degree of derangement in those who thought they could! She had not told Dan how she felt. In fact, she was slightly apprehensive to think their views might be strongly opposed on the subject. Neither of them attended church regularly but at least they were christened in the same religion and that had seemed enough. There had never been any reason to discuss it in depth but in every other way Elaine regarded Dan as strong-minded, reliable: more likely than not to be of sound judgement. Now, a twinge of doubt assailed her. His readiness to believe in ESP and the supernatural made him appear weaker – even gullible!

As if reading her thoughts Dan said, "Anyway, as well as launching a police search, we are even seeking help from Beyond The Veil!" Scrambling to his feet, he flung his arm wide with a flamboyant gesture, raised his chin and avowed, "Fear not sweet damsel, we shall leave no grave unturned, 'til the wench be found! ..." The slight tension was broken as they collapsed, laughing hysterically: a natural reaction after their morbid thoughts. Elaine felt much more buoyant by the time she went to bed – there was still time for Joyce to appear. Her faith in Dan was completely restored. He obviously had an open mind about the paranormal and she would try to maintain one herself – especially when they called in to meet Mrs Grey on Sunday.

32 – Empathy?

Sarah and Clarrie were again sharing the same sleeping quarters. Sarah was not apprehensive on her own behalf but Clarinda's experience of the paranormal was limited and of only recent origin. She had sufficient faith to know too that her daughter's own spirit guides would protect her but perhaps not before she had been subjected to a discomforting scare. There are, however, some things from which even the most caring mother cannot protect a girl!

Waking – or thinking she was awake – Clarrie was terrified to find herself in dense blackness. She felt an intense, penetrating cold and her limbs were inflexible. With will power and concentration, she succeeded in moving an arm. She clutched her stomach. To her surprise, it was bare and icy ... and running her hand up her body she found she was naked! Even more alarming – the body was not her own! She screamed and was appalled when no sound came! Was it real or a nightmare? She was at least rational enough to question her state of mind and the early years of conditioning by her mother proved their worth. Clarinda automatically resorted to prayer and soon began to feel warmer. The studio, now faintly visible in the moonlight was comfortingly familiar and she trembled with relief to be out of her insensate condition. Sarah was sitting up, watching. The faint sound of Clarrie praying had woken her. "I knew you must be experiencing something frightful," Sarah said, "so I prayed with you. You appeared to be coping with it well enough on your own so I made no attempt to interfere."

Clarrie, still numb with shock, said if it ever happened again she hoped anyone witnessing her plight would be far less reluctant to wake her up! Sarah shook her head with a slightly apologetic smile. "It was weird – you seemed to be speaking normally but the sound was muffled. It was as if you were buried under the quilt, but I could see your face was uncovered. Your voice gradually increased in clarity until you finally came out of it. Tell me what happened"

Knowing that neither of them would get back to sleep until she described her experience fully, Clarrie gratefully discussed the import of her dream. Sarah was fascinated. Her own ability was principally in the areas of clairvoyance and psychometry; she was rarely haunted by bad or prophetic nightmares. She thought it likely that Joyce had managed to take Clarinda over, when her guard was weakened by sleep. It followed from this that Joyce's body, wherever it lay, was probably in a dark cold place ...this was Joyce's sadistic way of telling them! How could she expect any sympathy! Had she been as vicious in life? Sarah wondered. What a devious, unpleasant person! She seemed more likely to be the murderer than the victim! Voicing her thoughts gave them a ring of credibility ...and they both fell asleep eventually with many more questions on their minds than were written on Sarah's list.

33 – Sleepless

He lay listening to her breathing. It was slow and steady ... surely, he could risk leaving her?

He moved to the edge of the bed but froze as she stirred and turned over.

She went quieter ...might even be partially awake: better not to risk getting up after all.

It was hours before he could be certain that his wife was in deep slumber and he crept out to the garage. It hadn't been in the least difficult staying alert himself.

With Joyce's absence still only partially explained and her silence even more disturbing, he had little hope of relaxing anyway.

The arrival of that blackguard, Todd, sent his brain into another spinning cycle of speculation.

Would the novelty of selling his paintings last long?

Even if it did, there were apparently two other local people who had also seen the snaps: Todd's wife and her friend!

Would they keep his secret too?

...It seemed unlikely!

It was risky, sneaking out in the small hours but he wanted to remove the two pictures from the trunk of the car.

He could never explain why he had paid money for paintings vastly inferior to those the children could produce; he put them out of sight in the tool shed.

He would burn them one day, when no one was around to comment.

Having succeeded in creeping upstairs and returning to bed without disturbing anyone, he lay quietly, thinking again about Joyce. If she had intended to occupy all his waking hours she was succeeding and he'd never forgive her for the torment and aggravation he was suffering.

What new catastrophe would today bring he wondered – surely things couldn't get much worse!

34 – Thursday 23rd

Cathy and Christopher both woke much earlier than usual. It was a miracle that the children had slept at all. They were so excited. To think that Ann had actually hoped they could all enjoy an extra lie-in this morning as there was no need to rush for school or work. Determined to ignore them – she shut her eyes tightly shut and tried to doze off for an extra half hour. There was nothing much left to do before the family departed.

Sensing she was awake, Eddie groaned heavily and climbed out of bed. "Come on my love, better get moving," he said. "I'm escaping before the invasion of the body bouncers! I'd like to load the car before breakfast, and then I can enjoy eating and a leisurely cup of coffee. You know I hate rushing but I won't leave until after nine anyway, I want to ring the office. There are a couple of messages I want to leave in case Jo telephones later. She said she would keep in touch in case her replacement needs advice in my absence."

The desire to sleep vanished... Ann climbed out of bed and left the room. She suddenly could not bear to look at him or let him see the expression of pain and disgust that she knew must be evident on her face. The measure of confidence she had gained the previous night evaporated. If he had to ring, why not do it later from a phone booth? Why bring up that detestable female's name in the presence of the wife he professed to love, but had been deceiving so despicably for so long!

It was flaunting his infidelity in her face – and yet her

heart ached, she loved him so much. Organising breakfast gave her something to occupy her mind while Eddie first loaded the car, and then went to change and shower.

The enormity of the task ahead had not been entirely out of her thoughts for days but by convincing herself there was nothing she could do until the family left, she had avoided dwelling on it. Now the dreaded day had arrived at last and Ann was shaking and jittery. An icy, hollow sensation in her stomach was spreading – rising to her throat – almost making her teeth chatter. She sat and clutched herself – lowered her head to her knees to banish the wave of nausea which gripped her.

Ann decided to abandon her previous plans for an early start... As soon as they went she would draw the blinds and go back to bed. If she could achieve a few hours' sleep, it would be the best preparation she could have, for what might be an all-night driving job. Even if only resting physically, it would be better than driving around feeling impotent. She could hardly dispose of a dead body in broad daylight!

She felt weak: helpless – hopelessly inadequate... Why must he speak with Joyce? Ann decided to eavesdrop when Eddie called his office. Her former calm slowly returned and as for sleeping ...No! It would be far more sensible to keep to her resolve – driving out to take stock of likely disposal spots. She could sleep after Eddie rang as he had promised, around six p.m. She would set the alarm for two in the morning – take the body to the car and drive it away. Simple! On no account would she be deflected again.

Dealing quickly with the children's breakfast, Ann firmly insisted that they ate properly, in spite of their protestations. Their excitement was natural but Ann couldn't help a stab of silly resentment when it was evident that leaving her behind did not appear to worry them in the slightest!

While Ann settled the usual argument about which side of the car Cathy would occupy – she always wanted the one claimed first by Christopher, Eddie made his call and she re-entered the kitchen in time to hear him say, "Yes, you are right, it is a bit early to expect anyone on leave to be ringing the office. I know she enjoys sleeping late when she can! No problems? Good ...you have my holiday number if it's needed. Yes, of course ...Thanks."

Within moments of his inquiries about his beloved Joyce, he was hugging her and kissing her 'Good-bye'. Ann could have screamed. Fortunately, Eddie took it for granted that she was bound to look upset, but he was sure she would soon recover and enjoy doing her own thing for a few days.

As Eddie turned the car, Mr Jones the postman cycled up to the box, saw him and handed it over instead. Ann watched from the front door as her husband flipped through the small bundle. He then reversed and gave it all to her.

"Just a couple of things for me to deal with when I get back: nothing urgent. I thought the picture postcard might be from Jo, but it's for the kids," he said. "Save it until they come home, we have enough rubbish in the car already!"

Ann stood forlornly as the car carried them away. Even Eddie's departing thoughts were with his mistress, not her.

35 – Another Family Outing

An hour or two earlier the Dean family next door had also been in a state of excitement. Bill, knowing how upset Matthew and Sally were about not spending last night with their friends, especially as Chris and Cathy were going away today, had surprised them by announcing a special treat. Jenny was equally amazed but happy to go along with the idea. After all, if Bill thought it was in order for them to miss a day at school, she was more than ready also to enjoy a visit to the zoo!

Monday was a Bank holiday and the village school was celebrating Founder's Day tomorrow – making it a good long break. Jenny regretted that they had not thought of going away themselves; a trip up to town would make up for the oversight. Of course Bill would be working, but he promised to take a long lunch with them and finish on time for once, so that the twins would not be too late returning. It would be a long day for them; they had to leave almost immediately although barely awake, but they were ecstatic. It was too early to telephone Ann, as Eddie didn't have to get up for work, so Jenny scribbled a quick note for her and dropped it into the Tillers' box on the way out; Ann would find it with the morning post later and not have to wonder at Jenny's unexpected absence from home.

36 – A Nice Day Out

In Mapledurham about ten miles away, another car was also setting out from home. At the junction with the main road, Clarrie waited to turn left towards Wallingford. The heaviest traffic was naturally going the opposite way, to Reading, at this time in the morning. Her mother sat beside her but turned constantly to chat with Polly who occupied a rear seat. Sarah was always reluctant to engage in conversation with anyone driving – knowing how distracting she would find it herself; the roads were inordinately busy these days, demanding a driver's full attention.

They had arranged to split up immediately on arriving in Farlow. Clarrie would drop the others in the middle of the village after a suitable pick-up spot had been selected. Polly and Sarah both wore stout walking shoes and were prepared to spend most of the day on their feet but Clarrie wanted to be sure they had somewhere to sit if she were delayed. They left the busy main road as soon as possible – travelling along country lanes was more pleasant – and were soon within a few miles of the village. It came in sight as they emerged from an avenue of trees. Clarrie pulled into a lay-by and stood looking down the hillside.

Farlow was spread below them like a colourful map. In the distance, a main feeder road poured traffic towards the M.40, and Farlow Hollow station – on a small branch line, was about half a mile from the heart of things: the car park adjacent to the locomotive sheds was larger than the station itself and more than half full.

Only one road, each end of it joined to the distant artery, looped to reach both village and station and, in turn, fed traffic to smaller lanes that fringed it like clustered veins wherever houses grouped together. From her lofty viewpoint, Clarrie appreciated that modernisation had not spoiled Farlow. There were no blocks of flats or slab-sided warehouses. The weathered houses looked quite picturesque from this distance and a church tower rose above the trees. She was assessing the view as an artist in search of a subject and was well satisfied. They had already crossed one river-bridge. Another lay ahead and Clarrie saw the sparkle of a stream, which leaked away from the main tributary to a pond over on her left. Smoke rose from what must be a tip, between the pond and the railway line. She could use artists' license and leave that out!

In the area immediately below the lay-by, were open fields separated by small lanes that were dotted with houses. The village was farther over to her right. It was smaller than she had expected and she wondered if her mother and Polly would find enough there to occupy them for a whole day.

Climbing back into the driving seat, Clarrie expressed her concern but also said that the view was good; if they did decide to stay for a few hours she could come back to paint it.

The side road they were on curved down to skirt the pond and they turned right to the village a few yards from the entrance to the station car park. With the square, colourless railway building behind them, they were all impressed by the surroundings.

On this side, anyway, there were no new estates – it was all delightfully rural.

Small areas of woodland broke up the flatness to the east and created interesting shadows across the grey road.

Where the road started to veer left on its way back to larger pockets of civilisation, a signpost pointed right and, following it, they were soon in Farlow Main Street.

In spite of being a small place, there seemed to be a dozen or so shops and even some of the old terraced houses displayed goods for sale in converted drawing room windows. It was quaint; Sarah and Polly didn't doubt that they could be happy there for the whole day.

"Look over there, Clarinda," Sarah pointed out, "opposite that little filling station is a small public house. We'll have lunch there if you feel like joining us around one-o-clock. What do you think, dear?"

"And we passed a bus shelter a little way back – we could wait there to be picked up later," volunteered Polly happily, "then if it rains, which I don't think it will, you won't have to worry about us."

"If it does rain," said Clarrie, "I shall be worrying about me! I'll be only too glad to join you in the shelter!" She pulled in, allowing them both to alight and added, "Don't expect me at lunch though, because I'm sure my picnic will be adequate and I would rather not waste time in the pub. I'll pick you up at six – OK?"

Because they were virtually at the beginning of the shopping stretch, Sarah and Polly decided to walk down one side and back on the other without being distracted, no matter how interesting it might seem across the road. Polly wondered if they should separate and compare notes from time to time but Sarah felt it would make them more conspicuous – they would be more obviously making enquiries rather than sightseeing!

The first shop in the row was a greengrocer and there was no way they intended buying anything weighty so early in the day. Sarah was reluctant to take up the owner's time in idle conversation but Polly noticed that there were dozens of postcards pinned to a small notice board inside.

"Come on," she said, opening the door, "I have an idea." The man who greeted them assured Polly that she could indeed put a notice up – it was 50p a fortnight!

He handed her a sheet of paper and a pen and while Polly wrote, he chatted with Sarah. He didn't have many strangers in and was curious to know whether they were newcomers or just visiting.

Sarah told him that a young friend had been in the village less than a week ago and told them how unspoiled it was – they were looking around while her daughter, an artist, was painting up on the hill. The greengrocer took the notice from Polly and glanced at it. "Oh – your friend lost her dog then?" he commented. "What a shame! Poodle, was it? I haven't seen anyone with a poodle around here!" Trying not to look surprised and avoiding Polly's gaze, Sarah improvised,

"It ran off before she reached the village! She walked from the station. Perhaps you saw her, even if you didn't see the dog?" She went on to give the description of Joyce that the porter had supplied but it was obvious the greengrocer had not seen her either. As they walked away, they both had a fit of the giggles. Sarah declared it was a stroke of genius, because now they had an excuse for stopping everybody in sight! Polly had put their telephone number on the notice to make it look legitimate but they were unlikely to be inundated with calls!

They went into a post office to buy stamps, a bookstore, where Polly bought a thin paperback (handbag sized), a wine shop, where they merely picked up a price list and a wool-shop where Sarah bought a crochet hook. She didn't crochet but knitting needles would have been more awkward to carry. They wandered around several larger shops where they did not feel so obligated to purchase anything at all, before crossing over the road to return.

On the stroll back, they thoroughly enjoyed browsing in two antique shops where they must be used to people looking without buying, and a few other establishments where they picked up things like torch batteries, scouring pads, a new toothbrush and some insoles. It was almost like a game in itself, buying the smallest items they could find which were also useful. When Sarah mentioned this, Polly reminded her of the crochet hook whereupon Sarah insisted that she did intend to learn; it was something she had always meant to do!

Everywhere, they used the lost dog and young friend story but no one had seen Joyce. Sarah wasn't really surprised. She merely wanted to eliminate the village as a possible source of information before going to the home of Joyce's boss. She had scheduled that pleasure for after lunch. They were almost back at the small hotel where they would be eating when they reached, and entered, Hoskins' Butchery and General Store.

As soon as she went inside Sarah saw her... Joyce!

She was standing aggressively, arms akimbo, in the gloom at the back of the shop. Mrs Hoskins was speaking to them and Polly answered but Sarah could only hear the irate voice of Joyce demanding to know why they were wasting time!

"What the hell are you doing here? ...Would I be caught dead shopping in a place like this?" Sarah could not help herself – she burst out laughing! Mrs Hoskins and Polly stopped talking, wondering at her outburst and Sarah apologised quickly. She left the shop and waited outside. When Polly joined her, Sarah informed her immediately that they had received their instructions... no more shopping!

As soon as they had finished lunch, they would ask the proprietor for directions and go to the house. Sarah still had no idea what they would say to the man's wife but inspiration might come, as it had to Polly when she invented the poodle.

Up on the hill Clarrie was making good progress with her work. There were few houses in the foreground of the picture. Only two older dwellings were in the left-hand lane, a few hundred yards apart, and a pair of more modern properties a field away, towards the centre of her view. They were quite close together and with the outbuildings and tall trees, they made an interesting group. She had not seen much activity down there – although a car drove away from one of the newer houses in mid-morning.

The older cottages on the left were undeniably scruffy – no real gardens or even many trees. As she watched, an old woman came out of the smaller one and walked to the other. A fat, black dog waddled slowly behind her. Something about the pair caught Clarrie's interest and she decided to include them in her painting... but she wouldn't put them where they actually were; she needed an interesting detail at the edge of the field. Yes – nearer to the new houses, just this side of the hedge... It made all the difference in the world to the composition.

The day was going well, so far, for everyone.

37 – Little Mary

Little Mary shadowed as ever by Blacky waddling slowly behind her, walked up the weedy track to the Todds' back door. She had dabbed perfume behind her ears and on her wrists. She knew from somewhere that it was better rubbed on the wrists, but didn't know why... it was probably just something the maker made up – so that people would use more. The scent bottle was very small so it wouldn't last long anyway! After today, she would use it only on special occasions.

Actually, Mary's special occasions were lamentably few... not like that woman who abandoned it with the case she thought, but you never knew. She might be invited to the boys' birthday parties like last year. She had helped Alice with the food and clearing up, but it was still special, wasn't it? Or – she might get an invitation to the Palace Garden Party! Mary found this thought hilarious, and was smiling broadly when Alice opened the door and let her into the steamy kitchen.

Alice had boiled the kettle several times while waiting impatiently for Mary to arrive – a new packet of chocolate biscuits with two plates stood ready on the table and tea-bags were in the pot waiting to be scalded. Mary was amazed. Sometimes it took Alice almost an hour to get organised when she called in, even though it was a daily event! Something was obviously up! More than tea was brewing for sure. Mary did not have to contain her curiosity for long. Alice was bursting to announce Elvis's artistic triumph, which she airily declared, had not really surprised her.

She'd always had faith in him and now it seemed that he was going to be able to sell his work as fast as he could produce it. Alice showed Mary the money that Elvis had given her for herself: not for housekeeping ... what did Mary think of that!

What Mary thought of that would not bear repeating. She certainly couldn't tell Alice, who was so simple and trusting ... and so stupid! As soon as she learned the name of the 'art expert' who had suddenly discovered Elvis's talent, she knew what had happened. That crafty swine had seen the photographs – her photographs – which she would never have used herself, to squeeze money out of the man. She was no low-down criminal – she had her principles and wouldn't resort to nastiness like that ...but Mary bitterly resented the fact that Elvis was making a profit out of her discovery.

It was unfair and she wasn't going to let him get away with it!

If she couldn't find any other way of stopping him, she would go and tell the poor man's wife about his goings on! But that was impossible! She couldn't: everything would have to come out – her seeing the woman in blue. She would have to give back the case and everything! It was out of the question – disastrous for her too. Although she could perhaps tell his wife over the telephone – just ring up without giving a name! Anyway, Mary wasn't letting Elvis Todd get rich that way when she couldn't. She would think of something!

Alice embarked on another topic and Mary's attention was suddenly caught by what she was saying. "What did you say? ...What was that about strangers?" she asked. Her voice was so sharp that Alice momentarily lost track. She went back to the beginning...

"I nipped into the village on my bike earlier and met two women I'd never seen before. Very pearls and tweedy, the thin one was; you could see the other a mile off in her bright orange dress. Nobody her size should wear orange! I always avoid bright colours myself ...dark stripes are much more flattering and... "

"For goodness sake!" Mary burst out. "What were they doing?"

"They'd lost something: or a friend had lost something. I can't remember what. They were talking about it in Hoskins' grocery; I was already there when they came in."

"Run out of cigs again 'ad you!" Mary couldn't help having a sly dig ...filthy habit, smoking, she sniffed.

"I thought you wanted to know about the two women, not my shopping," Alice retorted irritably.

"Of course I do." Mary hastened to assure her. She was in fact extremely anxious to know what the women were looking for – it might be the blue case. "Go on then..."

"Well, the smart one was more than a bit weird. I didn't think she'd seen me 'cause I was asking Mr Hoskins about some meat scraps for the cat and was at the back of the shop but she suddenly seemed to glare right at me and set off laughing for no reason at all! Then she went straight out again!"

Alice sensed Mary's breathless interest and paused, deliberately spinning out her tale, to light a cigarette. "The other," she eventually continued, puffing out a cloud of smoke, "asked if a woman they knew had called in while she was visiting the village a few days ago."

Mary was gripped. "Did they describe what was she wearing?"

"Oh, don't worry, I was only teasing – it wasn't your old tramp! It was a smart young piece in a blue suit and hat, blue gloves and everything ...must have caused a bit of a stir in Farlow! I wish I'd seen her – p'rhaps there's a reward!"

Mary wondered about that too, having actually seen the woman, but she still didn't tell Alice. She had to be sure first that it was worth admitting it. "Did they say how anyone could get in touch?" she asked.

"I think they left a card on the board at the greengrocer's but why are you so interested anyway?"

Mary hastily changed the subject. She made up her mind to take one of her very rare strolls into the village this afternoon... she could do with a few carrots and some mince – yes, she'd pull up a few spuds and have a nice stew for dinner tomorrow. It was a long time since she had been so excited about preparing a meal.

38 – An Unexpected Encounter

After her picnic lunch, Clarrie removed from her easel the canvas on which she had worked all morning and replaced it with a new one. The light was very different now from when she had arrived. The height of the sun produced shorter shadows, revealing other interesting possibilities for her to paint. Her second scene would be less dramatic, but brighter. The air seemed to shimmer as warmth rose from the shining road – she was lucky with the weather. The whole month had been pleasant so far. If she could work on both pictures again tomorrow, coming to Farlow would prove well worthwhile.

There had been very little traffic so Clarrie was surprised when an approaching car suddenly braked and pulled in beside her. A strikingly attractive head emerged as the window lowered and a rich baritone asked, "Surely you are Mrs Hunter ...I've seen you with a friend of mine, Algy Green. Aren't you Clarrie?"

Clarrie was startled but there seemed no doubt that the man must know Algy, so she smiled and agreed that it was quite possible he could have seen her with him, they occasionally ate out together. He seemed to know what she was thinking and said quietly, "You don't have to worry about my misinterpreting your association, I know all about his poor wife. I was 'best man' at their wedding. She was lovely. He still expects her to recover – waiting for a miracle – very sad!"

It seemed rather odd on such bare acquaintance to have come out with personal comment so Clarrie chose not to join in. She busied herself in the trunk again to ensure that nothing was pushing against the back of the wet canvas.

Not in the least discouraged, the stranger climbed out of his car and came to stand with her. She instinctively moved away slightly but not before she noticed the smoothness of his firm jaw-line and caught a whiff of expensive after-shave.

He studied the painting and nodded. "You are every bit as good as Algy said ...I think so, anyway, although he knows more about art than I do. Please don't imagine he would gossip about you to any odd bod! We go back a long way." He suddenly introduced himself. "He won't have mentioned me – I'm one of his darkest secrets, a newspaper reporter! Del Delaney is the name. You can judge my moral standing by the fact that, although I know about you and your mother assisting the police occasionally, I've never reported a word – unselfishly passing up many a world by-line!"

Clarrie relaxed and laughed, offering her hand. He sounded sincere and now that she took a closer look, she decided there was genuine warmth in his smile. His light-brown hair waved back from a wide high forehead. Taller than herself by at least five inches – probably around six feet – he was slim with broad shoulders. She wondered if she would ever have the chance to paint his portrait ...an outdoor study: in sporting gear, leaning on the roof of a car with fleecy clouds behind him. He would be a good subject. He stopped talking, suddenly feeling her calculating stare.

She could not avoid passing on her thoughts – or at least some of them! "Sorry, I was just thinking what good colouring you have for an outdoor picture – I hardly ever meet anyone new without mentally painting a portrait of them!"

"That's me, the out-door type," he smiled, "as long as

I'm on a horse, in a car or boat ...and in the latter case I like to hear an engine purring! You will gather that I am not energetic and definitely not into group sports!" He looked more serious for a moment and told her that it must be fate – coming across her so unexpectedly because he had intended asking Algy for an introduction.

Clarrie felt herself on the verge of cooling towards him ...surely this wasn't just a cheap pass after all? He had seemed different. Then she relaxed again – listening to his explanation. He was hoping to talk to her mother about a story he was covering. It had not yet hit the headlines because publicity might prove fatal for the victim.

Clarrie stopped fiddling with her easel and looked him full in the face. Was he genuinely asking for help or was he a sensation-seeker, who would only exploit her mother to advance his own ends? If someone was in real trouble, she would introduce him to Sarah; together they would do whatever lay within their ability but could he be trusted not to drag them under the glare of publicity? She looked away to clear her thoughts. She had perceived only anxiety in his expression so would reserve judgement. She adjusted the canvas, positioned it ready to work on, and started assessing the scene below. Filling a brush with a light wash of umber and turpentine, she began with free, sweeping strokes. As she sketched, most of her mind was on what Del was saying.

"The woman was abducted last week and her husband is so ill with worry, he has had a heart attack. There are two sons, both married and they have agreed to pay a ransom but for three days there has been no further word from the thugs who snatched their mother and they fear that she's dead."

Clarrie glanced at him quickly and started to reply – but as her eyes returned to her canvas she saw she had drawn something quite different from that which she had planned. Her sketch covered the area far more to the left than she wanted, including the railway station. What a nuisance! She picked up a cloth to sponge it out, but was unable to lift it from her side. Her arm felt paralysed.

Delaney could tell by her sudden stillness that something was wrong and interrupted his story to ask what it was. Clarrie looked at the station and concentrated her gaze beyond it until her eyes rested on the distant horizon...

Regaining the use of her limbs she waved him to silence. She could see what she afterwards described to Sarah as a hole in the sky edged with fog. It was like looking at a framed picture depicting a street crossing. There were no traffic lights – it was not in a town centre. On the corner facing her was a large building. She heard a name, Luke, and could also hear children: many children, who shouted and screamed as if in a playground. The building could be a school. It was the most prominent feature, but a little beyond, to the left, was a row of terraced houses... the third was the focal point of the whole scene. Without the faintest doubt, which afterwards amazed her, Clarrie knew it was the place he was seeking and described her vision to Delaney.

The woman was still alive, she informed him, and inside that terraced house.

Clarrie saw two other things that were likely to be of help. The street on the right was also lined with houses and in a ground floor window of the first was a poster – she couldn't read it, but thought it could be connected with a church. On the opposite corner, to the left, was a freestanding billboard – a soft drink advertisement.

If Clarrie had doubted his connection with Algy before, her misgivings would have been banished at that moment. He accepted her word immediately and was wild with enthusiasm. He ordered her to stay exactly where she was and not dare move a muscle. She nodded her agreement and he searched the ground for a few moments picking up a handful of small, white stones. He collected a screwdriver from his car to dig out a hollow in the earth where she stood and filled it with the stones, pressing them down hard to mark the spot. Standing behind her he said, "Now then, tell me exactly where you saw your street corner."

Clarrie pointed to the centre of the station building and moved her finger a little to the left, where a slightly taller tree in a field beyond it was prominent. It was directly above that tree, she told him, but she sensed that it was a long way distant and couldn't even make a wild guess as to how far.

"Don't you worry – I'll be back within the hour with an ordnance survey map and a surveyor. It's fine – you can move now, but don't move too far, I want to talk to you again! See you later!"

As soon as he left, Clarrie fetched a sketchbook from her car and drew, in detail, what she had seen. There could be many similar street corners and it was important that he be able to eliminate every wrong one without wasting time. Other small things occurred to her as her pencil flew over the paper – she even grew convinced that the poster was an advertisement for a garage sale. The church connection was with the large building – it was St. Luke's junior school.

Clarrie was staggered by the amount of detail when she at last stopped, knowing she had finished... Had she really had time to see and absorb so much, in so short a time! The brickwork of the school was old and chipped in places; an upper windowpane in one of the houses was broken and, in the same house, a ground floor window displayed a plant.

Clarrie saw that the huge hoarding obscured all but the black edge of an enamelled street sign fixed to the wall beyond it. It was uncanny, but she knew that if the angle had been a little more acute she would have known the name on it.

Everything she had on her canvas was rubbish, so wetting her cloth with turpentine Clarrie wiped it clean and started again. By the time Del re-appeared she at least had a sure foundation for her second picture but even he could see that it wasn't an hour's work. "You've been slacking while my back was turned," he accused, "I thought there'd be more to see by now!"

He turned away as another car drew in beside them and informed her that he had contacted his editor who put him in touch with a surveyor – the man approaching them now with a mystified look on his face.

"And you," returned Clarrie, "have more than your fair share of cheek! I suppose on the basis of our long-standing friendship you think you have a right to criticise!"

He treated her to a broad grin and as the stranger drew nearer whispered, "Don't tell him why he's here – I'll do the talking."

After a brief introduction, Clarrie carried on painting. She had moved her easel several yards away from the white stones and soon forgot she had company. The low voices were lost against the background of rushing river and bird song.

When the surveyor at last packed up his theodolite and left, Del came to talk again. He was sure that within hours he would have a triangulated section of the whole country to cover, from the grouped stones to the coast. The surveyor guessed the centre line would go pretty close to Wolverhampton and as the tree top swayed at least a couple of feet, the width of coastline at the base of the triangle might be fifty miles but that was nothing in comparison to the total area of the whole country! Del sounded extremely happy. He looked with approval at the painting. "My uncalled-for criticism inspired you – you are working a great deal faster now!"

"You don't deserve it, but I have a present for you," said Clarrie, handing him the sketch. She watched his expression with an uncharacteristic surge of smugness: pleased to see his astonishment.

A long slow breath whistled from his pursed lips. "I take back all reproaches lady and am suitably humbled, you are a genius. This looks like a week's work!" He studied it and picked out several things that might help to whittle down the search by telephone... it must, for instance be possible to find the location of all local schools quickly. It was easy to be infected by his excitement but Clarrie wondered, could the sketch really help his investigation; was it truly clairvoyance, or a figment of her imagination? She was almost choked by self-doubt.

In a flurry of thanks, he departed as quickly as he had arrived. He had not asked for her telephone number or given any indication that he would contact her again and Clarrie had to admit that she was disappointed.

She also knew why she was so worried about being wrong. She liked what she'd seen of Del Delaney and couldn't bear the thought of letting him down! Although she hadn't given her appearance a second's thought while he was present, Clarrie suddenly felt inadequate – a mess! She wished she had worn a pair of decently shaped slacks instead of her old jeans – and the loose blouse did nothing for her trim figure... Still, she was painting and he had apparently seen her better dressed when she had been dining out with Algy! Putting such vain thoughts aside, she went back to work. Below her, she noticed the same woman she had used in the other painting. The dumpy little figure in black left her cottage by the back door and set off across the field towards the village ...her fat old dog swaying along faithfully in her wake.

39 - An Unusual Day Out

Ann was hungry and looking for somewhere to pull off
the road so that she could eat her sandwiches. Even if she
hadn't cared about being seen she still would not have
considered stopping at a restaurant. She and Eddie hardly
ever ate out; it would have been wasting money needed
to meet necessary expenses. For the past three hours, her
anxiety increasing with every mile, she had been driving
around in ever widening circles without finding the
perfect place for disposing of a body. Very few had struck
her as suitable hiding places where it might escape
discovery for at least a few months.

She left the car once, to walk into some lonely
woodland, but the ground was like iron; she'd never be
able to dig a deep enough hole.

A bridge over a river interested her until she saw how
shallow the water was.

A few building sites that initially seemed ideal were
close to other sites that were occupied... there was no way
she could be sure of going in and out without being seen.

Before leaving, when Ann had tried ringing Jenny's
number she was puzzled. It was funny - Jenny hadn't said
anything about going out. Ann had not even seen her
taking the twins to school. Of course, they had no
obligation to keep each other informed of their
movements but they were both security conscious. Any
strangers wandering the lane would be watched more
closely if either one of the two houses stood empty. Ann
saw two unfamiliar figures window-shopping when she

drove through Farlow and but the women were a picture of respectability; not all strangers were potential housebreakers!

40 – Mary Lays Plans

Little Mary, in spite of her appearance, was fairly fit. Her daily rambling did her more good than jogging did for the energetic fanatics who often replaced lost fat with the next meal. She had deliberately left home the back way without going near Alice's house. Alice knew Mary hated shopping and meeting people – she would have wanted to know why and where she was going because Alice usually picked up Mary's few groceries; Alice might stop doing so if she saw Mary walking into Farlow!

The greengrocer's shop was almost the first in the street so Mary expected to be on her way home again within minutes. There were few people about as she ducked inside the shop where her eye went immediately to the notice board. A woman on the point of leaving was counting her change, and the slight delay allowed Mary to find the newest addition: *'A reward is offered for ...'*

The man behind the counter saw Mary enter his shop and was glad to see that the dog hadn't followed her. It was so slow these days; with luck, he could get her outside again before it reached the door and sneaked in with the next customer ...smelly thing! She seemed absorbed, reading the board, but he asked what she needed.

While he served her, Mary resumed her study of the notice with mixed feelings. There was no mention of a case or photographs, which was a relief – but the reward offered was for a dog – if you could call a poodle a dog! She asked for a pencil and scribbled the telephone number on the paper bag, which now contained her few purchases. Those women must know the girl in blue – they had described her perfectly. If Mary told them about Todd and the snaps, they would tell the young woman. That would put an end to his little blackmailing scheme!

"You seem very interested in the lost poodle, Mary," said the owner as she opened the door to leave. "If you know anything about it, the people who put it up are probably still in the village... I saw them going into The Bull for lunch. They might be there now ...it's still early."

Mary muttered that she wasn't interested in any poodle and hurried away, but outside she hesitated. She hated using the telephone but was reluctant to meet the two women face to face. Which should she do? In the end, the idea of ringing up won. Tonight, she'd go to the station where she could ask someone to do all the dialling for her – she would then be able to remain anonymous. No one must ever connect her with that girl, or she would have to part with her beautiful leather suitcase and all its contents. If she lay low, how would anyone ever know of the treasures hidden under her bed!

4l – After Lunch

Sarah and Polly were walking off the somnolence brought on by the excellent food they had enjoyed. The landlord recognised the name of the house they sought and had given them directions. It didn't sound very close, but they thought the exercise would do them good. They left the village behind and carefully facing on-coming traffic, walked along the narrow unpaved verge. In the distance, a small dark figure followed by a round black dog went down into a ditch alongside the road and clambered up into a field. When they reached the place where she had left the road, they saw her going through a hedge a few hundred yards away – very near the houses for which they were heading themselves.

Polly looked ahead at the long stretch of road and then at the ditch. "In spite of the fact that there seems to be a short cut," she said, "I would personally prefer to stick to solid ground!"

Sarah agreed. It was a pleasant day and they had three hours to fill before meeting Clarinda. She wondered how her daughter was progressing with her painting. She could not see the hill and lay-by from where they were but was happy about the area – it was not off the beaten track. No one would be likely to disturb her as she worked. Even as the thought crossed her mind she felt a fleeting doubt, but ignored it... Clarinda was not easily put off when working!

There were two lanes ahead and both cut across the fields to the left – it was the nearer one into which they soon turned; it was labelled, *'No through road'*. Above the treetops, they could see the chimneys of the new houses ahead. As they walked, they could see through the thinner parts of the hedge. The black dog was alone in the distance, head hanging low as it ambled along. Its owner must have already gone to the old cottage, one of two at the top of the other lane. It was remarkably quiet and pleasant after they left the main road and they soon reached the first house. Sarah hesitated at the drive entrance but Polly continued walking firmly.

Although Polly appeared overweight, she carried herself lightly and showed no sign of flagging. "What's wrong, Sarah? Surely, that isn't the house we want," she turned and called back, "the landlord definitely said it was the second." Sarah strolled to the wall where Polly pointed to a name board. Clumps of ivy were growing over it and trailing down, but she could see the letters *'AR ACRE '*.

Puzzled and still unconvinced Sarah moved the leaves to reveal the beginning of the name, *'NE'*. Happy to be proved right, Polly waited for Sarah to join her and they walked on to 'Far Acre'. She could see that Sarah was edgy and unhappy because she kept slowing down and looked perturbed. "Oh dear! What is the matter," Polly asked anxiously.

"I really don't know, I feel something pulling me back," said Sarah, "It is almost impossible to resist – like swimming against a strong current, but we have come this far and are certainly not going back now!"...

They were, however, disappointed.

At 'Far Acre', there was nobody home.

42 – Double Take

It was almost six-o-clock and Ann was in despair. There was no point in staying out any longer. As it was, she was going to have a hard time explaining to Jenny where she had been all day. If she were to be fit enough to drag a corpse around in the dead of night, she should return and grab a few hours' sleep. She had been unable to come to a final decision about how to dispose of it because no method had appealed to her as perfect. She had therefore lowered her sights. Instead of finding a permanent burial place, she would just have to settle for dumping it – a long way away!

A strip of new motorway being constructed had mountains of earth and rubble along one side of it. If she took the body there, she could throw stones over it. It might be found eventually but perhaps not for months. It wasn't a comforting thought, the prospect of having it found at all, but her only concern now was to distance herself from it ...as far as possible!

The traffic was much heavier than he had expected – they would be lucky to arrive before seven – and the kids were driving him mad, giggling and shouting in the back. He kept telling them to keep the volume down but they were still bouncing with over excitement. His mind was less on his driving than it should have been. It was on Joyce, damn her to Hell! Still, another day was over and nothing truly disastrous had happened. She would probably sail in after her holiday all sweetness and light, but she would have some explaining to do! How could Todd have got hold of those photographs for instance? Would he be paying Todd's price for the rest of his life?

An even more piercing scream from the rear seat interrupted his thoughts. This time it was too much even for Jenny and she turned to chastise them. Thank goodness they were nearly home Jenny thought, as they drove past the Tillers'. The place was in darkness and she wondered where Ann could possibly be. Still, with Eddie and the children off her hands, she may have treated herself to a day in town ...or even gone to a movie! No doubt, she'd hear all about it tomorrow. Now she had a pressing problem of her own: how to calm the twins before putting them to bed!

43 - Catching Up

Clarrie had picked up the others at the bus shelter and listened to an account of their day with interest, holding her own story back for the moment. She was a good driver but the roads were full of evening traffic and she needed to concentrate. When they all settled down after dinner, she would tell her mother and Polly about Del Delaney and her vision above the tree top: a new experience for her.

Part of her wanted to hold it privately, as if sharing it would diminish it in some way but her desire to consult with Sarah, so much more practised in the ways of the spirit world, was uppermost. It was difficult to accept that her own psychic power had increased so rapidly in the last year.

When Tom was alive, he had joked that fond as he was of her mother, he hoped Clarrie was not tarred with the same brush! She always assured him, she certainly was not – if he wanted to stay out late on the tiles, no friendly ghost would be able to get through to tell her!

She suddenly remembered what Algy had said once. He couldn't live with a wife who might know his every move!

Such thoughts naturally led back to Del – had she subconsciously known they would?

He was undoubtedly an interesting character ...but he no doubt shared with Algy a wariness of the supernatural, even though eagerly seizing the advantages offered by it. All the same, it was lucky for him that she was not on the lookout for a husband! If she had been, he might feature quite high on the list.

Clarrie pressed the automatic switch on the car key ring as she turned into the drive and the garage door lifted with a low rattle.

She stopped to allow Sarah and Polly to alight, and then drove in, lowering the door behind her.

Within minutes, she was letting herself into the kitchen and the aroma of food assailed her nostrils. Thank goodness for Polly. She had set the cooker timer before leaving and they could eat straight away. Clarrie was looking forward to telling them that whereas their day had been disappointing – hers had been exciting in comparison, and she ran upstairs to shower and change.

44 - Friday 24th

After an inadequate amount of sleep, Ann dragged herself down to the garage at two in the morning. By starting the car before opening the garage doors, she hoped to reduce the noise and then move it outside with the black plastic bundle hidden in the trunk. Apart from the engine ticking over, the night was quiet and she cringed as the doors scraped to a close again but she managed to bring them together without the usual clang.

Wherever they had been, she was sure that Jenny and Bill were home again when she returned home at eight - their lights were on. The houses were not so close that she really needed to worry about being heard but Ann preferred to take no chances. She drove gently down the drive, out of the gate and well away from the house without switching on her headlights. The faint moonlight was enough until she turned out of the lane, headed straight for the distant motorway and finally took the road parallel to it, which was soon to be superseded. She didn't dare risk driving on the unopened section and perhaps being seen by a police patrol.   Her first visit had shown the best approach to be from a picnic spot on the old road. Pulling off the highway, Ann was relieved to find the area quite deserted - no dozing lorry drivers taking a rest in the small hours and she had seen hardly any traffic for miles. She drove as far as she could away from the road and stopped under some trees... no moonlight penetrated to reveal her presence. Up to now, her plan appeared to be working well.

Knowing exactly where she was heading, Ann hauled out the body, balanced it over one shoulder and staggered into the trees. Although tall, Joyce had been incredibly thin ...like a yard of pump water! The derogatory comment flitted through her head unbidden – but even so, Joyce's dead weight was almost too much. Thank heaven she didn't need the fork or spade as well; it would have meant two trips and increased the risk of being noticed. The track she was following was narrow and almost overgrown in places.

On her exploratory trek, Ann had broken through the worst patches but it was even harder than she expected. Twigs and branches whipped her arms and legs ...stinging, even through her slacks. By the time she eventually reached clearer ground, she was hurting all over but thankful that the plastic had survived intact. All was well. She was within sight of the new road ...from here, speaking figuratively, it should be downhill all the way! For what she hoped was the last time, Ann adjusted her load more comfortably before leaving the protection of the wood. The clean new surface of the wide carriageway was a mere fifty yards away ...but suddenly, to her dismay, she saw a uniformed figure standing in the middle of it.

It was a man who appeared to be waiting for something so she laid the bundle over the bough of a tree and rested; surely, he would go on soon. It was intensely frustrating but the longer she sat the better perhaps ...up to a point. At least she was recovering her breath! Then he whistled and from left and right dogs appeared, silently hurtling over the waste ground. It was obviously a security man with his guard dogs – probably on a regular exercise route and as such, how would a body remain undisturbed for even a day? To them it would be fragrant dead meat!

Ann could hardly believe her bad luck.

Fortunately, the menacing little group – the handler

and his pack, moved away and eventually out of sight. Ann broke into a cold sweat imagining what might have happened had they come towards her or detected her presence on the faint breeze. Disappointment sapped her partly restored strength as she hoisted up her load again and returned to the car almost tearful with frustration – every muscle screaming. Her ghastly encumbrance seemed to have doubled in weight.

Before proceeding to her second most promising locale, Ann sat in the darkness of the car and drank some hot coffee from her flask. The thatched umbrellas over the picnic tables threw pools of deep shadow onto the ground. There is always something eerie about a place of amusement when viewed out of context, Ann thought: a fairground, still and empty after hours: a theatre when the show is over and the audience departed. The more she stared at her surroundings the more threatened she felt until she started shaking and just had to get away. After a couple of bungled tries, the engine started and she was on her way again.

Twenty minutes later, she arrived at a deserted stretch of road that ran through farmland. On one side, a high railway embankment ensured that until a train came by, the area was not overlooked. On her previous visit, the field gate had been open wide so it was a bitter blow to find it not only closed but padlocked. The deep, overgrown ditch she had found was miles away on the other side of it, beyond reach. She almost collapsed in hysteria and blind panic.

Appalled at the prospect of taking the body home again, Ann continued to drive around the narrow lanes frantic to be rid of it. She actually had it half out of the car, intending to drop it over a rail bridge in desperation – past caring whether it was found or not – when a disembodied voice spoke to her from the darkness, transfixing her instantly to the spot! ..."If that's rubbish

Missus, don't chuck it yet. It might be useless to you but give me a chance to look through it. I'll tie it up again and throw it away!"

Ann shrieked with terror – slammed the boot lid down and jumped into the car, fumbling with the keys as she locked herself in and tried to start it at the same time. The menacing figure loomed over her and appeared to be clawing its way through the screen. It was almost more than she could stand – tears blinded her as the wheels spun into motion. She was disheartened, weary, and felt like driving to the nearest police station to make a full confession. The rear mat was already soggy with melting ice ...how long would it be before Joyce melted as well? Ann made herself picture what her disclosure would do to Eddie and the children. For them, she had to be strong.

After returning home at four-thirty, it took Ann almost an hour to rearrange the freezer with her grim parcel again concealed in its depths; she then dragged herself upstairs, collapsed tearfully on her bed and fell into a shallow, troubled sleep.

When the strident jangle of the alarm clock woke Ann, at nine-o-clock, she regretted setting it ...her head felt like a lead weight on the pillow, but she reminded herself that to maintain her schedule she must be rid of Joyce's clothes today. The NSPCC branch committee members were probably already assembling in the hall, preparing for tomorrow's sale. The 'Prevention of Cruelty to Children' was a worthy cause but she felt cruelly treated herself! Floundering from the comfort of bed into the bathroom, the horror of the early hours returned to torment her.

She emerged from the shower feeling more awake but still with a headache and a sickly depression in the pit of her stomach. She faced a repeat performance tonight ...the same ordeal, but getting rid of the body at all costs. The sound of whistling outside drew her to the bedroom window and she saw a postman cycling away from the gate: not the usual man. As soon as she dressed Ann went to see what he had brought and was disappointed to find it was all for "Far Acre". What was the matter with the boy, couldn't he read!

She walked out to the other side of the wall and observed that the sign was partly obscured by ivy. She pulled it away and strolled to put the mail in Jenny's box, trying to think up an excuse for her absence yesterday. She was about to drop it all in together when she saw a piece of loose paper: Jenny's note. Well, one problem was solved – she could have been at home all day Jenny would never know! Now, she could go to the sale with the clothes ...the sooner she achieved at least one of her aims the better!

45 – Remorse

Bill was striving to keep his mind on his work – he could not shake off the feeling that Joyce was somewhere around, waiting to pounce on Jenny and tell all! He had succeeded in getting Jenny away from the house yesterday but his attempts at persuading her to come to town again today had failed. She wouldn't hear of taking the twins on another jaunt so soon. It wouldn't be fair; the 'poor little lambs' needed a quiet day at home to recover.

Wendy was doing well enough as his temporary secretary. He allowed himself to daydream for a moment … what a boon it would be if Joyce never came back …if she just disappeared in a puff of smoke …out of his life forever. Whether she did or didn't, he had learned his lesson – he would never cheat on his wife again… Never!

46 – Second Try

Sarah and Polly were on their way back to Farlow with Clarrie. They were anxious to visit the house where Joyce claimed to have been murdered and in no way disconcerted by the prospect of another full day trip. The weather was still good but to avoid wasting time they would be dropped at the end of the lane rather than in the village. If no one were home again, they would walk into Farlow. It would be, in essence, a repeat of yesterday: lunch at The Bull and being picked up at the shelter. Today, however, they would probably have time to spend a few hours in the antique shops they had found.

Sarah had been impressed by the clarity of Clarinda's extrasensory vision, when the young man had appealed to her for help. She suspected they would not have long to wait before he contacted Clarinda again. Polly, however, having always had faith in Sarah's psychic powers, was not surprised that her daughter took after her. It was tremendously stimulating to be with them, sharing and, she hoped, helping with the unusual problems that came their way.

Once alone, after Clarrie drove off, they started walking up the lane and almost immediately heard a car approaching on its way to the main road. Sarah hesitated as it came in sight – a young woman was at the wheel. Could this possibly be the woman they sought? She looked at them closely as if she recognised them but did not slow down. Sarah regretted not having raised a hand to stop her but said they would just hope that if she were Mrs

Dean, she wouldn't be out for long.

Sarah was startled when she turned to resume the walk. Joyce appeared – blocking her way! Oblivious to the drama behind her Polly strolled on. Joyce pointed after the car, speechless with fury. Sarah asked her what she wanted but Joyce was out of control... her image thinned, vibrated and faded, leaving Sarah mystified and irritated. Of the hundreds of spirits who had contacted her over the years, this one was by far the least predictable and consequently the most worrying – the sooner she was laid to rest the better. With this determination uppermost in mind, Sarah hastened to catch up with Polly.

Jenny answered the doorbell and was surprised to see on her doorstep two obviously respectable elderly ladies – equally obviously not selling anything. The younger, slightly taller one excused their intrusion and asked if she had a few minutes to spare. Without removing the chain from the door, she asked how she could help them. Sarah handed her one of Alec's personal cards, with his home number and turned it to reveal his extension at the CID headquarters.

Last night, Sarah had contacted Alec to arrange this little subterfuge; with luck, they would soon be inside the house having a cosy chat. "My name is Sarah Grey – this is my friend Mrs Bailey. We are trying to find a friend's lost dog; she visited Farlow and allowed her poodle off the leash in this area last Monday."

Jenny stared dubiously at the gilt-edged card and Sarah laughed dismissively. "The Detective Chief Superintendent is, of course, not in the least concerned with lost dogs, but I promised to ring him on a quite different matter at half-past-nine. I'm afraid I forgot, and now, half an hour late, we are so far from a public telephone – I wonder if you would be kind enough to ring him for me, with a brief message? ...Please reverse the call charge, of course."

Jenny decided to let them in and started to take the chain off, but Sarah stopped her. "Oh, please – there is really no need at all for me to call personally. You could merely say that Sarah is sorry to be late letting him know, but he will be expected at a quarter to eleven this morning. You can see why I am so worried – the poor man will have very little time to prepare!" Sarah turned away from the door and walked away a little. "We will be quite happy to enjoy the sunshine while you talk to him."

Inside, Jenny very sensibly checked the number in the telephone directory, dialled and asked for extension fifteen. Alec answered immediately and hearing a woman's voice said quickly, "Sarah is that you at last?" Within moments, Jenny returned to the front door. This time, confident that they were above suspicion, she invited them in for coffee.

"I hope my friend wasn't too upset," Sarah said as they followed Jenny into the airy sitting room, "I'm rather glad you rang for me. I don't know how I'll face him again, not having telephoned earlier!"

"He seemed much more worried that you were still tramping about in the wilds," Jenny laughed, so I promised I'd persuade you to have a little refreshment with me before sending you on your way"

After Jenny left them to fetch it, Sarah sat quietly – taking in the ambience, concentrating her thoughts. At last, she spoke. "There is unquestionably nothing to learn here, I am sure. I can discern no trace of Joyce or indeed any aura of violence – either in the past or present."

"But how can that be?" asked Polly with surprise. "I must say, Mrs Dean seems a nice respectable woman, but why should Joyce have made it all up. It doesn't make sense!"

Half an hour later, they left to resume their search for the fictitious wayward poodle. It had been easy to describe the attractive, blue suited, owner but no sign of recognition crossed Jenny's face and she explained that she spent every Monday in Reading. She always had her hair done, shopped for herself and Ann Tiller, her neighbour, and never returned until four in the afternoon at the earliest. She thought it unlikely that Ann had seen her either. They saw so few strangers around that Ann would have been sure to tell her. It was a shame they could not ask her but she was helping to organise a 'Bring and Buy' sale that would be taking place tomorrow and would probably be out all day.

During the conversation, Jenny mentioned her hard-working husband but there was no hint in her tone that she suspected him of having an affair with his secretary. It was puzzling but Sarah was convinced that, although Joyce was undoubtedly dead, it was not at the hand of Jenny Dean.

Sauntering away, past the property of the absent Ann, it occurred to them both simultaneously that Joyce went to the wrong house! They knew nobody was at home ...it must have been Ann they saw driving out earlier.

What harm would it do, they surmised, to walk around the garden? The gates were open; the poodle could be somewhere in there couldn't it?

For the sake of appearances, they rang the bell but while Polly walked about casually, Sarah stood like a statue, facing the wide bay window. If looking inside had been Sarah's objective it would have been difficult as the curtains were partly drawn but her eyes were tightly closed in concentration. Sarah was 'tuning in', prepared to receive a total impression of the house, or about anything significant which might have happened inside...

47 – News Hound

Clarrie had been painting for only an hour when a car swung into the lay-by and to her surprise Del stepped out. "Don't look so astonished," he laughed, "I am an experienced news-hound remember ...I have my sources, but refuse to reveal them! Threats will have no effect."

"You've been talking to Algy again, I don't need to ask." Clarrie retorted confidently. "My mother enlisted the help of his chief in a small subterfuge. She is actually hot on the trail of a murderer and needed to prove her bona fides to trick her way into his lair."

Del detected no hint of teasing in her expression and frowned a little. "I shall have to watch my step with you young lady. From what I've heard about you both, you could very well be speaking the truth and pulling a double bluff just to put me off!"

Clarrie wished she hadn't been flippant. He was no fool. "How did you progress with your search for St. Luke's?"

"Well, that's why I'm here really. I thought you would like to know how things are going. The surveyor did a fantastic job and triangulated the area of search all the way to the coast, on Merseyside." He reached into his car and produced a map, which he opened to show her. "At its widest it is very heavily populated – there must be hundreds of schools named St Luke, in that county alone. I was worried that by tackling it myself I would take too long and cost the woman her life!"

He acknowledged Clarrie's understanding nod – it was too big a risk. "But," he continued, the alternative was also out. "If I tried to explain my firm conviction that she was being held in that house, to the police already on the case, they would either refuse to act on a hunch, or they would find her and I'd then be in trouble for not telling them how I knew!"

Clarrie could see his problem and listened with interest.

He continued with a satisfied grin. "So, last night I rang Algy and persuaded him that he had to take me to his leader, there and then. He flatly refused until he discovered that I had vital information, provided by you, on a matter of life or death! We arrived at the Holme' residence within the hour which, by coincidence, was only minutes after your mother rang him." He stopped suddenly and asked, "You weren't joking about your mother, were you?" – Then immediately added, "No, that isn't fair ...but if there is a story in it, I hope I can rely on you for an exclusive ...which is the bottom line of the case I am on. I naturally didn't make any conditions but I don't think Algy will let me down if he can help it."

Del didn't appear to be in a hurry to go and although she usually disliked having an audience, Clarrie found his chatter quite entertaining and worked on steadily.

"I understand your mother is roaming loose in the village somewhere?" he stated with a note of enquiry in his voice.

"I'd hardly have put it that way, but yes – she and Polly are sightseeing and enjoying the fresh air while I work," Clarrie told him.

At Polly's name, he looked perplexed, not, apparently, having heard anything about her from his friendly police informant. Clarrie explained, "Polly was my parents' housekeeper until my father died. Originally, Mother intended taking an apartment and Polly moved to her daughter's but when my husband Tom died, soon after she was widowed, mother came to live in and look after me.

Polly came daily to help then, but it was too much for her really. Anyway, we thought it would give us more freedom if Polly moved in too, as a sort of companion. She has always been like an aunt to me – my mother and I are both very fond of her. Her niece was eager to take over the daily cleaning so we all benefit from the arrangement."

Clarrie flushed. Had she told him too much? She realised that she had incidentally managed to inform him of her own widowhood – but then, he must know about Tom from Algy. Del had been listening intently and in a more serious tone now, he confided that he had also been married – a long while ago. He had held a short-term commission in Army Intelligence and met this eighteen-year-old just before he went off to Singapore on secondment to their State Military. Ignoring all warnings, everyone advised against it, he married her by special license a month after his return.

Del was soon forced to accept that she was a cheap tramp and left her in sole occupation of their new flat while he went to live in the Mess. They separated officially and were divorced two years later. He threw himself into journalism when he left the army having made a few useful contacts. They pointed him in the right direction, but nobody gets a free ride and he'd had to work hard and long to stay ahead of the game.

Del said he enjoyed writing but planned to abandon the field of reporting soon, to concentrate on a book. "That's really how I first came to hear about your mother," he said. "I told Algy I was planning to write about haunted sites and travel round the country interviewing people. He swore me to secrecy and promised to introduce me to you both someday. When this woman was abducted my mental card index flipped immediately to your mother and I wondered if she would be willing to help." His face broke into a wide grin. "To be honest I had already seen you with him and begged for an introduction. He turned me down flat!"

"Well, if you would really like to meet my mother, she and Polly will be in 'The Bull' for lunch – you can drop in and introduce yourself. I have already told them about our meeting so they'll know the name."

"Now that is the best idea I've had all day!" he cried. "We will both go – lunch is on me! Come on. Pack up. You have done quite enough for one morning – a real masterpiece – absolutely fantastic!"

Clarrie tried to argue; she had a picnic with her; she had another canvas needing hours of work... she could do without a third trip to Farlow! It was no good; Del looked so disappointed that at last she gave in and re-packed her paints. Perhaps it was just as well, she thought – how could she keep her mind on her work if a party was in progress in the pub?

Their timing was perfect. As Del followed Clarrie, he saw her stop to pick up two people who had almost reached the village. So, he would soon meet the legendary Sarah... and wondered what she would think of him. He hoped he would make a good impression because now that he was getting to know her daughter she was likely to see quite a lot of him!

48 – Jumble

In the small hall hired for the sale, Ann stood with her bright orange plastic bag of jumble. This one really was jumble, but the other – unremarkable black – which she had left in the outer hall, was definitely 'boutique'. There had been three other members in the car park so she allowed them to see her with the more colourful sack. As soon as they disappeared inside, she nipped back for the other. Several more people arrived but it was ages before someone asked about it. "Whose is this large bag in the lobby?" A voice rang out.

Ann watched from a distance as the matching items met with cries of admiration. The member in charge held one aloft and asked who had made such a generous contribution.

There was no answer.

Ann considered saying that a ginger haired, six-foot tall, fat woman had dropped it off and immediately left, but on second thoughts decided it would be gilding the lily. The less she was associated with it the better.

The bored individual arranging the 'white elephants' snorted. "You watch, they'll price each piece of that lot out of sight, and then offer it as a set for 50% off! I wish I was about twenty pounds thinner, I would have bought some of it myself." She sighed as she looked down – trying to see her feet perhaps, and added, "Nobody on the committee will take it now that it has been waved about. They would be unable to wear it without everyone knowing where it came from."

Ann laughed politely. Most of the committee, she knew, wouldn't hesitate to pick up a bargain if it was a good fit. She waited only long enough to establish that she would not be attending tomorrow and was soon on her way, driving again through the countryside in search of a suitable burial site for the trash she still had at home! Tonight was the last chance she would have to dispose of it before the builder came and the freezer had to be moved. If he kept his promise and arrived early tomorrow she would certainly not be able to empty it under his eagle eye unless it was significantly less full.

Whatever happened, even if she had to drop it at the roadside – tonight she had to be rid of it. Ann tried to recall all the murder mysteries she had ever read where bodies had been disposed of, or successfully hidden. The trouble was that most authors allowed the villainous murderers to be found out in the last chapter, which was the very thing she wished to avoid. In real life, even bodies buried miles from anywhere were not safe from marauding animals; dropped into rivers, they became caught in fishing lines, or were seen by treasure-seeking skin divers!

Surely, some murderers must exist who had handled the problem successfully. How could one ever know how many? Ann remonstrated with herself as she drove; she must stop thinking of herself as a murderer. She was in this mess only because Joyce, a complete stranger, had tried to poison her but failed. Her own motive in hiding the truth was to save her marriage.

Last week she thought she was quite secure in Eddie's love and affection and when she succeeded in overcoming this hurdle, she would make him love her again, even if he had faltered a little.

If, at that moment, Ann had been able to see across the intervening miles, she would have witnessed the builder's lorry standing in her drive, several men dragging open the garage doors and the builder himself ringing her doorbell.

"Never mind lads," he shouted to them, "there's nobody in, but we know what we have to do. Let's just get on with it. It'll be a nice surprise for Mrs Tiller when she gets back."

"What about this freezer boss? I'll plug in the extension cable but it'll need lightening a bit to shift it out of the way."

"That's OK lad – leave it to me ..." ... If only Ann had been able to see across the miles!

49 – Del

When Clarrie drew alongside them, Sarah and Polly were perplexed, thinking something amiss had caused her to change her plans to paint all day. They were pleasantly surprised to hear that Del was in the car following her and they would be lunching together. Sarah was particularly glad that she was about to meet the man who had made such a deep impression on Clarinda – it was years since she had seemed so carefree – Sarah only hoped she would not be disillusioned.

As Polly and Clarinda talked, Sarah's mind was again on Ann Tiller for whom she felt immense sympathy. The poor woman had been involved in a situation from which she couldn't hope to emerge unscathed, by the vicious scheming of someone so blinded by her own desire that she had stupidly tried to kill the wrong woman. How had Ann coped alone with such an extraordinary experience? Sarah could represent her case to Alec but there was no way he would act merely on her psychic intuition. Unless Ann voluntarily told her own story, there was little he could do as yet, officially. There was not even any evidence that Joyce had broken her journey in Farlow!

The car park was behind the hotel and Clarinda drove under the deep archway that ran through the centre of the building, closely followed by Del's car, which he parked alongside. Sarah's first impressions of him were good and they were soon seated inside talking like old friends. His demeanour toward the two older ladies was easy but not familiar. Sarah noted his expression whenever he looked at Clarinda, especially when she was unaware of his gaze ...it held a glow of warm admiration, which pleased Sarah. She could understand now why he might prove to be special.

They were all on excellent terms by the time the meal was finished and, over coffee, Polly, remembering that he knew it from his army days, asked him what he had thought of Singapore. Her husband was there in the early fifties and in spite of the bandits 'up country' had loved it. Del said he enjoyed his stay in the mid-seventies but was saddened by some of the changes in character, which the island had undergone since he had lived there with his parents twelve years earlier.

It surprised Clarrie to hear that he was in Singapore as a boy and she exclaimed involuntarily, "Oh, how marvellous it must have been to live in such a romantic place. I have often wished I could see it for myself!"

"In that case, we'll go there for our honeymoon," said Del. Then he added, acknowledging the expressions on the faces of his audience, "Don't worry – I won't book the flight yet! I have no intention of proposing until I'm sure of the right answer ...my ego is far too fragile. I could never risk rejection!" Without pausing for a verbal reaction, he turned directly to Sarah and said, "I notice you always say Clarinda, never Clarrie. Do you object to its being shortened?"

"I don't mind others doing so, but I named her for my two sisters, Clara and Linda ...which one could I use without offending the other?" Sarah laughed, and then asked a personal question of her own. "You were surely not named Del by your parents – what is your real name?

"If you promise to continue calling me Del, I'll admit to being Clark Alan," Del replied, "probably after Gable and Ladd ...but as my initials might be thought to reveal my true nature, I have dropped the Alan completely and forever – I hope I can trust you not to reveal my dark secret!"

Del insisted on taking the check and as Sarah walked outside, she heard him invite Clarinda to dinner on Sunday. Calling her to one side Sarah remarked, "Don't forget we have guests coming on Sunday who might not leave before seven, I would be quite happy if you would prefer to invite Del to have dinner with us – it wouldn't be such a mad rush for you as preparing to go out."

When Sarah forestalled her Clarrie had been on the point of refusing for that very reason. She speculated briefly... just how much of her mind really was an open book to her mother? Anyway, it was a good idea. Clarrie sensed an underlying seriousness in his teasing references to his amorous intentions... Dinner at home, in company, would be more comfortable until she got to know him better! Del guessed that the suggestion had come from Sarah and immediately wondered whether she was unhappy about his interest in Clarrie ...but when Sarah herself approached to explain, adding that she hoped he would come, he accepted without further reservations.

They all went their separate ways for the afternoon – Sarah and Polly headed straight for the antique shops. In view of what she'd envisaged as she stood at the window of the Tillers' house, Sarah was no longer interested whether Mrs Tiller returned home or not. Sarah could not possibly approach her without jeopardising the girl's position – she would only be able to help Ann by avoiding all personal contact with her, which might hint at collusion.

Sarah had no doubt that Joyce was fulminating at the delay but closed her mind to communication. Waiting a few days more was a small price to pay for long-term peace of mind... She was sure the unfortunate Mrs Tiller would agree.

Del drove straight up to Wolverhampton as he had

reason to think that was where his story would break. When he saw them again he might have good news.

Clarrie went back up the hill and was soon hard at work, making up for the two-hour lunch break ...but she had no regrets; it had been well worth it and the company excellent!

The scene below was not as peaceful as it had been. There was a parked lorry and some activity around one of the new houses; it didn't matter – it was far enough away to ignore.

50 - Bill

When Bill arrived home after another frustrating day he was relieved to find Jenny in a good mood which indicated at least that the errant Joyce had still not shown up to denounce him. Now he had only to survive the weekend – well, three days until Tuesday. Joyce was sure to put in an appearance then and he could tell her about the business trip. It was certain to keep her quiet a bit longer. He needed time to ease his way out of this intolerable situation but if he managed to do so without sacrificing his family, he had learned his lesson!

Jenny reminded him that she intended going to the 'Bring and Buy' sale tomorrow and asked if he would mind taking care of the twins. To her astonishment and delight he said he would gladly do so if she really preferred to go alone but why shouldn't they all go to the sale together? It would be a pleasant day out if they stayed in Reading for lunch. Afterwards, if the weather was good they could walk by the river in Caversham. Bill was satisfied... one more day when nobody would be at home to receive unwanted callers.

He was almost happy until Jenny said, "By the way, somebody called here this morning." He couldn't answer and she continued with her tale about the two ladies looking for a lost dog. "I wouldn't have let them in of course, but the policeman I rang obviously knows them personally so I gave them coffee." He barely took in the details – he was so relieved she wasn't talking about Joyce – he poured himself a stiff brandy and breathed again.

51 - Cementing Plans

When Ann pulled into her driveway she saw immediately that somebody had been there since she left in the morning. Almost choking with dread she ran to the garage. The doors were jammed together more closely than she had been able to manage herself and she couldn't get a good enough grip to pull them open; they wouldn't budge. In a panic, she let herself into the house and hurried to the kitchen where she unlocked the door to the back of the garage. The whole area was covered with hard core - an even layer of tiny rocks. The builder had started work. But he wasn't due until tomorrow... and the freezer! Where was it?

In the darkness of the small lobby, which led to the garden door, Ann almost fell over it when she turned round. She switched on the electric light and saw a note on top weighted with a stone. With shaking hands, she lifted it and read:

"Don't worry about emptying the freezer - we will move it back for you when the floor is finished."

Ann collapsed onto a kitchen stool and gripped the table. They couldn't have looked inside it - it was locked... she had hidden the key, but she had to make sure! Shaking, she went to the garage shelf to retrieve it and lifted the lid. Thank God! ...It was exactly as she had left it, so she re-locked it and took the key back to the kitchen with her to read the rest of the note:

"Sorry not able to check with you before starting work. Can't come tomorrow. School wall collapsed yesterday so have to fix while children not there. Can't come Monday or Tuesday (Bank Holiday). Will concrete Wednesday."

Still unsettled, Ann drank coffee and looked at the Deans' house. It wasn't yet dark outside but their lights were on and she could visualise the cosy domestic scene. She felt so alone – would she ever be truly happy again? Ann had experienced an even more disappointing day than on her first foray in search of a gravesite and admitted defeat at last. As soon as she dared, she would again load the body into the car, drive it away as far as possible in the time available, dumping it in as deserted a place as she could find. She was now resigned to the fact that it would be discovered quickly and reviewed her own movements in case she was ever asked for an alibi.

It did not take long for realisation to hit her, like a thunderbolt. If an alibi ever was required, she was in trouble! Jenny knew she had gone to the sale hall this morning but someone there might remember her leaving again within a short time of arriving ...she would just have to say she had been shopping. It was seven-thirty now, but with luck, Jenny might not know that Ann had been away for hours so, looking on the bright side, at least those damned clothes were out of the house.

To avoid being disturbed by Eddie ringing later, Ann telephoned him. His father answered and told her how much he and Martha were enjoying the family visit – he hoped Ann was taking advantage of her freedom and putting her feet up. He passed her on to Eddie and she assured him, with fingers crossed, that all was well. After speaking briefly to each of the children Ann hung up. Now she could grab a sandwich and go to bed for a few hours.

Sleep would not come and in her restlessness she had a sudden amazing thought. The stony hard-core base in the garage was probably only a few inches deep ...if she moved it away from the middle – why shouldn't she dig a hole there, for Joyce? The ground might well be hard, but she had until Tuesday to get the job done ...it would be a perfect hiding place because, as long as she replaced the stones and levelled it again, the concrete would set within a week!

It was such an exciting prospect that her previous tiredness fell away and she went downstairs for a closer look at the floor.

52 – Pressure Mounts

Polly and Sarah were glad to be home after their second day walking the countryside. They were not used to being on their feet all day but had coped remarkably well. Noting how tired they were Clarrie volunteered to cook. Polly suggested micro-waving something from the freezer and gladly rested with Sarah while Clarrie went to work in the kitchen.

"What did you think of Del Delaney?" Polly asked.

Not actually answering her question, Sarah replied,

"Well, now that I've seen him I know why Clarinda is so favourably impressed. Did you notice anything in particular about him?" She raised an eyebrow at Polly and waited.

"If you are asking if he reminded me of anyone – then yes, I did think he looked a little like Clarinda's father when he was in his twenties."

"My impression exactly," reflected Sarah. "When Stephen was older, as Clarinda would remember him, he was not as fair and he carried more weight, but when we married, he looked like Del's younger brother might – if he had one! It took a while before I was able to ignore the resemblance and accept him on his own terms. It is possible that Clarinda is subconsciously aware of a kind of familiarity about him."

Polly smiled indulgently as Sarah launched into her pet theory. "It is often said that married couples grow to look alike, but," continued Sarah, "it is more likely that we are attracted to features similar to our own in some way –

either in shape or expression. I look at newly wedded couples in the newspaper and often think they look like brother and sister... but to answer your question – I like him."

Polly would have liked to discuss him further but the telephone ringing interrupted them. Sarah took longer than usual to push herself up from the deep comfort of her chair – the short rest had stiffened her tired limbs rather than restored them – so before she reached the hall the answering machine cut in.

Sarah waited. If it were anyone who might keep her talking for hours she wouldn't pick up. At the tone, an unfamiliar voice was bellowing in mid-sentence, "...don't know about the dog, but I saw your friend in blue and she lost something else as well. Give her a message from me. Tell her that Eric Todd has her photos and he's blackmailing her boyfriend. She'll find Todd at the garage outside Farlow towards Wycombe – he works there." There was a click as the line went dead.

Sarah reflected ...it sounded like an elderly person probably a woman – and unused to the telephone. It was most unlikely that she had anything to do with Joyce's death – or even knew of it – otherwise she wouldn't have left the message. She apparently hoped to cause trouble, for a man who had evidence of the girl's presence in Farlow, but who was probably not aware of what had happened to her; why otherwise would he become involved?

The woman hadn't given her name and Sarah wondered why. It could indicate that she had something to hide herself ...something that could possibly be of interest to the police – who would certainly want to hear the tape. What luck it had been, forgetting to switch the machine off. After playing it again for Clarrie and Polly, Sarah replaced the tape with another. Tomorrow morning she would telephone Alec and bring him completely up to date with all they suspected about the missing Joyce Hamilton.

Clarrie served the meal and cleared away before going up to her studio. It was several hours since she had carried her day's work from the car ...it had been out of sight upstairs and she was eager to see if everything about it was harmonious. When painting so intently, eyes could grow accustomed to small errors of judgement and ignore them ...but after hours away from the canvas they would be more critical. She set the painting on a display easel and stood back a few feet; everything appeared to be right. It had been a good idea to paint the old woman with the dog at the focal point of the picture; they added interest and movement to the composition.

Although she had expected to work on it for a while – a few touches here and there while it was still wet – Clarrie changed her mind. She was tired. It could have been the fresh air but, more likely, it was reaction after her stimulating encounter with both Del and the paranormal! She felt as though she had packed several days into one. Sarah and Polly wouldn't expect her downstairs again so she luxuriated in a hot scented foam bath before retiring and had to force herself to stay awake. Eventually she almost collapsed into bed and was soon fast asleep without even one more glance at the easel.

Several hours later Clarrie stirred – disturbed by cryptic, half-formed images that she tried vainly to suppress. She emerged reluctantly from the depths of slumber and gradually became aware that she could see the painting. It was as well lit as the actual scene in broad daylight yet with its back to the faint light from the window, it should have been impossible to discern. Pushing herself up slowly onto one elbow, bewildered by the inexplicable brightness, her gaze settled on the woman and as Clarrie watched, fascinated, the figure began to move.

The small round figure walked along the dry ditch and stopped for a while, crouching almost out of sight – then emerged, pushing something blue into a large bag. She had not been carrying anything earlier and the bulky parcel appeared awkward and heavy. In spite of this, the woman moved steadily across the field to the two cottages. It was wholly uncanny and, without making any mental effort to understand what she was witnessing, Clarrie stared, entranced... until the quiet scene was violently shattered by angry shouting!

Who else, wondered Clarrie, was out there in the valley with the scurrying old woman and the black dog? The wrathful yells increased in volume – became hysterical and closer! The unearthly illumination was instantly extinguished as Clarrie realised it was Joyce, but the voice lingered with her – it reverberated around the room. Horrified, Clarrie all but fainted, knowing she was not alone!

53 – Saturday 25ᵗʰ

Sarah rose early hoping to catch Alec before he became too involved in his routine but was disappointed to find he wasn't expected at all. Taking advantage of the long weekend, he and his wife had gone away for a few days. She didn't leave a message, other than that she had called and would like to speak to him when he returned on Tuesday. At first, perturbed, she considered talking to Algy, but after all, the girl was already dead ...a few days waiting would not alter the facts.

When Clarrie had showered, she hastened downstairs; she could hardly wait to describe her strange experience – eager to hear her mother's reaction. Both were still sleeping in the studio and Clarrie had almost woken Sarah in the middle of the night to discuss it, but it seemed such a shame to wake her. The waves of terror, when that awful voice still rang in her ears and which had threatened to make her pass out even after the vision faded, subsided as the cries became fainter and Clarrie perceived that Sarah still slept, undisturbed ...everything was normal.

Sarah was shocked, feeling she had let Clarinda down when she needed support but was more sanguine when they joined Polly in the kitchen where she was cooking breakfast. Sarah told Polly, with barely concealed excitement, "Clarinda had another of her strange dreams last night – it's probably wrong to call it a dream, but whatever it was, it has a definite bearing on our inquiries in Farlow." She pulled out chairs near the table and said,

"Let's sit down for a minute and hear all about it."

Polly said she was ready to serve breakfast, so why not have it in the kitchen to save time. "Why not indeed," agreed Sarah happily, sitting down, looking expectantly at her daughter who then began to describe what she had seen and heard in the small hours.

"After we returned last night I put the first of my Farlow paintings on an easel. I want to continue working on it today and was set for an early start. Do you remember the small figure with a dog, which is on the right of the field, near the two new houses?" Both her listeners did and pointed out that the more distant of the two houses from Clarrie's viewpoint was the one in which Joyce probably died.

"We saw that woman on our second visit," said Polly, "she took a short cut away from us, across the field."

"It may be of passing interest," Clarrie said, "that although I painted her there, I actually saw her outside the older cottages on the next lane. Anyway, placing her as I did improved the composition. Now I'm convinced she is connected to the events surrounding Joyce's death!"

Sarah's interest quickened. She leaned forward urging Clarrie to continue... "What makes you think so?"

Polly stood poised over the cooker – her attention no longer on the food she was preparing but riveted on Clarrie who shut her eyes, remembering. She described the strange behaviour of the woman after the painted figure moved.

They all agreed that the blue object, so incongruous, must be significant and when Clarrie described the shouting which had been far more alarming than merely seeing her picture come to life, they felt justified also in assuming that she was right, when she continued. "I'm absolutely sure it was Joyce shouting – she was watching with me, although at first I imagined she was out there in the field. I might have seen more but I suddenly knew she wasn't ...there, I mean! She was here in this house – in my room – yelling at me from inches away!"

"What did she say? What was it?" cried Polly excitedly.

"The voice was frenzied," declared Clarrie, "it was definitely a woman – shouting, *'How dare you! Drop it, it's mine'! ..."*

"This is fascinating," said Sarah. "I wonder whether Joyce – I think we can safely assume it was her – was actually shouting in your presence as you were observing, or whether her furious ghost was present, impotent, at the time her bag was being removed... shouting then, but unheard by the old woman of course. Your vision was certainly all encompassing, including even sound effects!"

It was an explanation that had not occurred to Clarrie and she accepted it with great relief. "I'd much rather believe that she was nowhere near me in the middle of the night. But the bag might prove she was in Farlow, so what is our next move?"

After some deliberation, they decided to leave Todd and his possible blackmailing activities to the police. They were more concerned about the possibility of their own inquiries alerting those concerned, leading to evidence being destroyed. The woman with the bag was a different matter, but, could they risk speaking with her if she was the one who had telephoned about the photographs?

Polly had to prepare soon to go to her nephew Dan's wedding – his brother Frank, who was driving her for the day, was due in an hour, so they decided to postpone their final decision until Tuesday. In any case, Sarah was reluctant to proceed without consulting Alec.

54 - Unwanted Calls

All was quiet when Ann woke up fully at around ten in the morning. She was exhausted after spending most of the small hours digging in the garage.

She had stirred earlier when the young postman skidded round on his bike at the end of the drive, whistling tunelessly. She had intended to catch him to make sure he left only their own mail, but couldn't move and instantly went back to sleep. About an hour later she heard Bill's car driving away. He couldn't be going to work so she guessed he'd taken the family to the sale... Jenny would be pleased. If they were all out, Ann could count on not being disturbed and could risk digging more, during the morning... but not yet! She relaxed.

Something did disrupt her repose at last; otherwise she would probably have slept much longer. What was it? A bell: not the doorbell, no. The ringing 'phone was far away, distant, no concern of hers. It was actually a mere eighteen inches from her head and stopped warbling the second she woke fully.

Ann wondered whether to ring Eddie in case it had been him. First though, she had to have some breakfast. The worry and physical activity was doing wonders for her weight – she hadn't had either time or inclination to eat for almost a week but couldn't afford to be ill – certainly not yet – so she cooked some bacon and eggs.

It was nearly eleven-o-clock when Ann reached for the telephone and she was startled as it shrilled under her hand. A strange voice, female, asked if she was Mrs Tiller.

Hearing Ann's affirmative, the voice asked, "May I speak to your husband please? I tried to reach him yesterday – about his secretary, but there was no answer."

Ann leaned limply against the kitchen wall... Just when she'd thought the nightmare was almost over... her heart raced. Incapable of speech she replaced the receiver. Whoever it was would not have an answer now either – Ann could not trust herself to speak yet! The woman would have to ring back...

She had almost recovered her composure when the instrument burst into life again. Taking a deep breath, she lifted it to reply and was astonished to discover it was Jenny, ringing from town.

"I'm glad to catch you at home," said Jenny. "I didn't call on the way out because there was no sign of movement. We thought you had already left and we'd see you here. Are you okay?" Ann muttered something about oversleeping and Jenny went on to say, "I'm sorry to disturb you, but we won't be back before six."

Ann swallowed hard, with relief... no strange woman worrying about Joyce and nobody home next door! ...But why was Jenny telephoning? She tried to concentrate again. "Will you be able to do a favour for us and baby-sit tonight?" Jenny was asking, "You know my birthday is tomorrow? Well, Bill wants us to celebrate – dinner out if we can be sure the twins are in good hands."

Ann had to say she would be happy to help out – Bill could go ahead and book a table. She privately hoped they wouldn't be very late home, as she might have to work through the night again. She didn't know whether to be glad or sorry the stranger hadn't rung back but before she could decide, the wretched thing sounded again. She considered ignoring it, eyeing it balefully until the sixth trill... then, very slowly, she picked it up.

55 – Birthday Surprise

When Jenny returned to the hall having telephoned Ann from a call box outside, Bill was handing out pocket money to Matthew who immediately looked secretive and agitated. He seized Sally's hand and dragged her away. "I take it they have found exactly what I want for my birthday!" Jenny laughed.

Bill put a finger to his lips looking beyond her as the children ran into the crowd. "Now don't spoil the surprise... What did Ann say?" Hearing that the birthday dinner was on, he also went out to call the restaurant. It was likely to be a very busy night – he might have to ring around to find a place able to accept a late booking.

Several people, knowing Jenny was Ann's neighbour asked where she was and why she wasn't helping at the busiest of their sales. Jenny found herself unable to explain. She had expected Ann to arrive eventually and was also puzzled but had been too pre-occupied with her own affairs to express any curiosity about what Ann intended doing. She could have decided to put her feet up: why not!

Trying to keep an eye on the twins, without being seen during the special purchase, was difficult and in the end rather pointless. Jenny saw the stallholder very kindly wrapping it for them, but it was a waste of the woman's time. They were incapable of waiting until tomorrow and brought it over to her immediately with cries of 'Happy Birthday' demanding that Jenny should open it straight away.

When she had unwrapped, admired it and proclaimed herself amazed at their cleverness – buying such a lovely gift for only fifty pence, as Sally informed her proudly – Jenny put it in her bag. In fact, she really did consider it a good buy; pleased that it was something she could actually use... it would brighten up her new suit.

Jenny had seen a leather handbag with a pair of elegant gloves displayed on one of the stands and had been tempted to buy them, but doubtful about the shade. They would match it perfectly if they were still there. The twins would be really thrilled by such positive proof that she really liked their gift. Bright blue was not a colour she would have chosen, but the scarf was, after all, real silk!

After handing the twins over to Bill when he returned, Jenny went immediately to see if the other accessories were still there ...yes – she was just in time to pounce as another customer picked up one of the gloves.

Ignoring the nasty looks, Jenny announced that she wished to buy the set and was soon carrying away her bargain in triumph. She wouldn't tell Bill she had bought them at a jumble sale ...he was far more snobbish than she was about picking up bargains and what he didn't know wouldn't hurt him ...but Jenny could hardly wait to show them to Ann ...perhaps tonight!

56 – All Going Well

The wedding was over and Polly was enjoying meeting many friends and relatives she hadn't seen for years. Everyone agreed that Elaine was the most beautiful bride ever and Dan looked so handsome... a credit to the family.

As was to be expected, his young brother Frank came in for the usual ribbing about being the next groom and when could they expect to be celebrating for him too! Partly because of this, Frank was eager to leave as soon as was decently possible. His speech had been well received but he had been too nervous to eat and his stomach still felt disturbed.

In any case, Elaine and Dan were calling in at Mapledurham tomorrow. Because he would meet them again so soon he could see no point in competing for Dan's attention now.

As soon as the happy pair left – ostensibly driving off on honeymoon, but actually to go to their own home – Frank sought out Polly.

She looked quite regal in a dark flowered brocade suit and a small matching pillbox hat, which, swathed in veiling bunched behind it, drew attention from her rather outsize figure and flattered her round homely features.

Her grandchildren – who were glorying in all the attention – and their proud parents, surrounded her.

They were in no hurry to depart as they were remaining overnight in Oxford and were trying to persuade Polly to stay also, but there was far too much going on at home for Polly to change her plans.

Elaine and Dan hadn't yet been told that her friend had died – time enough for that tomorrow. Today they were entitled to a happy wedding day unspoiled by any jarring note.

57 – Surprise Surprise

Ann was weary. The hole was adequate in area but needed more depth. It was placed as centrally as she could make it: a valley in a circular mountain of stones, making it difficult to gauge where the floor level had been when she started, but digging down twelve inches more should suffice.

Jenny and Bill being out all afternoon enabled Ann to work without fear of interruption and when she at last stopped for a tea break she had accomplished considerably more than she'd dared hope. Another hour should do the trick. She would only need half an hour to clean up and walk round to Jenny's; the mere thought made her groan. If only she didn't have to go out! She resumed work... the knowledge that it would be her first night of comparative peace fortified her.

Incredibly, the grave digging proceeded without a hitch and she was contemplating putting the body in it when the Dean's car returned. It drove straight past so she carried on. She hauled the black plastic bundle out of the cabinet, rolled it into the hole and within thirty minutes it was completely covered. The prepared ground now looked much as it had when the builder left it – fantastic!

In a buoyant frame of mind, Ann went upstairs to recuperate in a hot bath. At last she could afford time for a relaxing long soak – showering was refreshing but she wanted to pamper herself after the worst week of her entire life! Nestling deep in bubbles she recollected the strange call about Joyce and fought a wave of nausea, which rose to her throat. The woman had not rung back. She may have tried but would have found the line engaged anyway. First Jenny, then a long call from Eddie and the children had occupied it almost from the moment Ann had cut her off without ceremony.

Now, she was in little danger if anyone came looking for Joyce ...she was safely buried and no-one even knew she had been near Farlow, let alone visited Ann at the house. There was no way Eddie and his affair could come to light. No matter how much he missed her initially, Eddie would never admit it. Later, Ann – more glamorous, slimmer and fitter, in her new role of Cordon Bleu cook, would erase Joyce completely from his mind.

The doorbell chimed as Ann emerged from the bathroom but she was hardly in a fit state to go down so she grabbed a robe and flung open the window. A garden shop van was in the drive and hearing her overhead the delivery boy stepped away from the porch to look up. "Flowers for Mrs Dean," he shouted, "I'll leave them at the door."

"No! Don't. You have the wrong house," Ann informed him. "You'll have to drive up the lane a little farther I'm afraid.

"Are you sure," was his aggressive and inane reply. "It says 'Far Acre' in my book!"

"It might just as well say Buckingham Palace," Ann said, rather tersely, "...it says 'Near Acre' on the wall of my house! Take another look!" She shut the window sharply and went to dress, reflecting again on Bill's extravagance. Although Jenny was so lucky Ann had never envied her before this week. Bill was a few years younger than Eddie and had no doubt earned more, for longer. He would probably become a director of his firm within a few years. But Eddie was also quite successful ...he earned higher than average pay and was due for promotion soon. Bill was more flamboyant though and their homes reflected the difference between the two men.

Their houses, built at the same time by the same builder, were now quite dissimilar. Whereas the Tillers' was in its original form, surrounded by a trim but rather ordinary garden, Deans' was a show place. The ground floor had been extended to enlarge the sitting room, with double-glazed picture windows on three sides to take advantage of the professionally landscaped garden. No sliding doors opened to the outside ...they couldn't risk people tramping dirt straight in, onto the pastel-coloured Chinese carpets! Jenny's taste in furniture was also expensive and there had been no compromises – if anything did not match, it was out. She had an eye for antiques and the money to indulge every whim, but had she not been thrifty in other ways, perhaps Ann wouldn't have felt as comfortable with her.

They both enjoyed making some of their own clothes – small things for the children too, and took pride in producing homemade pies and cakes.

Both were careful shoppers and kept each other informed if they saw a bargain and this facet of Jenny's character, perhaps more than any other, endeared her to Ann. Jenny never flaunted her affluence in Ann's face and was not averse to saving money when the opportunity arose. Ready at last, Ann locked up and walked round to baby-sit.

Bill opened the door and greeted her; his better half was almost ready he informed her. They indulged in small talk until they heard Jenny approaching and both turned as she entered the room with a flourish. "I had to pop in to say good-night to the children. They were struggling to stay awake so I don't think you'll have any trouble with them Ann..." Jenny broke off as she saw them both staring at her with something akin to horror on their faces. "Good heavens – have I forgotten to zip something up?"

Bill and Ann both laughed off their embarrassment and

spoke together... "What? Of course not darling! You look stunning!"...

"Oh ...your outfit, I haven't seen it before, it's lovely! You should wear dark tan more often..."

Ann didn't know why Bill looked shaken, but she had lied about the brown suit; her attention was riveted on the accessories: the handbag, gloves and scarf ...she knew their late owner!

Fortunately, Jenny was too excited to suspect that neither of them had answered with sincerity. She was anxious to show Ann her birthday present from Bill and opened the velvet box she had brought in with her, to display a bracelet – the wide gold band was secured by a jewelled clasp: a square of rubies and diamonds.

It wasn't at all difficult for Ann to express her admiration – it was exquisite and she helped Jenny to put it on her wrist.

Bill watched them fiddling with the fastening ...but his eyes were actually on the brooch which held the scarf at her throat – a simple design based on the initial 'J', which he had last seen when he gave it to Joyce. He had removed it from Jenny's trinket box; she hadn't worn it for years and had never commented on its absence! How could it possibly be in the possession of his wife again! He swallowed hard – he dared not ask her, he could only wait until she raised the subject herself. Perhaps she was biding her time to torment him ...and if she was it was no more than he deserved.

The evening stretched ahead of him interminably now ...hours of torment, having to guard every word in case she was intent on trapping him... and if she was, it could only be because Joyce had, after all, carried out her threat. The wretched girl had ruined everything – not only his evening but also his marriage... his life. He had never felt murderous toward anyone before but ...if only he had his hands round her neck at that moment!

But wasn't the fault at least half his? How could he have landed himself in this mess? He looked at Jenny. God, she was beautiful! If only he could turn the clock back! Perhaps if he confessed before Jenny revealed that she knew... that might placate her... Perhaps, if only he could work up sufficient courage!

58 - The Betting Man

Eric Todd had taken the boys out for the afternoon to a football match and was in a good mood when they returned. His team had won and he also won a bet he'd placed on a race - he was not habitually a betting man but how could he resist risking a fiver of his unexpected windfall, on a horse called 'Modern Painter'! It had been an outsider at 33 - 1, so he had reason for his high spirits. He had even picked up a box of chocolates for Alice.

Mary had been with Alice while he was out. She wanted to find out if that woman had rung him up about her photographs. If she had, it was obvious that Alice knew nothing about it. Mary had to listen again to all the stupidity about Eric and his painting ...Alice even showed her a wet splodge on a piece of hardboard which would be instantly snapped up by the 'Art Expert'. Well, Eric might get a nasty shock when he tried to collect on it! When Mary heard his car arrive, she went home. The last thing she wanted to do was meet him face to face.

In fact, she felt a little ashamed now that it was too late. He had never done her any harm and she had often felt sorry for him having to put up with Alice. She let herself into the dark scullery and waited impatiently, holding the door open until Blacky caught up and waddled inside too. Mary made herself a sandwich, and then did as she did on most evenings now. She locked herself in, went to her bedroom and pulled the blue suitcase from under the bed, admiring again the soft leather. She was using it to hold all her treasures... mementoes of a lamentably dull life.

There were a few things that had been her mother's and a muddle of newspaper cuttings about weddings, births and deaths, which were almost illegible. There was a lace handkerchief she had found but never used, and an embroidered evening bag studded with rhinestones. Over the years, she had become convinced she had always owned it and carried at village dances, when young. Mary was pleased to have all her special things together in the splendid new case. The things it had contained when she found it were now dispersed. The dainty clothing was pushed to the bottom of an old trunk. She might give it to Alice, bit by bit, for birthdays or Christmas. There were skirts and blouses; she would keep them for a year or two in case anyone recognised them and a few bits of jewellery too which she hid. She fleetingly considered selling them one day, but that would make her feel like a thief so she dismissed the idea.

There was one thing that she was using already ...a lovely tray, real silver-plated. It was now in pride of place, leaning against the wall on top of a display cabinet in the living room. It was funny she thought – twice now it had rolled off in the night and she'd had to wedge it in place. If she found it on the floor again tomorrow morning she'd think she was haunted! Mary didn't know how right she was.

Joyce stood unseen. She watched, enraged, seeing her precious things in those coarse hands. That woman who had promised to help had better act soon or else...!

If she delayed much longer she would fix her too!

59 – More Problems?

After they left, Ann dozed in front of the television. She was far too tired to watch anything seriously and was thankful that the children, after their full exciting day, went to sleep quickly without the usual requests for drinks of water or a story!

The shock, which sent her head spinning when she saw Jenny wearing Joyce's things, had abated slightly. There was no reason why Eddie should ever see Jenny wearing them – and if he did, there was more than one set of blue accessories. Why should he ever make a connection ...but what rotten luck it had been, that the blue scarf should have attracted the twins at the sale. There was nothing Ann could do about it anyway, so she gave in to the weariness that assailed her.

When she was awakened by Bill's key in the door, she was startled to find herself in a chair instead of bed. Jenny went straight upstairs to check on the children while Bill walked Ann back home. She was finding it hard to keep her eyes open let alone make conversation and they were almost at her door before she realised how agitated he was. He was saying he couldn't bring himself to do something or other after all ...until he found out more ...she might be able to help him! It was all too difficult to follow. She opened her front door and was surprised when he followed her inside.

Ann suddenly detected the worry in his tone. "I simply couldn't believe my eyes and wondered if she had spoken to you about it," he said. Seeing Ann's puzzled look Bill repeated, "The scarf pin: where did it come from?" When Ann still looked blank he asked, "How long has she had it? A week... a day or two?"

"Oh, the brooch she wore tonight," Ann said, relieved finally to catch his drift, "Jenny mislaid it apparently and was thrilled to come across it again. She said it was one of your earliest gifts to her." Bill looked worried and agreed that it had been ...he said he knew it hadn't been in Jenny's possession for a long while. She never mentioned missing it – in fact, he had thought she'd forgotten it completely!

Bill perceived he was babbling, getting confused – and stopped abruptly. "Look, we can't talk now but would you mind if I came round tomorrow morning – I just have to talk to someone, or go mad!" He bade her goodnight hastily, and to Ann's relief, went. Whatever was bothering him could keep with her blessing – she had enough worries of her own without looking for more. Standing in the hall Ann hadn't been able to suppress the shivers which coursed up and down her spine – probably nerves. The sooner she was tucked up in a nice warm bed the better, she decided, dragging her aching body upstairs. Tomorrow, she thought, would be the first day of her new life ...Eddie would soon forget that Joyce had ever existed.

60 – Joyce

Sarah and Clarrie were sleeping peacefully ...the spectre hovered between them unseen. Time has no relevance in the spirit world but Joyce was still sufficiently tied to the earthly plane to count the passing days.

This idiotic female she fumed, looking down at Sarah, had actually walked right past the house where her poor lifeless body was concealed, without even attempting to confront her murderer!

Was that arrogant bitch going to be allowed to get away with it?

She had even called a second time and given up, just because the woman was out! It was beyond belief; what was the point of being able to communicate with her if she ignored everything she was told!

Her daughter was no better!

She even knew all about the nasty little person who had stolen her case.

Why had they done nothing about it?

They should inform the police!

What had either of them done to bring her murderer to justice?

Nothing!

All day she had waited for them to act but from the way they spoke it seemed they actually sympathised with Bill's wife who was apparently to be protected – allowed to get away with her crime!

No way! Joyce decided... If they weren't going to be any use, she would take her revenge on them. Her life had been snatched from her and somebody was going to pay!

Joyce immediately began to translate her threat into action. She stood over Clarrie, confident of penetrating her dreams ...a hypnotist establishing control over an unresisting mind. Clarrie's breathing grew more audible: shorter. She stirred and slowly sat up: then stood. She moved silently from the bed. She automatically started heading for the bathroom, but turned away before she was halfway across the intervening space. Instead, she moved stiffly towards the door to the landing.

Like a robot, Clarrie swayed slowly off the thick carpet across the floor of the studio, her bare feet making no sound on the polished wood. Her arms outstretched, like those of a sleepwalker, she turned the doorknob and went out. At the top of the stairs, her eyes still closed, Clarrie hesitated as if reluctant to descend, but Joyce willed her to walk down... resisting the temptation to make her fall; she had a much more ambitious plan in mind.

Polly was ordinarily a light sleeper, but even she was unaware of the drama being enacted outside her bedroom door.

Clarrie moved down softly, one step at a time – pausing on each. She reached the bottom, turned from the hall and entered the kitchen where she stood like a statue in the darkness for several minutes. At last, she went to a drawer and pulled it open. A slotted rack inside displayed a fearsome array of knives. Clarrie lifted one out, weighed it briefly in her hand then returned it and instead took out a bone cleaver.

Joyce was jubilant and sought to insinuate herself more securely into Clarrie's physical shell. She felt her hand closing over the short handle of the chopper and held it high. She exercised her control by bringing it down onto a wooden chair-back, splitting it with a sharp crack.

Clarrie lowered the cleaver to her side and stood like a mechanical toy awaiting the touch of a button.

Finally – looking neither to left nor right – she left the room with it and climbed the stairs back to the studio.

Sarah lay unsuspecting, peacefully asleep, her breathing almost inaudible.

Clarrie's eyes opened into a wide blank stare ...she walked to the foot of Sarah's bed, the cleaver now gripped in both hands. Standing over the sleeping form she swung the cleaver into the air ...the weight of it made her sway back slightly.

Joyce savoured the moment – she had mastered this girl – she felt all powerful. *Now! This is what she would do to all who dared cross her.* She made a supreme effort of will to bring the blade crashing down on Sarah's head but, to her chagrin, Clarrie spoke calmly and clearly, "Mother, wake up!"...

Almost simultaneously, there was a scream from the doorway – it was Polly, who had been alerted by the sharp snap of splitting wood downstairs. Clicking on the overhead light, Polly stared, unable to comprehend what she was seeing.

Sarah woke immediately and saw Joyce poised over her, her face twisted with hate. In a surprisingly cool voice, she spoke to Joyce. "Haven't you been wicked enough on earth to ensure a place in hell? Explain yourself! Why are you trying to harm us when we are doing our best to help you?" Sarah waited, listening, and then spoke again. "There is no point in lying to me – I know you died by your own hand! You took the poisonous stuff to that house intending to kill Mrs Dean."

Again Sarah listened and replied at last, "I didn't go to the house where you died because I knew she didn't live there ...if you had succeeded you would have murdered the wrong woman!"

Joyce abruptly abandoned her attempt to control Clarrie who, white and shaking, collapsed thankfully on her bed.

While Polly seized a blanket to wrap around her, Sarah was still pre-occupied with Joyce who had to be convinced that she must repent. Her only hope of salvation was to admit her faults and do her best to atone. Joyce was at first unable to accept that she had not met Jenny Dean; she told Sarah she had seen a photograph of the twins there... "No, the Tillers' also have a girl and boy!" said Sarah.

Joyce still insisted she had seen the name outside the house! But at last she understood and began to feel twinges of doubt, if not conscience. It was such a slow process that Sarah made a suggestion. "Clarrie, you had no difficulty throwing off Joyce when she thought she had you under control, so I have an idea. If you would rather not try it then please say so."

With her mother fully awake and in charge, Clarrie had no hesitation agreeing and was soon at her studio desk writing ...at least, that is what Polly saw. Sarah, sitting close by, witnessed Joyce making a statement of her own.

Sarah read the words, which appeared in a flourishing looped script, quite different from Clarrie's own writing. Occasionally she asked a question and the answer appeared with no hesitation. It was obvious that she had at last made an impression on the recalcitrant spirit. When Sarah was satisfied, she told Joyce that she must forget her earthly ties ...she should make a determined effort to cancel out the accumulated evil thoughts and intentions of her lifetime. They would all pray for her salvation.

Joyce almost faded but a flash of her old self surfaced and she asked, "What about that nasty old woman who has my case, my clothes and my jewellery?"

"Of what possible use are any of those things to you now? Why not allow her to enjoy them? She is too old for prison and couldn't afford a fine! Who would inherit them from you? I understood from Elaine that you were alone in the world." Joyce looked subdued and wavered slightly. Her image slipped away but Clarrie who still held the pen started writing again. When she had finished Sarah read aloud:

"She cannot keep the tray. It is a gift for Elaine. My wedding present."

Clarrie returned fully to normal and, having no idea what she had written, read the whole story according to Joyce. Strictly speaking, it wasn't evidence but, if Ann Tiller's version substantially agreed with it, Alec might be able to help her. As for the tray, Sarah was still reluctant to be in contact with anyone who might later be interviewed by the police, but had to devise a way of retrieving it!

She must keep her promise and deliver it. Joyce might be repentant at this moment, but who knew how she would react if crossed again!

61 – Sunday 26th

The ringing telephone woke Ann. Every bone in her body ached and she groaned aloud as she tried to roll over to answer it. It must be Eddie she thought, trying to focus her eyes on the bedside clock. Oh no: not at eight-thirty! He would not be so mean as to ring before ten.

It wasn't Eddie... She immediately recognised the voice of the stranger who had called yesterday. The woman apologised for ringing so early. "We were cut off yesterday! I tried again several times with no success. Then a friend came to take me out for the day so I couldn't try until last night but there was still no reply... I didn't want to miss you today too."

"What can I do for you," Ann asked, wishing she would get to the point. When the reply came, it was exactly what she dreaded.

"I am Mrs Ada Baker – you don't know me, but my niece is your husband's secretary."

Ann could scarcely believe her ears... so Joyce really did live with an old aunt! The cats were probably real too! She forced herself to pay attention. She must be careful of every word she said. "I'm afraid I don't know your niece either."

"He must have mentioned her though, but it doesn't matter – I just want to be sure he gets a message."

"Well, of course," Ann stayed calm, "But he isn't here at the moment. Is it urgent?" Ann said she would be glad to contact him if it was really important but the woman asserted that she didn't need to speak to him personally.

"Perhaps I can help you then," Ann offered.

"Oh, I'm sure you can," replied Mrs Baker. "Joan is supposed to be returning to the office on Tuesday, a day earlier than your husband, but she's had a minor mishap – twisted her ankle very badly and can't drive. She is in Wales you know. Anyway, she contacted the girl who has been standing in for her and she's sure she can easily cope for an extra day or two. Joan hopes to be better by the end of the week. She'll ring him at the office on Wednesday." As she chattered on, Ann was striving to grasp the fact that she was talking about Joan not Joyce.

"Did you say you were Joan's aunt?" Ann asked faintly.

"Yes. Joan Baker, your husband is her boss isn't he? … I am speaking to Mrs Tiller aren't I?"

Ten minutes later, Ann sat having a cup of hot sweet tea to clear her mind. It was quite obvious that she had buried a complete stranger in the garage! Who on earth was Joyce Hamilton? Where had she come from? This thought led to another. Who had Joyce really worked for? Whose wife had she planned to kill? She came to the wrong house …just like the new postman, and the delivery boy! All had made the same mistake. Joyce Hamilton was having an affair with Bill! and had come looking for Jenny. That accounted for his weird conversation last night!

As Ann was endeavouring to assimilate this earth-shattering truth, Bill was hurrying down the drive to her front porch. In answer to his ring she opened the door and fell back as he stepped inside. Bill began speaking with a desperation that made him breathless. His words came in staccato bursts and at first Ann couldn't grasp what he was saying.

"You'll probably think I'm mad – I know you'll despise me but I have to explain why I'm so worried. You may even know already, from Jenny. Oh, God I hope not!"

By the time they reached the kitchen where Ann switched on the kettle again, she had a feeling they would both need a drink before this ordeal was over. She had already heard about what he called his 'stupid fling' – hardly worth calling 'an affair' with his secretary who was now missing. Now Bill was telling Ann that when he last saw Joyce she threatened to tell Jenny everything herself if he didn't. Bill added that if and when Joyce calmed down after the weekend, he was determined to convince her that it was definitely all over.

Bill said he had suffered a few bad hours last Monday... (who hadn't? Ann thought grimly) wondering if Joyce was carrying out her threat and was with Jenny but later he'd discovered that she had taken a week off to go to a wedding. He had never, ever, intended to leave Jenny and the children; he would make Joyce see sense when she eventually appeared. Several things had cropped up however, which made him think he was too late – Joyce had visited Farlow already!

Without noticing the effect this statement produced in Ann's facial expression, Bill rattled on. Having at last started to release his pent-up fears and emotions, they spilled from him almost of their own volition. Had Joyce confronted his wife after all? That was his foremost concern! Not that he had noticed any change in Jenny's attitude towards him, not really, but that might be because he had been so blinkered by his own problems. She might actually know everything and be biding her time to accuse him!

Ann's throat constricted with fear. This alarming hypothesis made her feel faint; she busied herself with the coffee and waited to hear his reasons. At first, she had been dizzy with relief at having her suspicions confirmed – Eddie was not guilty of deceit and had never stopped loving her. How could she ever have thought otherwise!

Then the portent of Bill's words sank in ominously. The girl had after all left a trail. What had occurred to alert Bill to Joyce's fatal visit to Farlow? Had he told anyone else

– the police perhaps? Ann sat; numb with dread. Bill may have heard it from the police! Ann was instantly convinced that the trail would lead straight to her and to the grisly evidence she had so stupidly concealed in her own home and felt choked by her own stupidity. Dumping the body on the open road fifty miles away would have been better than coming back here with it. She steeled herself not to weep openly and eventually managed to speak.

"Why should you think Joyce has been anywhere near here? Surely she wouldn't risk antagonising you by speaking to Jenny herself. In her place, I would rather have *you* do it than risk having my eyes scratched out by an angry wife." She held her breath and waited.

Bill avoided admitting he was being blackmailed but went so far as to say that someone had shown him something belonging to Joyce, which she must have lost locally. Even worse – there was the scarf pin. He asked if Ann noticed it last night. Ann said she had, but did not inform him that for her personally, other things held more significance!

Looking, if possible, even more shamefaced than before, Bill confessed to having removed the pin from his wife's dressing table to give to Joyce on her birthday. "I'd forgotten to buy anything – the initial was perfect and Jenny never wore it."

Ann couldn't conceal her scorn and Bill defended himself. "It seemed such a good idea at the time – Joyce loved it and wore it often. Yesterday, seeing it at Jenny's throat, I couldn't believe it!" He shuddered. "How in the name of all that's Holy did she get it back? Could they have met? Are they conspiring in silence to punish me?" He paused long enough to drink his coffee, now cold. He speculated, "Perhaps they had an almighty row – Jenny saw the brooch, recognised it and snatched it from her lapel… Or did Joyce fling it at her?" He groaned heavily, his head in his hands, and then looked directly into Ann's eyes pleading for reassurance. "Could Joyce have been to our house on Monday? Did you see her anywhere around?"

Ann thought quickly. She had to dispel any fears that the girl and Jenny came into contact – it was all Bill really cared about. "Actually," she answered calmly, "There *was* a woman, quite tall I think, wearing blue ...I noticed her because it is unusual to see casual strollers in the lane. She was walking away towards the village."

Then, assuaging his sudden panic, she rested her hand on his arm to reassure him. "She couldn't have seen Jenny because Jenny went out half an hour earlier. Yes, I am positive it was Monday because Jenny had been with me – going over our lists together. I intended to mention the visitor when she returned but forgot. I had a little fainting fit, I expect she told you."

Bill's white face flushed with relief. He did remember, so he accepted that she had the right day. Ann explained that Jenny had shown her the pin, having found it during the week in the lane. It was not difficult to convince him when she pointed out that the recovery had probably been kept from him because the loss hadn't been confessed in the first place. He looked almost happy.

Ann was unable to curb her fierce resentment that Bill, whose selfishness had landed her in this ghastly mess, should feel happy about anything, but self-preservation was more important than revenge. "Jenny told me she mislaid or lost it ages ago," Ann continued. "She saw it glinting on the grass verge and was clearly delighted. She said it was one of your first ever gifts to her when you met ...I imagine that's why she never told you it had disappeared! Unless you bring up the subject yourself she need never know you are an Indian giver!" She couldn't resist the barb. He had done a miserable thing and Ann badly wished she could make him suffer as much as she had, since his folly had landed literally on her doorstep.

Ann had suffered the torments of hell all week – agonising over her own marriage and becoming criminally involved in the death – not to mention the disposal – of a complete stranger. She could cheerfully have strangled Bill. She wished he would go now ...just go home.

He started to rise, sensing that he was out-staying his welcome, but he turned to her suddenly, sat down again and resumed earnestly in a perplexed tone, "How can you explain this though? When the children bought the birthday scarf I didn't really look at it but when Jenny wore it with the bag and gloves, which she also picked up at the sale apparently, I remembered Joyce wearing an identical set. I was shocked; the painting on the silk is so distinctive, but how could her things have ended up in a jumble sale...?"

He saw the stunned look on Ann's face and thought it was one of derision. "Oh, very well," he grinned sheepishly, "I'm just paranoid, there must be hundreds of them about, but I can tell you, after the week I've had, just seeing it gave me a nasty turn." He ran a hand over his brow. "What with the pin – then the scarf on top of the other things I tell you I could have believed Jenny had strangled her and buried her in the compost heap – she has quite a temper you know, when provoked!"

Bill was at last inclined to be more philosophical about the fact that Joyce had not been seen since leaving London on Monday morning. "It need not mean anything more than that she is hoping I will be frantic with worry and declare my undying love when she comes back," he muttered with a frown. "No chance! Now I know she hasn't already ruined my life I wouldn't care if she stayed lost forever. I don't know why I let myself get involved. I think I detest her now."

After Bill left, Ann locked the front door and leaned

against it helplessly for a few moments. At last she staggered upstairs and crawled shakily under the eiderdown. She breathed deeply, trying to unwind the strings of tension, which knotted her whole body. What was done was done. She had behaved stupidly ...her panic at the thought of losing Eddie and the consequent break-up of her family had blinded her to the grossness of her own actions. The gravity of her situation was at last sinking in, but surely continuing the deception was less risky than confession? She would look forward positively to the return of her husband and family and what must be a good future for them all. She was paying a high price because she had been misled into thinking she should conceal the whole ghastly event in order to preserve her marriage but she had come through it so far. She had also inadvertently saved her friend's – the one that was really threatened! With this noble thought uppermost in mind, Ann slowly relaxed and slept for a few hours, until the telephone again shrilled in her ear.

This time, it *was* Eddie. Ann gave him the message and the first words on his lips – which she'd heard so often before were, "Poor old Jo!" If only he had been more communicative about his working life, Ann would have at least known his secretary's name! She would actively discourage him from keeping his two worlds so far apart in future: no more misunderstandings!

Eddie said that in spite of Joan's absence he would still have Tuesday off; it wouldn't be fair to his parents to take the children away a day earlier than promised. In reply to his query, Ann confirmed that the garage project was well underway and made him happy by saying she was enjoying her few days' rest but missing him.

Ann resolved to take it easy for the remainder of the day and ignore the layers of dust everywhere. Housework had been neglected while she solved her other dilemma but it wouldn't take long to bring back the customary shine to everything. By Tuesday lunch-time, when the family returned, it would be as though Joyce Hamilton had never been born, let alone the grim fact that she had actually died in the heart of their home.

62 - Polly

After the trauma of Joyce's visitation the previous night, both Sarah and Clarrie slept late. Polly had witnessed only the final moments of the drama but she was utterly shaken by the fury she had seen unleashed. Only the fact that Sarah retired afterwards to her own bedroom leaving Clarrie alone, reassured Polly that they had no more to fear from Joyce. In Polly's humble opinion, the departed soul deserved to rot in hell forever for trying to murder Sarah by using her own daughter! She thanked God for giving them both such strength. Today would be busy but Pat was coming to work, in spite of the fact that it was Sunday. As it was Pat's brother Dan and his bride who were expected she was eager to help. Frank too was calling in, and after Sarah had spoken to the newly-weds alone, they were all having tea together.

Clarinda's new friend Del was expected around seven-o-clock with news of the abduction so what had started as a casual invitation to Dan and Elaine had developed into a large-scale event. Polly was a little concerned about how Elaine would receive the news of her friend's death but although she had met Elaine only briefly, it was difficult to believe the two young women had anything in common.

It was after eleven when Sarah and Clarinda appeared for coffee. Now armed with a complete and abject confession from Joyce, they wanted to write out their own account and put everything on record with Alec before the police interviewed Ann Tiller. Sarah observed, anxiously, that the poor woman must have been suffering untold torment. Goodness only knew where she'd concealed the body but they dared not approach her. There must be no suggestion that even the briefest meeting with her tainted their version of the affair. There was no doubt that she had behaved very stupidly, not reporting the death immediately, but until faced with such a crisis, how could anyone be sure of responding rationally?

While they wrote out their joint statement, ready to be endorsed by Polly and handed over as early as possible on Tuesday morning, Polly baked. Young folk always had huge appetites and she wanted to make sure there would be enough to eat. She thanked her niece again for helping.

"Think nothing of it," Pat said. "It's good of Mrs Grey to invite Frank and me. When we left mum and dad in Oxford I promised to look after him, so this will save me cooking at home! He has a date later so he won't stay long but after all, Dan is our big brother, and we will see even less of him now he's married."

The written account was not finalised until after lunch and as their guests were due at three-o-clock they all had a last-minute rush to get ready. In spite of everything they were determined the visit would be happy. The tragedy that had overtaken Joyce had, after all, been of her own making ... Elaine should not be allowed to mourn too deeply, but Sarah was aware that this attitude would not sit well with Joyce even in her new frame of mind. Sarah wondered if the improvement in Joyce's disposition would last – especially if she was still around to see them enjoying themselves, apparently unconcerned about her recent fate...

There was nothing she could do about it either way, except hope that they had heard the last of her – forever!

63 – The Artist

When Bill returned home, Jenny was still out with the children. He had declined to accompany them on their usual Sunday morning walk over the fields, saying he had some work to complete for the office. He was safely back in his study with an impressive pile of paper spread over his desk by the time he heard them coming. From his window at the rear he could see them at the garden gate beyond the orchard. He heard something else too... a car crunching over the gravel in the front drive. People didn't usually come without a prior arrangement on a Sunday morning so he went immediately to look.

His heart sank when he saw it was Todd ...what was the man thinking of, calling when he wasn't alone! He must get rid of him quickly he resolved, before Jenny reached the back door, and he hurried outside, desperate to prevent their meeting. Jenny might invite the man in!

Before Todd could alight he said, at the car window, "I didn't expect to see you again for a while," His tone was far from welcoming. Eric Todd, confident that he would not be refused said he had brought with him another painting for approval. Bill was furious and attempted to persuade him to go away – he would look at it on another day. It was not convenient now – out of the question! Unfortunately for Bill, Jenny and the children, full of curiosity, arrived to greet the visitor. Jenny was obviously bewildered. She recognised Eric's face, having seen him at the service station, but had no idea that he and her husband were so well acquainted.

Todd took advantage of Bill's confusion and climbed out of the car to shake Jenny's hand and meet the children. He patted Sally on the head and said, "What a little beauty. I have two boys myself. Just think, you might break their hearts one day!" Bill felt sick, and even sicker when Todd added slyly, "I'd love to paint your portrait – your brother's too."

Jenny looked even more surprised and asked if he was a professional artist. Keeping his eyes averted from Bill, Todd told her he was only an amateur and was grateful to have found a sponsor as knowledgeable as Mr Dean. One day, who knew, he might be famous, and all because her husband was taking such an interest in his work!

Without waiting for Bill to comment, Todd lifted out his latest masterpiece. Jenny was speechless but Matthew greeted it with great enthusiasm ...he loved the colourful splotch and declared that he knew what it was. Sally studied it closely, frowning, and challenged him to tell her.

Bill, anxious to end the encounter, drew Todd aside, out of earshot. "How much this time, you leech?" he demanded. Todd replied with no attempt to whisper,

"Oh no – really, I wouldn't hear of it – the usual fee will be acceptable. I only hope your faith in me will be justified one day and make you a rich man. I'll be happy with a cheque and if I have time I will paint another one or two next month."

After his departure, Bill picked up the painting and took it inside. Behind him, Jenny was howling her dismay, having just discovered both children covered with paint – their clothes were a mess. "The wretched thing is still wet! Bill, I simply can't believe you have actually bought it ...and where are the others he was talking about?"

Bill turned away. He now had to put a good face on things – pretending to see merit in them. He went to fetch the two he had put in the shed and showed them to her. "I'm not sure about them at all really," he told Jenny, "but it was over a drink in the pub one night. I foolishly promised to take a few pictures from him... encouraging a struggling artist – you know!"

"How could you?" Jenny could not help saying. "They are atrocious. He certainly should not be encouraged. What on earth are we going to do with them?"

"I don't *know* what to do with them," said Bill irritably, "that's why I pushed them in the garden shed! I suppose I didn't want to admit that I must have had one too many when I said I would buy them!"

Jenny suddenly laughed at his look of self-loathing. "For goodness sake, cheer up," she put her arms round him and planted a kiss on his cheek. "It's not the end of the world! Who knows, he might be right about making good one day. In the meantime, I vote we hide them in the attic!" Bill began to breathe again. He didn't deserve such luck. He certainly didn't deserve Jenny either. He just hoped she'd never find out!

64 – Revelation

After lunch, Dan and Elaine Bailey set off on their honeymoon, a week in London. They had both wanted to spend the wedding night in their own home. They had spent months making alterations to the house since buying it when they became engaged: decorating and furnishing it had been great fun.

Elaine was now resigned to the dreadful possibility that Joyce might have met with an accident – perhaps even a fatal one. A few nights ago she had a strange nightmare, which for some bizarre reason she associated with her missing friend. She was in complete blackness, icy cold and something was shaking her – bouncing her. It wasn't in itself particularly frightening, but she woke with a tremendous explosive anger inside her, a sensation quite foreign to her usual amiable disposition. Elaine dismissed it but when it happened the following night she mentioned it briefly to Dan over breakfast.

As they drove, Elaine reminded him and said that last night she'd had a similar odd dream but on waking felt entirely different. Instead of anger, her mood had been calm, almost happy.

"Perhaps our friend Mrs Grey interprets dreams as well," laughed Dan. "Personally, I would be mortified if you hadn't woken up happy this morning!"

Thinking of Mrs Grey, Elaine's heart sank. The idea of life after death was one she could accept as long as she didn't have to deal with it personally. What would the woman be like? How would they be expected to react when she started seeing or hearing things? Would she be wearing dangling earrings and long, flowing robes? Elaine mentally chided herself... of course the woman would be quite ordinary... Dan's aunt was normal and Mrs Grey was her friend ...but psychics went into trances didn't they? Eventually Elaine admitted that what she really dreaded was her own embarrassment. She would be the only unbeliever in the midst of the converted.

Leaving Frank and Pat with Polly, Sarah and Clarrie sat with the young couple alone for more than an hour after they arrived. It was difficult deciding how much to reveal without knowing the official attitude to the case, so they kept the story short without even mentioning the involvement of Ann Tiller.

"It has been an interesting and somewhat alarming experience as far as we are concerned," said Sarah. "The police gave us a description of Joyce and what she was wearing but even before that, we knew she was no longer alive. Telling you then would have been pointless. We had no proof and it would undoubtedly have cast gloom over your wedding." Dan murmured his appreciation and put his arm round Elaine to comfort her as Sarah continued. "Most of the information I am giving you now we learned from Joyce herself – she has come through to us many times during the past week."

Elaine's eyes widened, in disbelief.

Sarah saw the look she gave Dan and decided to provide her with proof of their credibility; otherwise Elaine would not really listen to what she was saying. She closed her eyes for a moment. Mentally, she asked Joyce – if she sincerely wanted to make amends and achieve peace in the afterlife – start now. Sensing a change of mood Elaine watched nervously. Sarah smiled and there was reassuring warmth in her voice. "I understand your friendship with Joyce went back to your childhood. Joyce is here now, speaking of those far-off days and wants to tell you how sorry she is for being the cause of your illness."

Elaine was confused. How had Joyce ever made her ill? Sarah went on. "She asks if you remember their cat dying... it was found in the garden, poisoned."

"Yes of course. Joyce hated it, yet it was the only time I ever saw her cry. She seemed inconsolable, but when we were alone..." Elaine's voice trailed away. She recalled the barely concealed sparkle of glee in Joyce's eyes when she described how it lay, with rigid limbs twisted into visible evidence of its agonising death. Even after so long she still remembered her own stirring of distaste, that Joyce could dwell on such a hideous end to a family pet.

"Joyce has just confessed," said Sarah, "that she was herself responsible for the animal's death." She paused briefly for this to sink in. Before Elaine could comment, she resumed. "Think back to the day you both sat in your garden shed eating fallen fruit. Joyce was alone for a while when you went to fetch more... she sent you away because she wanted to steal some weed-killer from a tin she had seen behind you on a high shelf. Do you remember using a flat stick to dig out wasps and stones from the plums? Joyce had used it to prise off the lid. She also used it to scoop some of the powder into an empty crisp packet ... "

Sarah could see a slow dawning of amazement in Elaine's face. Dan reached for Elaine's hand and obviously didn't share her incredulity at Joyce's cunning.

"When you returned with the fruit, she left without eating any," Sarah continued, "but you must have consumed them yourself because later that day you became very ill. It was decided that you had over indulged in the plums, but she guessed you had digested some of the powder which still clung to the damp stick."

Elaine was absolutely stupefied as Sarah brought that

long ago episode back to her vividly. "Joyce at last accepts full responsibility for having caused you pain... and seeks your forgiveness," added Sarah.

Elaine was not totally surprised about the cat or that Joyce, always impulsive, was capable of behaving so recklessly, but she was appalled that Joyce could have continued to pretend a close friendship with her afterwards. Would she actually have let her die too? She distinctly recalled her suffering, which could have been lessened if Joyce had told someone the reason for it!

Answering her unspoken thoughts, Sarah said, "In view of what happened to the cat, Joyce admits that it might have been fatal for you too. She has the temerity to say she would have been very sorry to lose you as you have always been her only real friend." Glaring sternly into the empty space beyond the young couple, Sarah commented, "I must say Elaine – she still sounds far more concerned for her own position than yours! But please try to forgive her." Sarah shook her head knowingly. "As a newly reformed character, apologising apparently doesn't come easily! Should you have anything to say, or ask, she will hear you as she is still with us." Sarah sat back and waited.

Elaine tried composing herself, to think clearly. She looked at Dan, a keenly interested observer. He would want her to ask something that Mrs Grey could not possibly answer without Joyce... something for which Elaine personally had no explanation – thus ruling out telepathy. Opportunities like this never came to most people; it mustn't be wasted.

After a few moments Elaine said, "We were once punished at school, when Joyce and I handed in identical homework. She must have copied mine but I never did find out when, or how. Is she prepared to tell me now?"

Sarah's head tilted slightly, appearing to be listening, looking away from the others. Eventually she smiled. "I'm afraid Joyce's first reaction, characteristically, I'm sure, was to blame you! She says you were good at arithmetic and usually got all the answers right." Elaine nodded, slightly embarrassed and began to speak but Sarah raised her hand to prevent the interruption and went on... "For once, you had two wrong and, as hers were exactly the same, your books came under extra scrutiny... you both suffered!"

"Yes, but how did she copy my paper? We weren't even together that night and the following morning I was late for school! I took the homework from my school-bag and handed it in during the first lesson with all the others, including hers!"

"Apparently, the exercise was a straight-forward group of fractions to solve. Joyce cunningly wrote out everything except the answers so, when she handed her book in with all the others it was incomplete. Your teacher was in the habit of taking them home to mark, so Joyce had the whole day to sneak into the staff room and copy your solutions into her own blank spaces."

Dan could not stop himself bursting out, "Well I'm damned! That seems absolutely typical of Joyce! I tried so often to warn you about her. I never believed she really was any friend of yours Elaine. Now you have to accept it. She was a self-centred opportunist. You were punished along with her... Tell us – did she make any attempt to exonerate you – to accept the blame for cheating?"

Elaine admitted that Joyce had not confessed. If she had, she would have had to explain how she had done it; Joyce obviously preferred Elaine to remain puzzled and slightly in awe of her.

The remarkable demonstration of mediumship impressed Elaine who was now completely convinced that there was an afterlife and accepted that she had been in touch with Joyce. "You knew I was sceptical Mrs Grey, didn't you? I can only say I am sorry I doubted you before we came. But you still haven't told us how Joyce died."

After saying they need not address her so formally, Sarah explained that Joyce either had retained or obtained the same powder she'd used on the cat, intending to use it on someone else when she left home last Monday. Unfortunately for her, she had accidentally consumed it herself.

Dan gasped and immediately said he'd lay odds that it was her boss's wife Joyce planned to be rid of. Sarah hastily told him that although he was right, Joyce had made a terrible mistake. Had she succeeded, a perfectly innocent stranger would have lost her life. It was obvious to them both that Sarah intended saying no more about Joyce and her murderous intentions. They had to accept that the police would be handling things from now on.

Clarrie went to call the others and tea was soon served.

It was impossible, under the circumstances, to banish the subject of psychic phenomena and the four young people were eager to be told of other things experienced by Sarah over the years. She was reticent about doing so herself, but perhaps in reaction after the tension of the previous night, she was not as firmly opposed as usual when Polly volunteered a story of her own. The event had made a deep impression on Polly because she was then unaware of Sarah's mediumship.

"It was just after you married Master Stephen. We had been shopping together and were returning home by public transport because Stephen needed the car, do you remember?" she asked. "You reached the empty barrier first and I wondered why you stopped about ten feet from the sign."

"I do remember quite clearly," Sarah said. "I stopped because I thought we were joining the end of a queue – I saw people already waiting."

"Well, you turned your back to the stop as we talked and although I didn't notice, other people were lining up behind me and getting mixed up with the next queue by the time our 'bus arrived. When it did, you suddenly whirled round as if you were shot!"

"I recoiled because I heard a roaring engine, screeching brakes and people behind me screaming in terror," Sarah said, "It was enough to make anyone jump!"

"That is the whole point," Polly finished the tale. "The 'bus had arrived normally, with no undue noise and nobody was there to scream! You looked thoroughly shaken Sarah, and we later discovered that a runaway coach killed eight people there, ten years earlier! Talk about uncanny!"

Pat shuddered. "I'm glad I'm not psychic," she said, "I couldn't stand the strain – how do you know whether the strangers around you are real or ghosts?"

"One of the first tales I ever heard about you, Sarah," said Dan, "was about old Mr Grey coming back from the dead, to tell you where to find some family documents. Was it true?"

Sarah looked puzzled and frowned, casting her mind back. "I don't think so Dan. I'm sorry to disappoint you – it sounds so theatrical: father comes back from the dead to reveal secret will! I have seen him though, much to his own surprise." She smiled affectionately as she thought of him. "He never believed in life after death and has actually told me he still doesn't believe it!"

Time flew by and they were all surprised when the doorbell sounded to announce Del's arrival. Pat and Frank left immediately but Elaine and Dan lingered. Guessing they were far too keyed up to think of going, Polly had a quiet word with Clarrie and with her agreement invited them to stay for dinner. She hastened off to cook, leaving the others to their eerie tales.

Del will probably be eager to join in, Clarrie thought, as she went to greet him, it was just what they needed – a happy evening with friends telling ghost stories in the lamplight! She was unaware of the subdued spectre still watching from the shadows ...the confused but still not completely harmless spirit of Joyce.

65 - A Sociable Evening

Clarrie welcomed Del on his first visit to the house. "I hope you had no trouble finding us," she greeted him warmly.

"No problem," he laughed, "you missed your vocation – you should have been a cartographer!"

There was little time to talk as other guests were waiting, but he informed her quickly that the school and the house had been found and Algy was likely to ring up during the evening to keep him abreast of developments. "He wasn't in the least surprised to hear that I could be reached here – he says we were made for each other and gave us his blessing!" Clarrie laughed, refusing to be embarrassed.

"I would hardly expect him to do otherwise. He's very discerning – a good friend with my best interests at heart! You told him, no doubt, that you were coming at my insistence because my life is meaningless without you!" Before Del could reply, Clarrie ushered him into the sitting room to meet the newlyweds. Introductions were brief but he gathered it was Elaine, the friend of the woman whose disappearance they had been investigating. Apparently, it was now solved. In consequence, she and her husband totally accepted the validity of the paranormal and like new converts to anything, their thirst for information was insatiable.

Being equally fascinated by the supernatural, Del settled down quickly, encouraging them to continue talking. Knowing from Algy that Sarah and Clarrie rarely indulged the idle curiosity of sensation seekers, this was an occasion not to be missed.

Elaine asked if Sarah had ever been contacted by anyone famous – like Rosemary Brown who communicated with musicians. Sarah said she had no skills to put at the disposal of such eminent people. The closest she had come to any historic figure was not with the man himself but with his grandmother, to whom she had spoken at length and learned a lot, not generally known, about the man's early years. Sarah had been enthralled but thought others might consider it rather dull. Their instant protestations persuaded her to continue.

She explained first that Stephen, her husband, was an artist. He had a small battery tape recorder – quite a novel device then, in 1962 – to record impressions as he painted. It was easier to speak as he worked rather than scribble notes on colours and tones. He had it with him the day they visited the man's birthplace. "I took Clarinda outside – she was only a toddler – while Stephen stayed in the house to do some sketching." Sarah told them. "Eventually he came into the garden to join us, but the woman and I were deep in conversation."

"How did he know?" Dan asked, mentally putting himself in a similar position.

"He could hear my voice but not hers," explained Sarah, "and with great presence of mind he handed me the device, set to record. He picked up Clarinda and carried her away without interrupting me and waited until I joined him. The tape helped me to remember her answers… I had tried to repeat them after her anyway, so we were able to reconstruct the conversation, but I'll never forget her… I was so thrilled". "Who was she?" cried Elaine, "You haven't told us who her grandson was, or the name of the place where you met!"

"Well, let me first tell you a little of what she said… see how long it takes you to guess." Sarah laughed, beginning to enjoy the game. Her audience concentrated, wide eyed. "The lady's name was Alice. She was born at the turn of the l6[th] century and grew up with her brothers in the English Midlands. They were the children of Joyce Leigh of Burton, Buckinghamshire and Edward Griffin who was born in Warwick in l585," Sarah frowned in concentration. "He became... now let me get this right – Usher of the Chamber of the King and the Parker of Berkeswell. Her Grandfather Nicholas was Sergeant-at-Arms at the Queen's Court where he had been the Queen's Attorney." Sarah paused, to see if any of her audience wished to speak but they all looked completely baffled.

"Oh, don't stop, please give us some more clues," urged Dan. He had studied history at 'A' level and was sure he would be able to place the grandson, given time.

Polly, unknown to them had been listening for a few minutes. Now she said they could relax a little longer – dinner would not be ready for another fifteen minutes.

Returning to the kitchen Polly remembered hearing about Alice: she was wearing a hooped, brocade dress lavishly embroidered with autumnal leaves and flowers: a jewelled girdle around her hips from which hung a large gold cross and, on her head, a simple velvet cap edged with pearls. Polly understood the thrill felt by the youngsters as they gathered round Sarah, sensing a small part of death's veil being pulled aside. She had never lost her own feeling of privilege and awe at being in such close contact with the afterlife.

Joyce, now that she was beginning to comprehend what had happened to her was slowly losing her grip on earthly things. She had revelled in the contact made with Elaine ...feeling still, in a strange way, that she had the upper hand. Elaine was so naïve – so unworldly!

No, she grimaced, it was herself who had left the world, but where was she? Sensing with growing alarm the pull of a powerful force that wanted to drag her away, Joyce stubbornly resisted it. In a way, it would have been a relief to give in to it but, if she did, her death might go unavenged; these two sanctimonious women might let her down. No! She would not yield yet.

Joyce was bored with Sarah's story ... she knew the end of it. How? She was then intrigued to find that she knew what Polly was thinking and discovered that with little effort she knew what everyone else was thinking too.

She was equally surprised to find she didn't care ...it was all trifling, immaterial: of no interest to her. She almost lost her grip and the force pulling her grew stronger... until she pictured her poor body again: maltreated, in its ignominious grave. Her rage returned in full strength.

The savage passion, which had tied her to the earthly world, would bind her until it abated.

She watched and waited – waited to pounce if things did not go her way!

66 – Past Revelations

Her listeners were less interested in food than in the mystery grandson as Sarah resumed, "Alice Griffin's uncle John had four sons and several of her cousins married into the Spencer family. Her cousin Nicholas, who became the Sheriff of Northamptonshire, had three distinguished sons ...and one, Bartholomew, was a poet and author. One of his sonnets, 'The Passionate Pilgrim', was mistakenly published under the name of his better-known kinsman."

Although Del had read history at Brasenose, Oxford, literature was his greatest interest and he suddenly interrupted, "Could that possibly be the one reprinted around 1815 ...are you telling us that it actually wasn't by..." he stopped abruptly, not wishing to ruin the game for the others and added, "him?" to round off the question.

"I am merely repeating what Alice told me ...you have guessed the name of her famous grandson?"

"Good God," exclaimed Del, "I believe I have! What a story!"

Dan and Elaine were even more eager for Sarah to carry on. "What happened when you first met," Elaine asked, "who spoke first?"

Sarah told them how, as Clarrie played on the grass, she saw the spirit form of Alice who was delighted when she perceived they could communicate. She lost no time in introducing herself as 'dear Will's grandmother'. She was anxious to speak of him and had tried many times, to others. There were immediate cries of recognition.

"You were visiting Stratford-upon-Avon and Will can

only have been Shakespeare!" Dan cried in amazement.

"Yes," confirmed Sarah, "and you can't be any more astonished than I was myself at the time."

"I've never thought of Shakespeare having a family at all, if you see what I mean," Elaine mused, "except for Anne Hathaway of course. Who was Alice's husband?"

"Alice married Richard Shakespeare whose aunt Lady Isabella was Prioress of Wroxhall Priory. She appointed him Bailiff of land the Griffin family was leasing from the Priory; that's how they met – it was a love match. Their son John married his step-mother's niece, Mary Arden of Wilmcote and had eight children. Will, the oldest son was their third child. He was only eighteen when he married twenty-six-year-old Anne."

Sarah paused again, feeling she must be boring her listeners, but they wouldn't allow her to stop. "William and Anne had two daughters, Judith and Susannah but their only son died."

"It is absolutely fascinating," Elaine whispered earnestly. She now had complete faith in everything Sarah said.

Clarrie turned to Del and said, "You realise that this is all off the record don't you? No by-lines for you I'm afraid!"

Del groaned aloud. "I don't believe it! I have inside dope on the life of Shakespeare and can't use it!" He was equally gripped and eager to put a question of his own. "Many people say it's much more likely that Sir Francis Bacon was the real author the plays and sonnets. What about that angle Sarah?"

"Alice had a great deal to say about that," Sarah nodded.

It had been for that very reason that Alice was seeking to communicate. She'd overheard such talk – it hurt and infuriated her. She also said the language of the midlands was monstrously difficult to follow now and was amazed that people of so many races came to visit her grandson's home.

Remembering her kind, but slightly haughty demeanour, Sarah was again transported to the quiet garden on that long ago, sunny afternoon. Alice was a proud woman, annoyed by the suggestion that her grandson was a barely literate yokel who produced his writings by luck or larceny. Her family, boasted several Knights with access to, and office in, the Royal Court. Will had been a pupil at the Guild School in Stratford ...his Latin and Greek, *"No better or worse than most young gentlemen of his day"*. He was put to study law for a while and also helped as a teacher in local schools

In spite of the fact that Alice had never been known to William, he was obviously a favourite – she spoke of him indulgently. "He was no more a lad than most – going on 'boy-rambles' to neighbouring villages. He oft-times took home mushrooms, blackberries and crab apples or, for his mother, flowers from the fields."

Alice's husband Richard had a close friend – Robert Arden and when Robert married Mary Webb, Mary and her younger sister Abigail became friends of hers too. Alice was distressed to have passed into the spirit world after the birth of John her second son, William's father, when he was only two years old.

She said, In 1535, Richard took dear Abigail to wife, to mother my two darlings, and I heard her many times speaking of me to them, and was greatly pleased that they were not permitted to forget me."

Sarah suddenly realised that they were all waiting for her to speak. She tried to explain why Alice was offended by such talk of Will's status – references to his being a butcher, a wool-stapler or glove maker were, *"All and none true"*, to quote the lady herself! Will's father John was High Bailiff, Chief Alderman and a Burgess of Stratford who owned grazing land. The stock was sold at several locations, including the ground floor of one of their houses in Henley Street where Will sometimes helped in his father's business. Sarah also told them that Alice mentioned the story spread by, *"A wordy man not then even born",* which referred to Will having to leave the area because he stole a deer from Charlecote Park.

Del again commented. "She must have meant Dr. Samuel Johnson who, in his day, was regarded as an authority on Shakespeare. Are we to hear the truth of it?"

Sarah repeated Alice's own words, illustrated as Alice had, with a shrug of contempt, "Will did raise his bow and shoot the beast. Straightway, he fearlessly confessed and was discomforted for one whole night, in the Lodge, under the keeper's eye ...but he was no common thief to flee in shame." According to Alice, William's departure was already planned. He was to go to London to stay in Southwark with her cousin, a respected wine merchant.

Alice had said, proudly, "He did well indeed there, his plays pleased many and on his return, he purchased New Place – an envied Great House of the Clopton family. A Mulberry tree did he plant in the garden which, to his delight, grew well. Sadly though, a certain Reverend Gastrell hath later caused it to be removed, to discourage the many pilgrims which did annoy him!" Sarah imitated Alice's disapproving frown.

"I've been there several times and seen a Mulberry tree," said Dan, "it must be a re-plant." He turned to Elaine. "Do you remember it? I think we even have a photograph of it."

"Yes, we have! How wonderful it must have been to hear of it first hand," said Elaine, "Did Alice say anything about all that has happened since her own day!"

"I can tell you one sad comment she made," said Sarah, "and then I think we've had enough of ghosts, we'll have dinner. Alice usually sees the countryside as she remembers it, but occasionally the present intrudes and she is bewildered by the noise. She asked me: *'Where? Oh where, are the quiet lanes of leafy Warwickshire?'*..."

Del mentioned Will's often quoted memorial verse, supposedly proving his simplicity and Sarah was able to tell him it had been uppermost in Alice's mind as she denounced his detractors. Will first saw the verse in the possession of the Sexton of Holy Trinity Church and said that, if it would succeed in keeping his earthly remains safe, it should be *'Chipped into mine own stone'*! The thought that his bones might one day be tossed into the nearby bone-house with the cartloads already there appalled him.

They all stirred at last when Polly re-joined them, but Clarrie suddenly spoke of an episode, which she had always treasured.

"Do you recall the tale Alice told you, mother, of Will in his teens, when he courted most of the village girls in turn – wrote verses for them and had to fight other boys to prove he was no sissy!"

"I know that part of his life interested you the most," Sarah smiled. "I wonder if you could you still repeat the sonnet which Alice recited for me?"

Everyone immediately sat again except Clarrie who looked embarrassed, wishing she had not raised the subject.

"Oh Clarrie, do tell us," Elaine begged. "You must be able to remember it."

Sarah explained, feeling a little guilty at having put her daughter on the spot! "Will's father was impatient with his wenching and disapproved of the boy's latest passion... a girl *'no better than she need be'*. He had intercepted the missive but nevertheless was extremely proud of his son's way with words. He showed his step-mother, Abigail, who admired it enough to keep the scrap of paper in Alice's 'memory casket' for the rest of her life. If you can bring it to mind Clarinda, we can satisfy the curiosity of our young friends and get on with the most important business of the evening – eating!"

Clarrie took a moment to collect her thoughts but didn't really need to strain herself to bring to mind that sweet sonnet:

"Why is my love a thing of piercing sorrow;
An ache on parting, a longing fevered pain?
My eyes are moist, wishing for that morrow
When I may glimpse thee yet again.
The Winter's nights blew long and cold;
At last they shorten now, as Spring
Brings out May buds, the young, the old,
The birds to buss on soaring wing.
Observe the many things that grow
And feast on Summer's warming sun;
There is a love that conquers woe
And does not fade when Autumn's done.
Yet I am anguished when we part
'Til thy 'turning footsteps lift my heart."

As Clarrie's clear, well-modulated voice died away almost to a whisper, she felt Del's eyes gazing earnestly towards her and was disconcerted by his silence.

With murmurs of appreciation and wonder, Elaine and Dan went out of the room with Sarah. As Clarrie followed, Del held her arm and pulled her to face him.

His eyes gazed down earnestly into hers and he said quietly, "If I could have written anything to bring that light into your lovely eyes, there's no way I would have wasted it on any other village girl."

Clarrie, for once, was lost for a flippant reply... then, releasing the sudden tension, Del dropped a quick kiss on her forehead, turned her round firmly and propelled her through the doorway to join the rest of the party.

67 - Kidnapped

It was after ten when Elaine and Dan left. Sarah helped Polly in the kitchen and then they both tactfully retired to their rooms, leaving Clarrie to entertain Del in the sitting room. Algy had telephoned an hour earlier and it was obvious that Del was anxious to discuss the case. Sarah expressed her willingness to help if necessary but was more in favour of Clarinda's continuing without her, as she'd had such a strikingly successful start.

Once alone, Del explained that the police had good reason to believe the woman was being held in the house that Clarrie had described. The man who lived there was known to them - as was his brother who had recently been released from jail. Neither man had been in nor out since they started watching the place but it was definitely occupied. If the victim was inside she was not alone, so they were assuming she was alive and being looked after by another member of the man's family - probably his wife.

Clarrie was gratified and greatly relieved at having been proved right but was not at all sure how she could be of any further help. Del had to admit that he was also uncertain, but thought she would be fascinated to see some 'blow-ups' of photographs taken on the spot by an associate of his. It was quite uncanny, Del commented, how little difference there was between them and her own drawing.

He went to fetch his briefcase, which he had left in the hall and produced two large photographs together with her sketch which they studied together as they talked.

The woman's family still hadn't heard from the kidnapper since agreeing to pay the ransom and were frantic with worry.

Although predisposed to believe that the householder and his brother were involved because they had been suspects in a previous attempted kidnapping, the police needed to be sure before they revealed their own presence and went in. The victim's safety was all-important.

Only when they were convinced she would not be harmed would a rescue attempt be made and until they verified the whereabouts of the two brothers, they dared not make a move.

Clarrie stared at the photographs, which had been taken from two different angles. One coincided almost exactly with the drawing but revealed the name of the street and the other must have been taken from a house opposite. "How did you find it so quickly?" she asked.

"Alec Holmes, Algy's boss, Faxed the drawing to every CID office in the triangle and within two hours someone contacted him from Wolverhampton ...at that stage he had not even hinted to them why he was interested. Things went incredibly smoothly from then on." Del looked smug as he began collecting everything together again intending to put them back to his case. "Alec's opposite number there is an old friend so he accepted without question an assurance that the grounds for suspicion were solid, but could never be disclosed." Del stopped and grinned disarmingly.

He gave her an admiring sideways glance, "He could hardly draw attention to his favourite witch and her crystal ball could he?"

Before Clarrie could retaliate he went on to tell her that since Friday evening the police had been trying to find the two suspects but no-one on the streets had seen either of them since last Monday afternoon.

A series of visions kept intervening between Clarrie and the image of the terraced house, but she found it impossible to hold on to any of them for long.

After a few moments she asked Del, "Is the man's name Barry ...Barry Evans?"

Before he answered she said, "Another name just flashed into my head too... Jeb, I think, but with a different surname... Jeb Smith – they would not be brothers in that case would they? I must be way off beam!"

Del wrote the two names in his diary and smiled. "Well, the brothers are Jeb and Albert Jones so you might be a quarter right! I am impressed enough already by your sketch not to ignore anything else you come up with, so if you don't mind, could I ring Algy back?"

As he rose to go to the telephone, Clarrie had another flash of doubt and told him again that she must be wrong because she was suddenly convinced that they were already in prison. She closed her eyes and could almost feel the walls pressing in on her. Del wasn't at all put off and went to discuss it with Algy.

In a few moments he returned and said that Algy was circulating the two names and would contact him again in the morning. As soon as he had news, Del in turn promised to ring her. They were completely at ease with each other as they sat talking – learning about each other's likes and dislikes and the pattern of their lives.

Del's parents, he told her, were both well and living in Spain. They had lived in the Far East for most of his father's working life – in shipping, and couldn't face retirement in the damp UK climate. Del went over to see them several times a year.

He spoke of his brief, miserable marriage and Clarrie spoke with no reservations about her own very happy years with her husband Tom, whose tragic death had almost destroyed her own desire to live. The time flew by and they were both startled when the hall clock chimed two.

It was after two-thirty when Del eventually left but as he rose to go he gave Clarrie some news that made her feel suddenly empty. He would soon be working overseas. "I didn't mention this assignment before although I had already accepted it," he said, "because, ever since we met last week, I've been hoping that I could persuade my boss to send someone else."

Del took both her hands and she couldn't hide the consternation that she knew he must be able to read in her expression. He said mournfully, "I'm going to be in the Middle East for twelve months – from the first of July."

Clarrie had known Del for only a few days and even that short time was enough for her to know that he could become someone special in her life – but he had to want that too. Apart from light-hearted teasing, he had made no attempt to present himself as seriously interested in her and she tried now to put things into perspective. This rather nice ...no – this extremely attractive stranger, had crossed her path briefly and would soon belong to the past. She was still glad to have met him and was sincerely sorry he would soon be on his way again.

Del still held her hands tightly and looked earnestly down into her eyes. "I am so terrified of frightening you off! We met less than a week ago so I'm not asking how you feel about me. I just want you to know that I can hardly bear the thought of leaving you. I'd rather stay to be with you as often as you will let me, in the hope that you will fall madly in love with me. I am, already, hopelessly besotted with you."

Clarrie opened her mouth to speak but he placed a finger on her lips and whispered... "No, please don't say anything. Sleep on it and if you decide I stand a chance we will talk about it next time we meet ...how about dinner on Tuesday night?" She nodded and he promised to pick her up at eight-o-clock. Almost immediately he turned and walked resolutely to the front door. It was just as well... Shakily, Clarrie appreciated that he had not expected her to give him an answer... she was stunned. She stood and waved as he climbed into his car and drove away smoothly. No hooting, no fierce revving of the engine... No fanfares! She reflected with some surprise, and a twinge of disappointment, that he hadn't even attempted to kiss her goodnight.

It didn't matter. He had said enough to lift her heart and leave her with a sense of contentment. Even if he did go away, she was sure their futures would be linked ...it would be a marvellous, exciting future and all good things were worth waiting for.

68 – Windblown

A blustery wind blew in Farlow. Outside the Deans' house, something small and square fluttered in the garden.

Occasionally it flew into the air and was once trapped in the branches of a bush. A sudden gust released it, blowing it across the lawn and dancing it in cartwheels to the porch where at last it came to rest, sheltered, wedged behind a potted plant.

A mile away, Eric Todd was on his way to bed after watching a late film, wondering how he could have lost one of his precious snaps ...he only hoped it hadn't fallen where Mrs Dean would find it! If it had, his latest, most lucrative business venture might come to a sudden ignominious end! He cursed quietly.

Joyce's upsurge of anger carried her back to Farlow... What right had her murderer to sleep in unruffled calm? She tried to disrupt Ann's peace but failed... foiled perhaps by Ann's clear conscience! Her lack of success increased her fury and she sought another victim: Bill.

Lying awake, already prey to his own stupidity he was oblivious of her attempts to make contact with him and she screamed with frustration, *"Insensitive swine!"* His wife was hazy and almost invisible to her, as if lying beyond a protective veil ...conceivably because she had not known her in life. But then – she had never met the thieving old woman either and she would have no trouble reaching her. By stealing from her, she had eased the way: created a bond: a thread she could follow.

As Joyce thought of it, the cottage loomed before her and she hovered, a wrathful vengeful ghost, staring in outrage at the shining silver tray.

69 – Monday 27th May

Algy's promised call woke Del from deep sleep. The telephone, barely a foot from his ear, shrilled several times before he stirred and reached for it. Hearing the note of excitement in Algy's voice he was immediately wide-awake and sat up on the edge of the bed.

"Are you ready for this?" Algy asked.

"Get on with it man, of course I am!" Del glanced at the bedside clock. "I'm always at my best before six a.m."

"Well ...she's done it again! The two brothers were arrested in the early hours last Tuesday near Paddington... they gave false names: guess what – Barry and Jeb! Look, do you feel like coming with me to Wolverhampton today? Can you be ready in twenty minutes?"

Nothing would have stopped Del from accepting – he'd already planned on going there anyway. "Your car or mine?" he asked.

Half an hour later the two friends were on their way, Algy at the wheel of the red coupé, his pride and joy. Driving was no chore for him and like most good drivers he was a poor passenger. Knowing Del felt the same he glanced sideways and grinned broadly. "Shut your eyes if you like; catch up on your beauty sleep, but keep your wet head off my upholstery ...there's a towel in my grip on the back seat!"

Del ran a hand through his damp hair: unconcerned. It would soon dry. "You know damn well I want the whole story so get on with it – why on earth weren't they identified by their fingerprints? As known criminals, they had to be on file!"

"The first thing you should have asked is, why were they arrested? They were in a stolen car, which was found to contain drugs, so there was no way they could make bail. They may have used it just to pick them up or deliver... anyway, because they obviously expected to dump the car and didn't want to risk leaving fingerprints they had painted their fingers with glue which was far more difficult to remove than they expected."

Algy laughed wryly. He had once tried to remove a similar substance from his own hand and in the end had allowed it to wear off. "Once we had traced them by the names you gave us, they were identified quickly and are now being escorted back to the midlands. They have no notion, of course, that they are suspected of abducting the woman, who may or may not be in their house!"

They soon lapsed into a comfortable silence in which Del found his thoughts constantly returning to Clarrie. He wanted to talk about her but didn't quite know what he wanted to say. Algy had known her a long time but how could he raise the subject casually?

As though reading his mind Algy suddenly gave him the opportunity by asking, "So, you are obviously quite infatuated by our friend Clarinda."

Del was taken aback and when he didn't reply instantly Algy said, "You had better watch your step if your intentions are other than honourable, I have a high regard for her and, as I was instrumental in your meeting, I shall have my eye on you!"

Del grinned and asked what Algy thought he could do about it if they were not honourable... "If I wronged the girl in the good old-fashioned way I would be much more afraid of her mother!"

"There's nothing frightening about Sarah," Algy declared, "she is one of the best balanced people I have ever met. On the other hand, I admit that she has a formidable invisible army supporting her – you could be haunted to your grave!"

Suddenly serious, Del admitted that he had never been more certain about anything in his whole life. He intended asking Clarrie to marry him; the only question was, when? In spite of his teasing, Algy was surprised.

In all the years he'd known Del, he couldn't recall his being enthusiastic about any woman, after his first let-down. He was no womaniser; there had been very few casual girlfriends hanging on his arm. The absence of female companions didn't seem strange to Algy, virtually alone himself since his wife became ill; if he couldn't have her, he craved no other partner.

Algy recollected joking with Clarrie once, about the impossibility of her husband's deceiving her or sneaking off with his mates for a secret drink! Even though they laughed, Algy recognised that his facetious comment revealed a deep-seated fear in himself, of having his privacy invaded: not actually, but mentally. A degree of telepathy usually exists between married couples but if one were psychic, wouldn't the other feel inadequate: inferior even; could the male ego withstand the challenge?

He could not resist pointing out the risks to Del, curious to hear his reaction. Del didn't laugh. He confessed that similar thoughts had occurred to him too but as he could foresee no circumstance under which he would wish to deceive her it wasn't worth worrying about.

It surprised Del to think that Algy would feel his masculinity threatened. Personally, he had no qualms about his own ability to cope. Psychic she may be, but Clarrie was sufficiently confident in her abilities and place in life to relax... at least, with him! Beyond her obvious physical attraction Clarrie was a good companion: bright, witty when appropriate, but able to enjoy silence too. They had much in common. Del wanted her friendship but needed a great deal more and was confident he could make her happy.

It was almost seven-thirty when they reached junction l7 on the M40 and turned on to the M42 toward Bromsgrove. After the early morning mist patches on the Oxford - Banbury stretch it had been a pleasant drive, but now the weight of traffic was increasing. It was a relief, having covered eleven slow miles, to cut away from the main stream.

Even though the road was busy with holidaymakers, there were not many lorries for a couple of miles until they joined the M5.

They had been discussing politics but, as soon as they were heading irrevocably down the slip road onto the motorway, Del's thoughts flew to Clarrie.

He had such a pressing urge to contact her that he almost suggested they head for the nearest telephone.

Talk about besotted!

He chided himself and tried to concentrate on what Algy was saying. Clarrie would probably be asleep still ...he wondered if she was an early or late riser.

There would be more point in ringing her when he could report on the kidnapping; later, he promised himself. They covered the eight-mile stretch of motorway in seven minutes in spite of the heavy traffic.

70 – The Victim

Only ten miles away, in a darkened room, a thin middle-aged woman was waking fearfully to face yet another interminable day of captivity. She desperately needed the lavatory but they made her use a bucket and the burly female who brought it always watched her closely – her expression alternating between scorn and impatience. The woman's hands weren't tied but her feet were padlocked to the iron bed frame and the chain had chafed her ankles badly. She tore strips from her underskirt and bound them as well as she could but the painful throbbing convinced her that the injuries were septic. The worry took her mind off the rawness of her lips where one of the brutes had ripped the skin off with the adhesive tape. It had been strapped over her mouth when they brought her here, in a wardrobe box. Terror still gripped her... she re-lived the shock of opening her front door and being attacked by two masked men. The door chain wasn't on – she never bothered to use it during the day. In the secluded drive, an instant before the sack was thrown over her head she had glimpsed a small van but doubted if she would be able to describe it ...if ever she had the chance ...if she came through her ordeal alive.

She had screamed for help after the initial shock wore off, but they laughed, confident that no one would hear. An eiderdown hanging over the window was kept in place by a large wardrobe, which seemed to occupy most of the room. Because, out of her reach, a radio was left permanently on, it was equally impossible for her to hear anything outside her airless prison. She knew only that she was in a terraced house.

They advised her that on the other side of her shared bedroom wall the place was occupied by a couple who were old and deaf, and in the property on the other side there were six kids in the family who screamed all night and day themselves …one more scream would not be noticed!

In answer to the clanging hand-bell she had been instructed to use, her jailer came and dropped the bucket near the bed with a crash. Over her head, she wore a scarf, which was pulled closely over her lower face and she rarely spoke. There was actually little need for her to speak at all and when she did it was in a whisper. Identifying her in future would be next to impossible but the captive was slightly comforted by the precautions being taken. It must be their intention to let her keep her life if not her dignity!

Her chains were now on again. Little interest had been shown in her wounds but when her breakfast came there was a tiny brown bottle of iodine on the tray with a bundle of cotton wool. It would probably not help as much as it hurt, but using it would give her something to do, taking her mind off her family. She wondered why they hadn't paid the ransom that must have been demanded. It was a week since she was taken from her home... Why was she still suffering this humiliation?

Downstairs, Jeb Jones' wife Edna looked anxiously up and down the street. Where the hell were they, she wondered. Jeb and his brother Bert had gone off, God only knew where. They were supposed to be back within hours, and that was last Monday! She wondered if they'd taken the ransom and left her holding the baby. Some baby! There was no unusual activity outside: just an estate agent bringing a couple to view the house opposite. They weren't inside long. The upstairs curtains opened, swished about and were left closed – inviting burglars for sure, Edna thought. They shook their heads at the agent on the way out, evidently unimpressed.

If Jeb didn't get in touch soon what should she do, Edna wondered. So far, his precious scheme had cost her more work, more worry and money for extra food. She'd get nothing out of it in the end, at this rate. Her young son Harry thought they were sheltering a friend who was hiding from her husband – a story he could understand and accept with no hesitation. At ten he was already a man of the world, willing to keep their secrets because they included him in their adult conversation.

Hearing his mother call, Harry dragged himself downstairs yawning and scratching himself as his skin crawled awake to the sensations of a new day. What did she want now? Wasn't it supposed to be a holiday? He had plans of his own; he hoped she wouldn't interfere with them, messing up his day!

Edna, still at the front door, looked round at him sourly. "Have you washed?" she asked. "It doesn't look like it! Your clothes are a sorry sight ...as if they've been slept in too... wouldn't put it past you!"

"Aw, come on mum; don't start ...wha'dya want me for? I 'ave stuff to sort out for the gang ...they'll be 'ere soon."

"Your Dad's not back yet so I can't leave the house with her upstairs. Go round to your aunt Flora and borrow some spuds and eggs. Running out of everything we are and the shops are shut. Keep your eyes open for strangers too, on the way round." She pointed upwards. "Her old man might have sent some spies out after her!" The hint that he was on an important secret mission took the sting out of the mundane errand and Harry ran out with no more complaints.

Not many people were about; all having a lie in, he thought – not much else to do around here. There was a car parked just round the corner with two men inside it.

He looked behind him and saw another across the street. Was it suspicious? What were they waiting for? As he watched, the second car started up and drove off: nothing to worry about there. He drew level with the first car and observed the men inside.

Without any embarrassment, he stood staring and saw one light a cigarette. The window opened suddenly; the driver stuck his head out. "Hey, boy... You want to earn twenty 'p'?" he asked.

"What do I have to do for it?" Harry sniffed in a disinterested tone. He wasn't that short of petty cash.

"Can you nip through the school gate to the quadrangle...? See how much longer my son will be – he's doing a bit of ball practice with his mates."

"He's 'avin you on mister," Harry chortled, "When it's an 'oliday school's always locked up! No way could 'e get in!"

"I'll kill him," the man roared angrily, "been waiting here for an age!" He flipped a coin at Harry and added, "Thanks anyway son." As they drove off the two policemen grimaced at each other, hoping they had got away with it. When the call came over the radio from the house opposite the boy's, one team had left, but it hadn't seemed necessary for them both to move away from the observation post.

A third team still watched from a safe distance as Harry entered one of the nearby houses and after a few minutes emerged carrying a plastic shopping bag. They waited until he turned towards his own house before taking over the position at the corner. This time, one stood with the bonnet up, fiddled for a while and left it propped open. In case they were being observed he strolled over to a phone box then rejoined his mate in the car. Occasionally he stood outside on the pavement checking his watch but it was probably a waste of theatricals. No spectators were around. Not even a curtain twitched. It was still too early to expect much activity on a holiday – not yet nine. All the men on watch were alert but not impatient. Waiting when something was likely to happen, was nowhere near as tiresome as it would be otherwise.

Edna looked inside the bag that Harry dumped on the table. She pulled a face when she saw how few potatoes her sister had sent but noted that at least she had spared six eggs and added a frozen packet of fish fingers with half a loaf. "You didn't tell her we had a visitor did you?" she asked anxiously and was re-assured when Harry shook his head scornfully. "See anything suspicious around?"

"Naw!" Harry growled as he stuffed his mouth with a couple of pieces from the sliced loaf... "Put the boot in though for some kid who's givin' 'is dad the run around! That was worth going out for!"

Edna paid no attention to the story. She was used to her son boasting about his own cleverness: just like his dad! If Jeb himself had to carry all the overnight slops downstairs, down the yard to the only loo, he wouldn't get clever ideas like keeping a stranger locked up all this time! She was sick of it. Still, she dared not risk letting the woman go outside. Jeb scared her stiff. What would she do if he didn't come back soon? Set the woman free? If she did, he'd be bound to arrive within the day and kill her for sure!

Upstairs, the captive viewed her breakfast dolefully. The runny jam had soaked through the dry bread on its journey from the kitchen and was much too messy to eat.

She wondered why they bothered to deny her anything but plastic crockery and spoons ...she had nothing to cut her way out of and could hardly throw them through the window to attract attention. It was just one more nastiness to endure.

Downstairs, Harry's gang – seven assorted urchins – banged on the back door. Their presence was reported by a tramp, apparently sleeping it off in the back alley. One of the boys had kicked the bottle out of his hand on the way past, put it to his mouth and heaved it away in disgust ...it had, after all, been taken as a prop from a nearby bin!

When they returned, Harry in the lead, the tramp stretched his limbs and rose unsteadily. He waited until most of them had passed by, and then spoke to the lad at the rear. "Any use calling there for a drink," he asked, pointing to the yard gate.

"No way," said the boy. "I'd keep away from Mrs Jones if I was you, 'er old man'll kill yer when 'e gets back."

"On her own, is she? I might try my luck."

"Don't risk it mate – on 'er own she might be but she'd make two of you!"

As the boys went out of sight the 'tramp' spoke again. "Did you get that? Any comment?"

He waited.

His radio, without a crackle, relayed quiet confirmation and a few moments later informed him that it was almost certain she was in sole charge.

"Go back to sleep," said the disembodied voice facetiously. There was no way he'd do that in spite of his long uncomfortable night... something would break soon.

Like many of his colleagues he wondered how they'd got on to this place and why they were so sure the victim was here. The information must have come from a pretty reliable source though ...an operation this size would take some explaining if they came up empty handed!

Nearly two more hours elapsed before the faint whispers from his radiophone became more interesting and he cautiously raised the volume.

They had a search warrant.

Stand by!

The 'tramp' stood, flicked the worst of the dust off his clothes and was reassured when he saw that at each end of the alley a group of 'workmen' lingered. One waved a newspaper and they approached slowly; after hours of inactivity he was glad of an excuse to stretch his limbs and walked to meet them flexing his muscles. When something did happen, he wanted to be fit and ready.

71 – Jail Again

At headquarters, the two sorry-looking Jones brothers were in separate cells after being interrogated. They had not been in touch with anyone since their initial arrest because they hoped to remain unidentified for as long as possible.

Just their luck, Jeb thought, that the second van they nicked to pick up the loot had belonged to some drug dealer!

He'd planned perfectly and carried everything out just as he said he would, without a hitch. The only thing he asked his dummy brother to do alone was to find a vehicle... something inconspicuous.

Bert had an eye for flash sporty jobs and without such clear instruction God only knew what he'd have turned up with!

Now, in spite of all his precautions, their real names were known.

Jeb wondered exactly what Bert had said. He would naturally have denied knowing about the drugs – like he had himself, but Jeb hoped the big ape had not let on why they stole the van; surely even Bert wouldn't be that stupid.

Jeb was furious that after all his masterly planning they had not been able to collect the ransom.

He wouldn't let himself worry about what Edna would do with the woman. She was no fool so she'd probably find a way of getting rid of her – letting her loose somewhere, one dark night!

If only he could talk to Edna! He was fairly confident about getting off the drugs rap. Neither of them had ever been convicted of anything other than petty crime and now that they had the van the cops were bound to find the owner too; he was the real drug dealer!

Such cheering thoughts put Jeb into an almost relaxed frame of mind and when the door opened to admit two smiling detectives he grinned back.

When they informed him that they had a warrant to search his house, his smile faded and he crumpled visibly. "You won't find any drugs there!"

It was all he could bring himself to say.

72 – Meanwhile

Miles away, in Farlow, Ann Tiller had slept until late and, determined to restore her usual calm before tomorrow, took some coffee back to bed with a book for a further hour. While she made a light lunch for herself later, she couldn't prevent her mind from going over Bill's duplicity. She tried not to worry over the fact that someone other than herself knew of Joyce's visit but she had admitted seeing her... Why should she ever be suspected of knowing more? What had this unnamed person found? She hadn't dared question Bill. He wouldn't expect her to care and she could not take the risk of setting him thinking.

In the early afternoon Ann heard the Deans' car driving away: another day out! Obviously Bill was trying to keep Jenny away from the house in case Joyce turned up, but tomorrow he'd have to go to work. He probably expected Joyce to appear in the office and would be frantic again when she didn't! Ann despised herself for being glad he was suffering, even though in only a small way compared to her own tortuous week. She refused to let herself dwell on how she would handle Jenny in future ...how could she appear normal, knowing of Bill's duplicity? What a mess he had made of all their lives!

By the end of the afternoon, the house shone and lunch for tomorrow was prepared, ready for slow cooking while she was out. Her laundry basket was empty too ...at last she could enjoy an evening of complete relaxation. All the horror was behind her now: forever.

73 – Raided

Before the police descended on the small terraced house and the hapless Edna, the house in the next street, which Harry had been seen to visit, was checked out and found to be occupied by Edna's sister Flora and her husband. He was a plumber; they had no children. It was considered safe to interview them both and Flora's help was enlisted. When she agreed that her nephew, Harry, had to be kept away from his home the youngster was delivered, by the police, protesting loudly. "That woman's husband must want 'er back real bad," he commented bitterly.

As soon as Harry was under the watchful eye of his uncle, his Aunt Flora walked round to her sister's house. Having identified her sister through the letterbox, Edna had no hesitation opening the door. Immediately, two policemen and a woman officer rushed inside and, showing her their search warrant, confronted her. She made no protest. As Jeb said, Edna was no fool: she was almost relieved – the game was up!

After her rescue – so low key that it is doubtful whether any neighbour was aware of the drama before reading of it in the local paper – the victim was rushed to the local hospital where she was later reunited with her family. She had not been badly treated and they were able to take her home within an hour or two of her being rescued.

True to his promise, Algy arranged an interview for Del with the Chief Superintendent and gave him full credit as the source of the vital information leading to the successful outcome of the case. Del had consequently filed his story ahead of all the other media reporters and been congratulated by his editor. He had also been introduced to the captive's family as the one they should thank for the happy conclusion, but to no one did he reveal his own source!

By seven-o-clock in the evening, Del and Algy were on their way home. They were still unable to stop talking about the day's events; it wasn't often that things went so smoothly. Del was tempted to ring Clarrie, but there was so much to tell her that he decided it would be more satisfying to talk face to face. They would be back in Oxford before 8.30 so he'd ring ahead to warn her before he freshened up and he would be with her forty minutes later. The decision made, he put the matter out of his mind.

When they were going through Dudley, about to join the M5 he found himself again unable to stop thinking, with increasing agitation, about Clarrie. Algy glanced sideways. "You OK? You've gone very quiet! I think I'm being ignored."

"Let's stop for a drink somewhere – a bar snack or something," Del found himself saying. He knew he was principally interested in getting to a telephone but didn't want to explain to Algy ...he knew it would sound ridiculous.

"Good idea," Algy agreed, ignoring the junction signs now and heading off on a side road. It had just begun to drizzle.

"I don't mind missing eight miles of motorway at the moment," he added, "after such a warm day the surface will be like glass in this shower."

The pub was bright and time was not pressing so they were glad they had broken their journey. Leaving Algy in the bar, Del mentioned casually that he was going to ring Clarrie to tell her what had happened and Algy agreed, she deserved to hear as soon as possible. When Del dialled, the telephone was answered before the end of the first ring. He didn't even announce himself before he heard Clarrie saying, "Del, at last, thank God! I've been frantic all day." He was stupefied. Intuitively, he'd known he should call and could have kicked himself for resisting. In answer to his appeal for an explanation, she said she had an overwhelming conviction that they should stay well away from main routes – it was imperative. She was thankful that, although they had been over miles of motorway during the day, they were all right.

He promised they would stick to minor roads even though it would take longer and rejoined Algy. Del was gratified, as he related the conversation, that his friend was equally disposed to take Clarrie's advice without question. Half an hour later they were rounding off their meal with coffee, when a group of badly shaken people entered the bar and explained how they had just escaped being involved in a nasty pile-up near junction three.

Del and Algy would have been on the move between junctions two and four if they had not broken their journey and they looked at each other with horror. Neither doubted that they'd had a lucky escape. While Algy settled the bill before leaving, Del rang Clarrie again.

As they drove out of the car park he was able to say all was well now. They had Clarrie's blessing to use whichever roads they liked. "She said her oppression vanished about twenty minutes ago and if I had not already contacted her she would have been frantic with worry." He went very quiet. After a moment, he laughed. "Do you imagine it's possible that she actually cares about me?"

"At the risk of making your head even bigger, I think she probably does," said Algy. "I must admit that for two people who hadn't even met a week ago, you are amazingly tuned in to each other's wavelength!" Del didn't answer and Algy ventured to comment again. "Even so, don't you think you are rushing things a bit? You have been in this position before. You were away for years and married immediately you came back, when you scarcely knew ..."

"For pity's sake! You can't compare Clarrie to..."

"No, of course I'm not! Don't get excited. I just mean that, as a soldier, you should know that time spent in reconnaissance is seldom wasted! You could enjoy getting to know each other more fully before taking on the responsibilities of marriage ...and by that, I'm not suggesting you live together first. I know you both well enough to know that such an arrangement wouldn't appeal to either of you."

"I would take Clarrie on any terms, but I wouldn't insult her by offering anything less than total commitment." Del said, before lapsing into silence for a while. Eventually, before Algy spoke again, he revealed the direction of his thoughts. "If I hadn't been posted so soon after meeting my first wife, she might not have changed so drastically, from naive young girl to hard-bitten, self-seeking floozy. Who knows?"

"Come on, you can't put all the blame on circumstances," Algy retorted. "Her true character would certainly have asserted itself and you would have lost interest quite quickly if you had given yourself time to get to know her! Anyway, I wouldn't dream of putting you off marriage to Clarrie ...if she'll have you!"

"That's my fear," Del pulled a wry face. "I can't risk proposing on such short acquaintance and I'll soon be too far away to do so in style!" His attempts to have someone else sent in his place had failed, he explained. "I'm sure we will write to each other but I wish we had more time to establish our relationship on firmer ground before I leave. I must go to Spain for a couple of weeks before I take up the post, it wouldn't be fair on my parents not to spend some time with them."

"Why don't you take Clarrie with you?" Algy suggested. "She'd probably jump at the chance to capture the Mediterranean sunshine on canvas."

Del stared at him open mouthed. "Do you really think she'd come? What a brainwave! She could meet the folks and stay on after I leave to paint as long as she likes."

Algy looked smug. He did not doubt that Clarrie would accept both proposals and could not have been more delighted.

74 – Scoop

Del had a late supper with Clarrie and didn't leave until well after midnight. Her mind was in too much turmoil to relax so she made herself a cup of hot chocolate and sat nursing it at the kitchen table.

Ten minutes later, as it was cooling, untouched, Sarah joined her... "I knew you were alone and wondered why you hadn't come up to bed. Is anything wrong?"

Clarrie was pleased to have company and switched the kettle on to boil again.

Everything was fine, she said, but her restlessness contradicted her words.

She chattered animatedly about the rescue and Del – and Algy and Del – and Del's 'scoop'.

Sarah could tell by the way they acted and talked in each other's company that Del and Clarinda were incredibly close already and was pleased if her daughter had found real companionship again, even though a little bewildered by the suddenness of it all.

Sarah was aware of an underlying disquiet in Clarinda's mood but refrained from comment or asking what had caused it.

"What do you think of Del, now that you are getting to know him?" Clarrie asked.

"Whatever I think, personally, is immaterial, he seems to be brightening your life and that's all that matters to me, I want you to be happy. But yes, of course," Sarah added hastily, "I'm not avoiding the question, I like him very much."

"He talks as if he has no doubt that we were made for each other – our destinies entwined for the rest of our lives, almost jokingly – but has made no proposition: marriage or otherwise. I don't mean that I particularly want him to, not yet anyway. I enjoy his banter." Clarrie paused, a little embarrassed. "I'm telling you this because he has invited me to visit his parents with him before he leaves for the Middle East and I have accepted." Seeing Sarah's astonishment, she added hastily, "You mustn't read any more into it than that he wants to show me Spain and I will be staying on to do some painting after he leaves."

"What a marvellous idea, Darling. You need a change and what better way is there to see a new country than having a native guide!" Sarah enthused, then added, "But you must both be careful not to shut his parents out too much. They must miss him and your presence in their son's life might be somewhat of a surprise! Give them a chance to get to know you because I have a feeling it will augur well for happy family relations!"

A faintly alarming thought then occurred to her. "I take it they are quite willing to have you staying on alone ...it isn't just Del's idea?"

"Would you believe that the suggestion came originally from Algy? Del rang his parents before he came tonight. He says they are absolutely thrilled ...his actual words implied that his mother left him talking to his father while she rushed off to write a guest list for the wedding ...but yes, I do think they are happy to have me."

Clarrie laughed, recalling the casual way Del threw out this, and other indirect lines, hoping to catch her unawares and have her rise like a hooked fish.

If he thought she could be caught so easily, he was mistaken; it was an amusing game she was quite happy to play until he was ready to risk a formal approach. She was, anyway, reluctant to increase the pace at which the relationship was advancing; things were moving so fast already that she felt it was all a little unreal. His going away for a year might not be a bad thing ...but already she dreaded his enforced absence: after years of being self-sufficient she would be terribly lonely.

75 – Tuesday 28th

The telephone extension in the studio was at Clarrie's bedside and when it burst into life she hurried across from her easel to pick it up. Her mother and Polly were still in bed but she was far too excited to sleep well after Del's visit the previous evening. She had been up, working, since six! As she answered, hoping the ringing had not disturbed the rest of the household, she looked at the clock – just after eight: it was Alec.

He immediately apologised for ringing so early but was anxious to speak to Sarah, having heard that she had been trying to reach him. Clarrie gave him a brief outline of the reason and he offered to visit them rather than ask Sarah to come to his office, if the matter could wait until after lunch. Clarrie immediately invited him to eat with them and he accepted. Sarah had in fact heard the telephone ring and tapped on the studio door. "That was Alec wasn't it? I hope he didn't waken you." Then stepping inside the room, she saw that Clarrie was dressed and already hard at work. "Good Heavens, do you start as early as this every day?"

"I wouldn't say I always feel so energetic," Clarrie admitted, "but I didn't sleep well and if I had allowed myself to drift off after six-o-clock I wouldn't have come round until tea-time!" Sarah refrained from commenting. Instead, she asked if Alec wanted her to ring back and was delighted to hear he was coming at midday.

Before she left the studio, she stood and watched Clarrie putting the finishing touches to the first of the

Farlow landscapes. It had a fresh morning glow, which immediately reminded Sarah of her initial glimpse of the valley and was a charming contrast to the more colourful, almost identical view that had been done in the afternoon. In the latter, the heavy shadows cast by the trees created more drama but Sarah preferred the romanticism of the first, and said so.

"I'm not really happy with the second picture yet," confessed Clarrie, "I intend to paint more texture and detail into the darker patches. In my own defence, I must say I spent less time on it than this one. If you remember, I abandoned it for a long lunch!" She laughed as her mother's brows rose knowingly, and started cleaning her brushes.

Sarah went downstairs to put together the notes and statements in readiness for Alec's visit and, as she did so, considered how best to approach the person who had found Joyce's suitcase.

By now she must be feeling quite safe with it.

As soon as Alec permitted, she and Polly might devise an excuse to call on her. It was going to be very difficult but Joyce would undoubtedly haunt her forever if she didn't keep her promise to retrieve the tray.

There was no point in worrying; when the time came, they would probably receive Divine Guidance! She fervently hoped so anyway!

Having worked herself up into a state of contained excitement and anticipation, Sarah was disappointed when Alec rang again to postpone the meeting, if possible until tomorrow. An unexpected visit from his Chief Constable must take precedence. He hoped she would understand – unless it really was a matter of life or death!

Sarah consoled him, "The death has already occurred so of course my tale will keep for another day, but if you have time, will you read any reports you can get hold of about a young woman who was reported missing last week..." She gave him all the information he needed to track down the details, mentioning also Terry White's involvement. Of course Alec knew that it was connected to the mystery which had first taken Sarah to Farlow and would appreciate that until now Sarah hadn't wanted to involve him too deeply. As she put the receiver down she smiled. The unexpected delay might be a necessary part of the grand design. Hers not to question why!

76 – A New Woman

Ann had nothing at all on her mind except arranging a fresh display of flowers from the garden and preparing lunch, so she made an appointment with the village hairdresser. As most of her clientele had been in just before the holiday weekend, the owner was happy to squeeze Ann in …she was a new and potentially regular customer.

The hairdresser would not be disappointed; even though Eddie wasn't cheating on her after all, Ann had been scared out of her complacency and was determined to become more trim and better groomed. She still had some good clothes, unworn for years, ready for when she lost another stone in weight! Her booking was for eleven and as she was on the point of leaving Jenny called round with the children. Ann greeted them warily but Jenny didn't notice her reticence and the twins, ecstatic that Chris and Cathy were coming home, eagerly invited them for tea. Ann solemnly accepted on their behalf and, as she walked out to her car, she explained where she was going.

Jenny was really amazed. "My goodness," she laughed, "Eddie won't recognise you. In four or five days you have become a new woman! I haven't seen you wearing this outfit before, I like it – and I think you've lost a few pounds too." Jenny stood back to admire the result …"Yes, you are thinner. Have you eaten at all since he went away? All this *and* a hair-do …he'll think he's come to the wrong house."

It would have been easy to be offended at the inference

that she had been fat and dowdy before, but Ann knew Jenny only meant to encourage her and was pleased. Jenny asked if Ann would come for coffee tomorrow. They had hardly seen each other for a week and the men would both be back at work.

"Anyway," Jenny said with a rueful shake of her head, "Bill has bought some paintings – the most terrible daubs I have ever seen in my life – painted by that man Todd who works at the garage. Believe me, I've seen more artistic creations by the twins! He is such a pushy character too: over familiar. Personally, I think Bill has flipped but I would value a second opinion!"

Ann was intrigued and actually began to look forward to going. Her recurring fear, since Bill's confession, about being unable to face her friend again with a degree of equanimity was forgotten. It suddenly seemed possible that life would soon return to normal and perhaps in the years to come she would convince herself that the past week had never really happened. With a light heart, Ann drove away to be made beautiful ...in just a few hours the family would be home and her world was settling into some semblance of order.

77 – The Blackmailer

The children, laughing and chasing each other, ran ahead of Jenny as she approached the house. Seeing them race up the steps to the porch she shouted a warning to slow up but it was too late. Matthew, looking back to see how close Sally was, knocked over a small plant pot. It was not damaged but soil scattered over the shiny floor in all directions. They were both immediately subdued, then Matthew timidly said, "I'm sorry mummy ...I can put the flower back in. Look, it isn't broken!"

"I will I will! Let me do it mummy," Sally cried eagerly. The sight of all that mess and an excuse to get her little hands into it was a chance too good to miss. "Don't let Matthew – it was his fault!" Matthew glowered at his sister but couldn't deny that he hadn't been looking where he was going.

"Neither of you will. I'd rather tackle it myself," said Jenny firmly. "Keep away from it and come to the back door."

After unlocking the house, she sent Matthew for a broom and Sally for the dustpan and brush while she put on her overall and rubber gloves. As she filled a bucket with water the children stood waiting quietly. They were wondering if they were going to be punished, and if so, how? They need not have worried. Jenny knew it had been an accident. "You can come and watch me. It will give you time to calm down before you play inside," she told them as she led the way to the front.

The worst of the damage had been put right and Jenny

was about to swish water over the tiles when Sally spotted something white wedged near the doorsill. She ran to remove it, ever helpful, and took it to Matthew. They both examined it admiringly. "Can I keep this please?" he asked Jenny. When he held it up to Jenny's face for an answer she was momentarily speechless. Recovering, she told him to put it in her pocket.

"I wonder how it got there," she muttered.

"Oh, I know that," Matthew volunteered, "That man was holding lots of them."

"What man?"

"The man who is going to paint Sally and me."

Blood pounded in Jenny's ears. She was overcome by a dark dizziness and clutched the porch rail for support. So... that explained it! Blackmail! The fact that Bill was giving in by buying those terrible daubs proved beyond doubt that he had something to hide. She couldn't wait to take a good look at the woman he preferred to her. The children, sensing something was wrong, were looking frightened so she managed a smile and sent them off to play while she finished washing the tiles.

Later, still shaking, she stared at the snapshot into the laughing eyes of the beautiful girl in Bill's arms. It was not just a party pose. He was gazing at her with adoration and holding her too close.

What was she to do? Confront him or pretend she didn't know? The children were sure to mention it, so it was bound to come out into the open. Perhaps it was for the best – at least that odious man wouldn't be able to squeeze any more out of Bill for keeping quiet.

The more she looked at the girl, the more sure she was that she'd seen her somewhere. Eventually she remembered two women who called the other day about a lost dog. They had shown her a photograph but she had scarcely looked at it, knowing she hadn't been at home that day.

Now, she was sure it was the same woman. If so, what was she doing in Farlow?

Had she come to meet Bill?

Jenny made herself a strong sweet cup of tea and lay huddled on the bed, listening to the children's voices rising and falling happily as they played in the garden below. Tears ran uncontrollably down her cheeks. She had thought theirs was the most perfect marriage in the world. He appeared to be an ideal husband. Their home was constantly admired and the twins were adorable. They had everything. It was Eddie Tiller who had once seemed likely to stray, not her Bill.

This last thought sent her mind racing back to the day she had made an unannounced trip to town. She'd walked into the bar and saw Bill with Eddie and a strikingly attractive girl. Now it slowly dawned on her that what she had seen was Eddie with Bill and Bill's girl – this girl! Jenny felt like a complete idiot for accepting so readily his hints that the girl was with Eddie. To think she had felt so sorry for Ann! Jenny wished Ann had not gone out. She wanted to apologise to her immediately, as if Ann could possibly have been aware of her private thoughts ...she wished she could talk to her before facing Bill but it wasn't fair to spoil Ann's pleasure at the return of her family by burdening her with her own misery.

Perhaps after all it was best to sleep on it. Ann would be coming for coffee tomorrow and by then she might have shown Bill the photograph. Perhaps he would laugh and tell her it was all a storm in a teacup ...perhaps!

The children had gone very quiet – an indication perhaps that they were up to no good – so Jenny forced herself to her feet and went downstairs. Her eye fell on the telephone and beside it, half tucked into the pad, was a small white card ...the one Mrs Grey had given her: the police superintendent's.

Fear began to grip her stomach.

Surely it was very unusual for someone to come looking for someone else's dog! Perhaps they were more interested in the girl than the poodle; could they actually have been checking on behalf of the police?

Really, she gripped her throat briefly; she was allowing her imagination to get out of control. She must appear as normal as possible tonight.

She would watch Bill more closely than usual and might bring up the subject of the awful paintings to assess his reaction. If remotely possible she wanted to save her marriage but only if he was finished with this girl for good!

In a stupid, inexplicable way Jenny was beginning to feel already that, if he had deceived her, it was all her own fault. Was this how battered wives felt? So fervently did they desire their husbands to be ideal, that they preferred to look for imperfections in themselves? She knew it was the wrong attitude, but was prepared to sink her pride to save their future. Perhaps, after all, it would be a mistake to tell Ann anything at all. Jenny had twenty-four hours to decide.

78 – Sweet Dreams

Driving back home from the salon, Ann felt good. She had allowed the hairdresser to re-style her hair as she judged right, and was delighted with the result. It made her look years younger. Jenny was right: Eddie wouldn't recognise her! It had taken longer than she expected so it was fortunate that she had prepared a casserole for lunch; by the time she arrived it would be cooked. If it hadn't been so late she would have driven on to show Jenny her new look but couldn't risk being out when the family arrived. She had just finished setting the table when she heard the car outside. Ann felt like an excited teenager as she rushed to the door to greet them.

Eddie was startled by the enthusiasm of her bear hug and the way she kissed him. He held her at arms' length and gasped. "Good heavens! I'm glad you missed me, but let me breathe woman! You look absolutely radiant: did being without me do you so much good?"

"After just one day alone," she laughed, "I looked so awful I had to do something drastic to restore my self-respect. Do you approve?"

He certainly did, hardly taking his eyes off her while they attempted to exchange information, in between the excited chatter of the children vying with each other to give her their own special news.

"Yes, the parents are both fit and well."

"No – nothing much has happened here." (May God forgive me she thought!)

"We didn't do much other than watch TV."

"Yes, the sale went quite well. No, I didn't buy anything."

"Yes, it was a really good drive, both ways."

"By the way," Ann managed to say at last, "The builders have started work." This last piece of information stopped everything. They all ran to view the foundations.

"Well," Eddie said with a satisfied air, they are making a good job of it." He eyed the low wall, which neatly enclosed the layer of hard-core.

If walls do have ears, Ann thought, it's a good thing they don't speak as well! She stared at the middle where she had done the work herself. It looked no different from the rest. Next time we want a floor laid, she decided, we'll do it ourselves and save a fortune!

Eddie walked over it, tamping a few small stones flat with his heel. He echoed Ann's thoughts. "Really, I don't know why we didn't tackle the job without them. We could have had a cement mix delivered."

"Too late," Ann replied, "they'll be pouring concrete tomorrow." Laughing, she led the way inside for lunch.

The rest of the day went extremely well. Eddie didn't seem at all put out to hear that he'd have to manage without his secretary tomorrow. "Poor old Jo," he shook his head in sympathy. "Trust her to do herself an injury – if she lost any inches at all she has probably put them back on, being forced to rest!"

The children did not need much persuading to go to bed. After their long drive and eating more than usual at teatime with the twins, they were thoroughly exhausted. Having finished their own evening meal Ann and Eddy sat together contentedly mulling over events past and present in a more leisurely way.

Eddie suddenly said quietly, "I don't know whether it's because I haven't seen you for a few days but you really do look rather special tonight ...I do believe you are wearing your war paint – are you aiming to seduce me?"

Ann went across and crouched at his feet.

"This is your new lover," she whispered. "Are you going to let me?" He gathered her in his arms and she needed no verbal answer. In spite of everything, Ann couldn't remember when she had been so perfectly, blissfully, happy and she soon fell asleep that night, sure that all her troubles were over.

79 – Last Chance

Jenny lay listening to Bill's heavy breathing. She had given him several chances to come clean about his feelings. She even invented a story about a wife who forgave her husband a torrid affair because he'd been honest, implying that she'd be inclined to do the same ...but she suspected he wasn't really listening.

He had seemed preoccupied and she was sure he was only pretending to be absorbed with his newspaper. The only time he took any interest was when she asked if Eddie was still seeing the redhead he had been with in the bar! He hastily told her to forget she'd ever seen them together; she could take his word – there was nothing in it.

Jenny thought it was probably the only true thing he had told her for a long time, and was miserable. Several times, she'd been on the point of making a direct accusation but something held her back. She still had not come to terms with his double-dealing ...she wanted to talk it through first with another woman – Ann.

In spite of the overwhelming evidence, Jenny couldn't believe that Bill didn't love her. He adored the twins and his home meant a lot to him, if only as a visible sign of his success. She needed to hear him confirm his love though, and if tonight was anything to go by, he had no intention of discussing anything. Eventually weariness overtook her and she fell into a fitful sleep.

80 – Clarrie

Clarrie was ready a good half-hour early for her date with Del and Polly couldn't resist commenting. "When the bell rings, you go straight back upstairs and I'll answer. Your mother will give him a sherry while he waits. You shouldn't appear to be over-eager!"

Clarrie laughed, saying that she was far too old to indulge in such childish games but when she heard his car arrive she announced that as it might be cool later, she was going for a shawl and would be down in a few minutes.

Polly and Sarah exchanged approving glances and Polly went to welcome Del. It was marvellous to see Clarrie looking radiant and they unreservedly approved of anyone who could make her so happy. She had been devoted to her husband and not looked at another man seriously since he died ...they both wanted her future to be secure with a man they could both admire.

81 - Wednesday 29th

Ann enjoyed the best night's sleep she had experienced for well over a week. Eddie rose early without disturbing her and came in with a cup of tea before he left the house. He shook her gently, planted a kiss on her nose and said, "There's no need to get up yet, I have had some toast and I'm just on my way out, but the builder has arrived so I thought I had better warn you. They won't need you until coffee time so you can turn over and go back to sleep until the monsters disturb you!"

When she protested that it was far too early for him to leave he said he wanted a good start to the day... Jo would not be in and the other girl was incapable of acting on her own initiative. She needed more supervision than he usually had to give. As he went out, he called back, "I want a word with the builder before he starts mixing - I've had a great idea - see you later!" Ann snuggled down into the duvet sighing happily. She could afford to relax until the children woke up.

She heard his progress downstairs and the firm clank of the front door lock ...then voices under the bedroom window. "I'm sorry to spring this on you, just as you were about to concrete - I know it will add to the cost, but better to consider it now than later!" Eddie's words floated upwards. The builder replied, apparently agreeing to comply. He didn't sound at all perturbed. Then Ann heard Eddie's voice again "Good, so you can go ahead digging and shuttering today and cement the lot tomorrow. A plot 6' by 3' and 4' deep should do it... right in the middle."

As Ann sprang upright in sick horror she heard him say, "I've always fancied an inspection pit."

Before Eddie's car reached the gate, Ann was clambering out of bed into her clothes. She didn't know how, but she had to make the builder stop work and go away... what on earth was she going to say?

When she ran outside he was issuing instructions to his men who were poised to drag the stones away from the hidden grave. She babbled hysterically for a moment and they all looked at her with open disbelief. "I just heard my husband talking to you, but he's never mentioned the pit to me and I am completely against it ...with the children about you see ...please don't do anything ...in fact, go away until I've had a chance to speak to him about it. I really feel very unwell ...I can't have men working here at all today!"

They stood silently, looking at her as if she was quite mad. Ann was behaving like a maniac, she knew. She felt wholly deranged and couldn't quell the hysteria rising in her tone of voice as she insisted again that they must leave.

The boss had a quiet word with the two labourers and they started to pack up as he turned to Ann. "This is a very bad business Mrs Tiller. I promised your husband we'd do the job today, and I take my instructions from him. I'm afraid I'll have to telephone him the minute I get back to the office, but there's no way we will be back on this job again until next week ...and all this inconvenience will add to the cost!"

Eddie would certainly be extremely upset when he heard and completely baffled. Should she ring him first? What could she say on the telephone? Anyway, she didn't need him to tell her that it was all over – she must contact the police immediately and confess. It would be better if she coped with the initial unpleasantness alone, as she had at the beginning of this mess. Poor Eddie! He would be absolutely devastated. Ann steeled herself to bear the brunt of things herself, allowing him to work on in ignorance until she took official advice.

First, she must get the children out of the way; she would take them to Jenny. It would all come out now. How was she going to break it to her friend that her husband was a louse? Together, they would decide what to do. Surely, after all Ann had endured, she could rely on Jenny to support her.

82 – Jenny

Jenny, after a rotten night, was up and dressed having coffee in the kitchen while she waited for the twins to appear, demanding breakfast. They were still quiet until they heard Cathy and Christopher whooping eagerly as they ran round the side of the house. Her heart sank. She was astonished to be visited so early but, on the other hand, was anxious to speak to Ann so she hastened to let them in with mixed feelings.

One look at Ann's white face told Jenny that something was badly wrong and she immediately sent the children upstairs to play. As coherently as she could Ann described the arrival on her doorstep of the young woman who turned out to be Bill's secretary. Before she reached the traumatic climax, Jenny held out the snapshot she had been holding and asked, "Is this her?"

"It would be more correct," said Ann gazing at the girl, "to say it *was* her!" Before Jenny could question her she asked, "Where did you get this? Did you know what was going on then?"

It took them an hour to sort out the tangle of what had happened and finally they were both in tears. Their emotions were mixed. Jenny, who had feared that her husband was completely lost to another woman, was relieved to learn that even the girl admitted her failure to lure him away. She trembled, knowing she could so easily have been dead now, if fate hadn't led the murderer to the wrong house. Albeit inadvertently, Ann had saved her life!

Ann was glad her news had not come as a complete shock. She felt drained and had no reserves of strength left to offer moral support. Uppermost now, was her abject fear. She was almost in shock and Jenny, recognising this, took her into the sitting room where she made her lie on the settee and wrapped a blanket round her. While the kettle boiled again for a hot drink, she sat holding her hand and described the visit of the two strange ladies. They had police connections and Jenny now convinced they must have been on Joyce's track.

Remembering the visiting card, Jenny insisted that the best thing to do was to telephone the same man again ...at least he must know the background to the situation whereas the local police would not and explaining would be much more difficult.

Ann was in no condition to think clearly. Now that Jenny had taken control she subsided into a state of near collapse and lay wanly, tightly crouched, hugging her stomach. She nodded without speaking. Leaving a fresh cup of hot sweet tea within Ann's reach, Jenny went to the telephone, picked up Alec's card and dialled with a shaking hand.

83 – Emergency Call

Sarah glanced at the clock. It was unlike Alec to be late, not without ringing to explain anyway. Polly, beginning to grow anxious about the meal being spoiled, had switched everything off; it would be safer to re-heat things than have it all dried up. Clarrie was also put out. She'd been happy to stop work for an hour or so but at this rate it would hardly be worth starting again after he left. She was on the point of announcing that she would have to resume work when a car arrived and to their great relief it was Alec.

They were surprised to find he had come in an official vehicle which, having dropped him off, drove away again without waiting. He hurried in making abject apologies but was assured that as long as he was well, and here at last, it was of no matter. When, earlier, he received Jenny's call within minutes of arriving in his office, he had been intrigued, guessing it was directly connected with Sarah's visit to Farlow. He was aware that she had been inquiring into the disappearance of a young woman and as she had suggested, had since looked through all the reports on the case. From what Clarrie had told him he knew the girl was dead and that it was in this connection her mother wished to see him. Alec was now keen to hear what Sarah would say.

It wasn't often that he felt one jump ahead of her so, before she could give him any hint of what she knew, he told her that the body of Joyce Hamilton had been buried in the Tillers' garage after being stored in a freezer and carted in the boot of a car over half the county of Oxfordshire! Alec explained to his rapt audience how, after the call from Farlow, he went there immediately to investigate. In view of the circumstances he felt that he owed it to Sarah to take a personal interest.

He had taken with him a female officer and Detective Sergeant Terry White who appeared to know the person who first reported the girl's disappearance. Mrs Dean had told him little over the telephone but it sounded extremely serious. Within minutes of their arrival, as soon as he gathered the gist of things, he rang Eddie Tiller himself, from the Deans', and asked him to return home. By the time Alec left the village the body was being exhumed and Eddie was comforting his wife under the sympathetic eye of the policewoman. Detective Sergeant White was with the local force to watch proceedings at the Tiller house. It was out of their hands officially but Alec had many friends in the senior ranks and he knew no further action would be taken before he reported back.

After listening with ill-concealed excitement, they could hardly wait to show him their own documentary testimony and Sarah handed him the two sheets of paper. Alec had taken his own notes while Ann and Jenny made their statements and he compared them with Clarrie's automatic writing, which gave Joyce's version of events.

It was quite uncanny and he felt the hair rise on the back of his head. He would never get used to being confronted by the incredible truth that there really was a life after death.

Finally, he sighed. "Poor Mrs Tiller! I wonder if she'll ever get over the trauma. She certainly went through the mill – and back! She must have been at her wits end."

"I agree," said Clarrie. "First the shock of thinking her husband had been deceiving her for years with another woman, then being terrified into believing her own life threatened. Her first emotion after the horror of the girl's violent death must have been relief that she had escaped such agony herself."

"It would have been infinitely more sensible to call the police immediately, without question," ventured Polly, "but I can understand why, in her confusion, she resolved to conceal all knowledge of her husband's infidelity."

Alec sighed again with a wry shake of his head. "So can I," he admitted, "but we can't allow people to go around burying each other indiscriminately! I don't know how much luck I'll have convincing my Chief that Joyce Hamilton only got what she deserved and trying to make him understand that Ann Tiller is the real victim, but I'll do my damnedest."

He informed them when they reached the coffee stage, that in spite of his late arrival, he would be dashing away... the car would return within minutes. Alec was reluctant to take Sarah with him as she might then be stuck in Farlow for many boring hours but there was no reason now why she should not speak to Ann Tiller. "It might cheer her up," he said, "knowing someone is on her side."

In consequence, Clarrie offered to drive her mother and Polly to the village. As it was a nice sunny day again, she would be better employed looking at her painting on the spot, instead of struggling to improve it at home. They were all eager and ready to go when Alec's driver arrived, so they followed him within minutes. Alec had told them to come straight to the Deans' and when they pulled into the drive, he came out to meet them. "I have explained that you are able to back her up but it's up to you whether or not you wish to explain how. I'm leaving now to see if I can pull a few strings. Wish me luck!"

Jenny was waiting at the door to let them in, so Clarrie also drove off without delay. Sarah and Polly went inside to meet Ann.

84 – Art in Context

Ann was subdued but had recovered a little of her composure. After meeting everyone, when Eddie had assimilated the gravity of the circumstances, he asked her if she would be all right. He wanted to check the situation at home and would then return to his office for what, after all, would be only very few minutes at the end of the afternoon. He had left in panic and was therefore worried about the state of things there. She agreed that he should go; there was nothing he could do for the moment and she had company.

The young woman officer, who it transpired had met Sarah previously on another case, was delighted to see her again. She knew that Alec, her boss, trusted Sarah's discretion and was consequently content to sit in the hall while the four women spoke together. She could see them through the open door but was out of earshot and did not intrude.

"I just don't understand how you knew Joyce had been to see me," said Ann. "If she had told anyone she was coming to Farlow – which would be surprising as she was planning to commit murder – she would surely have said she was coming here, to Jenny's."

In the few minutes before Sarah's arrival Alec had allowed Ann to read the paper written posthumously in Joyce's own hand and Ann was shaken to see that it contained some minor details that she'd left out of her own statement. In her immense relief – having her story backed up, she had not immediately questioned its source.

The man had been in and out of the house in less than five minutes – there had been no time for questions but now she naturally wanted to know how and when it was written.

Ann's penetrating questions indicated that she possessed a very clear, logical mind that only the truth would satisfy. After a few minutes of trying to avoid doing so Sarah eventually revealed that she was psychic and sometimes helped the police.

Ann and Jenny were stunned, but couldn't deny the truth of what they had themselves witnessed. Discovering that Sarah's daughter had written it, controlled by an entity from the dead, Ann shuddered. Never having believed in ghosts her first thought, as conviction sank in, was, "What about Joyce? Will she come back to haunt me? I will be terrified of ever being alone again."

Sarah sought to assure her that Joyce really repented and meant her no harm. Ann looked unconvinced and asked, "I met her! How can I believe that?"

Polly saw Sarah freeze slightly to complete stillness and close her eyes, and held her breath. She knew from experience that some new revelation was about to take place. Immediately, Sarah smiled and turning to face Ann asked, "Are you prepared to accept a gift from Joyce as a token apology?" The look on Ann's face was wary. She didn't answer until Jenny nudged her excitedly whereupon she nodded with a puzzled frown. Sarah said, "Cast your mind back to the day this dreadful thing happened. You worried how to dispose of some clothing." Ann stared wide-eyed. Sarah continued, "The least difficult items to conceal are still in your bedroom drawer ...lacy things, easily obtained by anyone and not traceable to your late visitor."

Ann gasped, covering her face with her hands. She suddenly felt like a thief. The death of the girl wasn't her fault – she felt no guilt about that, but taking possession of the clothes, even though she could hardly bear to look at them was different somehow. Sarah patted her hand, "Don't be upset my dear. Joyce knows you'd never have used them but she says she really hopes you will, one day. Please tell her if you can, that you understand and forgive her for all the trouble she's caused."

Forgiveness was a large step to take when Ann still didn't know how Joyce's murderous intentions would affect her entire future, but if the alternative was the return of Joyce's animosity towards her she had no choice! "I hope Joyce really understands that at the time, I did try to stop her drinking from that pot... although I thought it was only some kind of drug. Anyway, as she has tried to put the record straight I do forgive her." Ann was at a loss as to what else to say... one could hardly expect the girl to be happy with her reply, or indeed be happy about anything: she was dead! After a moment, she asked Sarah, "What will happen to Joyce now? I mean, as she hasn't actually completely gone! I thought, if I thought at all, that souls went straight to heaven or hell."

"Well, as I understand it," replied Sarah, "the after-life consists of a series of planes. Souls are accepted into the highest one possible according to their state of grace. Each is a place of learning and progression. We ascend gradually until we become pure love and are absorbed into one whole Supreme Being."

"I suppose the really good people who die have less to learn," said Jenny, "but who teaches them?"

"I wish I had all the answers," Sarah laughed, "but I can only surmise that up there, they all help each other, perhaps by example!"

Jenny was not to be put off, and asked, "Where is hell then?"

"Some say that hell is right here on earth," rejoined Sarah, "but for our purposes I think we can presume that the unrepentant evil never ascend past first grade, which may be a very uncomfortable place."

They all relished the relief of talking of something other than the exhumation going on next-door and it was something of a shock when the police officer tapped at the door to say it was all over. She could take Ann back to 'Near Acre' if she wished.

Ann looked entreatingly at Jenny who immediately insisted that it was out of the question until Eddie came home. She went upstairs to telephone Bill who would be preparing to leave his office within a few minutes. She asked him to be sure to come home as soon as possible – no drinks with the boys tonight; she had decided to explain everything to him in person. As she replaced the receiver she thought of the snapshot and the others, which the loathsome Todd still possessed.

The last thirty-six hours had brought about a subtle change in Jenny. The light hearted little housewife who had been content to let her husband run her life – the person who happily allowed him to make all decisions with complete faith in his judgement, had gone. The efficient career girl who acted confidently in the best interest of her boss had returned. With scarcely any hesitation, she picked up the directory and looked up the number of the filling station. When she eventually had Eric Todd on the end of the line she announced clearly, "This is Jenny Dean. The arrangement you have had with my husband is at an end. I am well aware of the situation and if you know what's good for you, you will put the rest of the photographs in an envelope, together with the money you have already received from him... and drop them into our post-box on your way home."

Todd was at first stunned and then protested that the money was payment for the paintings. "If you think you are going to get away with that, then you are a fool," Jenny said firmly. "I have already spoken to the CID and am expecting Detective Chief Superintendent Holmes to arrive here at any moment." There was an audible gasp from Todd, then silence. "Make up your mind," Jenny ordered curtly, "shall I leave your artwork at the gate or show it to him?"

"Okay, okay... I'll do it, but I've spent some of the money," he whined. Realising she had won went to Jenny's head.

"We'll be happy to take a cheque to ease your cash shortage, but just make sure it doesn't bounce!"

As luck would have it, Alec arrived in a police car barely a minute before Jenny saw Todd's van turning in the driveway.

He must have had a shock when he saw it – she doubted if he had really believed her about the CID! They shouldn't have any more trouble with him but she would not tell Bill yet.

There were a few other matters she wanted to discuss before she gave him anything to smile about!

In due course she would let him off the hook, but not until she had seen him squirm a little. She would tell him she was willing to continue as normally as possible for the sake of the children and perhaps one day she would forget the deep hurt she felt, but he had a lot of explaining to do before she could forgive him ...she only hoped he had learned that the game wasn't worth the candle!

85 – Progress

Below Clarrie as she worked, the shadows lengthened gradually. As the angle of the sun changed, the solid darkness under the trees began to lift, revealing mysterious hints of life. An old oak sheltered a kissing gate she had not noticed before and large patches of rust-coloured fern glowed in the warm light. This was the fleeting moment she had hoped to capture... the splendour of strong sunshine with a hint that it was about to fade. She painted feverishly but soon realised the futility of continuing: to do so would ruin what she had already achieved.

As she started to pack up she saw the little woman with the black dog leave her neighbour's house and start walking slowly back to her own. It was such a calm peaceful scene in the faintly orange afternoon light that she felt inspired to tackle another painting to complete a trilogy.

Before leaving, Clarrie took a few more photographs to help her decide. Later she would consider seriously whether it would be worth returning to this same spot.

Little Mary waddled to her back door. The front one had not been opened for years and it was beyond her strength to un-wedge it anyway. She would have stayed longer with Alice but she was fed up to the back teeth with hearing how clever Eric was.

"He paints things ever so quickly but they must be good because they are selling on sight". Alice boasted of his natural talent... "Thousands of artists work at it day in – day out for years and never get anywhere!"

It had been on the tip of Mary's tongue to tell Alice that her husband was no genius – just a common blackmailer but she hesitated. If it ever got back to him that Mary suspected him of using the photographs to get money, he would know who had pricked his profitable little bubble. If only she hadn't made that telephone call she might have spoken to him and got something out of it herself; it was too late now. Anyway, she thought, she was no cheap crook... then, with a stab of guilt, she remembered the suitcase she still had.

She should never have kept it. They called it stealing by finding didn't they? Mary gave an involuntary backward glance and her step quickened. Her stomach lurched at the mere thought that her dishonesty might come to light so it was no wonder that she almost fainted with shock when she walked into her kitchen...

Sunlight cut into the gloom and, shimmering on the swirling dusty air – in its bright shaft, stood the woman Mary had robbed.

86 - Little Mary

The sinister female confronting Mary was undoubtedly the one she had seen across the field. She appeared in the very clothes Mary had taken from the bag! The long fawn raincoat hung over her thin woollen-clad legs almost down to her clumsy plastic shoes. Her outline, topped by the wide brimmed hat was quite unmistakable.

Mary first yelped with shock then howled aloud in dismay. She wanted to turn and get away – anywhere, until the menacing female had found and removed all her things! Having to face the woman and her accusing scowl was too much for Mary to endure and as her legs were incapable of flight she sank to her knees, gasping, fighting for breath, and yet she couldn't look away from the sinister gaze. Behind steel rimmed glasses the eyes flashed angrily and seemed to burn into her own until they radiated a glow which consumed the paste-white face and blinded Mary to everything else... she could no longer discern a countenance or sense anything at all other than the glare of mute, scornful accusation.

Still staring into those glittering eyes, Mary saw them fade in intensity ...the twin circles of the spectacles took shape: not a pair of glasses after all! They were on a shelf... merely part of the pattern on an old jug. Mary stared as if concussed at the empty room around her and slowly crumpled into a faint on the kitchen floor.

When she came round and relived the whole experience, she doubted her own senses; she must surely have imagined the whole thing ...being overcome suddenly by the burden of guilt! Anyway, people had definitely to be dead before they became ghosts! There was no reason to think the woman she had seen was dead! Was there? Struggling against panic, she attempted to rationalise her situation. What could they do to her for keeping goods that were abandoned in a field? She was, after all, just an ignorant old woman!

Mary felt a sneaking unease, which she had not allowed to surface before. It was clear that the woman in blue must have changed clothes and abandoned the tatty stuff, but why would she have left the new things hidden too, yet failed to return for them? In her desire to keep all the goodies and feeling safe from discovery, Mary had fantasised about the loss being reported and the police not caring – after all, only a fool would expect them to be safe in a field! A Gypsy or any passing tramp could have picked them up! With the aid of a nearby stool Mary pushed herself to her feet shakily ...before she did anything else she needed to sit properly and allow her limbs to untwist.

Entering her small living room the first thing she saw was the silver tray, which in spite of the wedges was no longer leaning where she had left it. It wasn't on the floor where it might have rolled again, it was on the table in the middle of the room! She quivered fearfully, her stomach churning. The only way it could have got there was by careful placing... someone was trying to tell her something. She was undoubtedly haunted!

Terror lent wings to Mary's feet. She scrambled to put everything back in the suitcase and get it out of the house! If she didn't, those terrible accusing eyes would be on her constantly in the dark of every night. Even the thought was chilling: she dared not risk being pursued to the end of her days.

When everything was bundled unceremoniously back into the case – and oh, how she grieved to be parting with it – she concealed it with an old blanket, hoisted it over her shoulder and left the house.

High on the hillside, Clarrie looked through the camera lens and adjusted the exposure. A figure was crossing the field and she lowered the camera to watch ...it was the old woman, moving much faster than usual in spite of the fact that she had a bundle on her back. The dog, unable to keep up with her, was yards behind, not far from the cottage.

Their presence was unimportant, so Clarrie took a couple of snaps at different settings, before driving down to pick up her mother and Polly. Throughout the afternoon, she had witnessed the ceaseless activity around the two houses on Old Farm Lane. It had quieted in the last hour and she was anxious to find out what was happening to Ann Tiller. It would be a tragedy if she was taken from her family and punished.

It was odd really, how little thought she had given to the situation during the past few hours. Her mind had been dwelling more on Del and the promised visit to Spain. Apart from the prospect of seeing a new country, it would allow them to get to know each other better. Whether he proposed marriage, or whether she would accept if he did, was unimportant. Marriage, in any case was out of the question for at least a year. She was looking forward very much to meeting his parents and had no doubt that it would be an interesting, exciting holiday. She was so exhilarated, in such a magnanimous mood, that she wanted a happy ending for everyone – even Joyce!

87 – Aftermath

Sarah and Polly were totally exhausted after their unusual, enervating afternoon and were extremely relieved when at last Alec returned to "Far Acre". He greeted them with an encouraging, re-assuring smile. He was unable to make any promises, but there was at least a faint possibility that, although she would have to give evidence in the Coroner's court, and submit to some lengthy, harrowing questioning to satisfy the powers that be, no charge of murder would be made. It was a unanimous decision that she had behaved in a reckless, foolish manner and would have to face the music – no matter how muted, for her treatment of the deceased, but for the moment, she was not considered to be a threat to the community and would be allowed to remain at home. The welfare of the children had figured largely in this decision, as had her previous good character; the circumstances were, after all, extremely unusual.

Alec looked fatigued and accepted Jenny's offer of tea and sandwiches gratefully. Not long afterwards, Eddie returned to take Ann home and Bill came within minutes of their departure. Sarah, feeling their presence was now intrusive, asked Alec if he would mind taking them up the hill to Clarinda but in fact there was no need, her car arrived as they walked outside.

Jenny stood on the porch step and saw them all off, with deep relief; what a day it had been! Had she not been so anxious to have Bill on his own, Jenny would happily have entertained them all for longer, but she needed to confront him.   Bill had treated her shabbily and she wanted to make sure he would think twice before ever doing so again!

88 – Home Again

Clarrie followed the circular drive round the central flower bed and halted behind the police car. They sat waiting quietly until it pulled away. With a final wave when they started moving, Sarah sank back into her seat. The small convoy moved out of the gate but almost immediately they had to wait again, near the Tiller house where the last remaining police car was emerging from the drive.

Sarah suddenly sat upright, her eyes drawn to the hedge, a little way beyond them and she tugged Clarrie's arm. "Clarinda Stop! Look, do you see her?" she asked. "Joyce is standing there – pointing to the ditch behind the bushes. Slow down until the others are out of sight, then stop."

Clarrie couldn't see anything, but wasn't surprised; it was still more remarkable to her when she did!

"I'll go over and take a look?" she offered, switching off the engine and climbing out of the car. The other vehicles disappeared and Clarrie walked along the lane until Sarah called out for her to stop.

Pushing aside the foliage, she immediately saw the blue leather case, which she retrieved quickly and carried back to the car. "I would have had some explaining to do if the police had still been around," she said. "What on earth shall we do with it?"

"We will leave that decision until we get home and examine it. Put it out of sight in the trunk" Sarah instructed. Having complied, Clarrie nervously re-joined them and repeated her question.

"My present feeling is that we should hand it to Elaine who, after all, was closer to Joyce than anyone else," Sarah declared. "We know that Joyce wants her to have the tray and I imagine we will find it inside. We also know from experience that if she has anything else in mind Joyce is quite capable of letting us know!"

"Personally," Polly remarked with feeling, "I hope we've heard the last of Joyce."

Sarah's prediction proved correct.

Of course, they didn't know whether anything was missing, but there were a few toilet articles and some clothes. Some bits of jewellery and make-up were loose amongst the jumbled contents, which had been thrown into the case with little regard for their worth.

The silver tray was at the bottom and having assured themselves of this Sarah decided to contact Elaine and Dan. They were still on honeymoon but had mentioned the name of their hotel in case they were needed. She rang up immediately and it was agreed that they should call in again on their way back to Oxford. The household at last returned to something approaching normality for a few days. Clarrie had handed her film in for processing as they passed through town so Polly collected the photos when she went shopping and took them up to the studio as soon as she returned. Clarrie was eager to see the shots of the valley.

The more she thought of it, the more the idea of the project appealed to her …three pictures of the same area in different moods – apparently on one day. It might even be possible to sell them as a set. Spreading the whole collection of photographs out on the table Clarrie immediately saw that whereas she had seen only one person, hurrying across the field, there were in fact two! The taller, but equally drab figure of the second woman was close on the heels of the first and Clarrie hastened with great excitement to show Sarah who examined the snaps eagerly.

Sarah burst out laughing as she handed them back. "Well, now we know why the things were put back so conveniently in the same place! Joyce must have terrified the poor old thing out of her wits." Clarrie wondered why Joyce was, so to speak, in disguise, but as Sarah pointed out, for identification purposes she would appear to each person, as they had known her on earth.

Polly, hearing them laughing as they came downstairs, glowed with contentment. She could never have hoped for anything better... Instead of a lonely retirement, she was living with true friends: completely accepted as part of the family. There was even the added bonus of excitement. In an environment where the so called paranormal was an acceptable part of daily life, who knew what would happen next? Ghosts didn't frighten her – Polly had absolute faith that Sarah could cope with anything!

89 - The Wedding Gift

When Elaine and Dan arrived at the weekend, they were eager to hear the complete story about Joyce's disappearance but Sarah refrained from giving them any information that they would not eventually hear from the police. Despite this, there was quite a lot to tell and it was some hours before they were ready to leave. They glanced inside the case and admired the tray.

Elaine sighed as she placed it on top of the clothes, face down to protect the patterned surface. "I shall always treasure it," she said, "but I am not at all sure what to do with these other things." She looked questioningly at Sarah.

"I'm sure Joyce would want you to use anything you can - but dispose of it however you wish. She has no more use for earthly things," Sarah assured her as they took the suitcase out and put it with their other luggage in the car. They drove away with all the customary promises to keep in touch.

Sarah followed Clarrie into the house and was immediately aware that the atmosphere had lightened; she felt comfortable and relaxed. There had been moments when even her confidence was shaken... she should have had more faith. Next time ...yes, next time she would not waver.

90 – And Then...

Conversation on the way home was somewhat desultory. Elaine was saddened by the re-awakened knowledge that her friend had come to such an awful end... driven to madness by falling for the wrong man. Dan remained quiet, allowing her to mourn in peace. When they reached home, he carried the small blue leather case from the car first and put it on the sofa where Elaine immediately opened it to take out the tray; the other things could wait until tomorrow. He was turning away to continue unloading when Dan heard her gasp of astonishment. Elaine was staring at the gleaming silver surface and slowly lifted it, to show him. He had put the tray into the case himself and it had not been opened since. It had then been, quite definitely, blankly clean.

Now, as if in answer to Elaine's question, repeated so often during the last hour: *"What would Joyce want me to do?"*...Dan saw a message written in lipstick – boldly red, in contrast to the tray's silver white base:

Be Happy - Love Joyce xxx

The Ghostly Echoes Series

If you enjoyed reading "A Poisonous Echo" and "Ghostly Echoes" – the first in the Ghostly Echoes Series, then look out for books three and four and five (Restless Echoes)!

Dangerous Echoes

A young medium arrives in the village and is soon the object of much interest. So much so that she is welcomed into the household of an elderly relative of Dan's wife Elaine. Concerned, they need to enlist help to discover if the medium is as genuine as she seems and his Aunt Polly decides to investigate. Clarrie and Sarah are too involved in their own crises to realise the risks Polly is taking and Polly is so enjoying the thrill of immersing herself in old friendships and researching past romances that she is unaware of the dangerous path she may be treading...

Haunting Echoes

Clarrie is on a painting break, soaking up the atmosphere of the English Countryside, with her canvas at the ready, when she is senselessly attacked by a complete stranger... Her barely started painting is stolen from its easel and Sarah is left to put the clues together while Clarrie fights for her life on a hospital bed...

The Background to 'A Poisonous Echo' / 'Ghostly Echoes'

Sarah

As the wife of a successful artist, achieving normality for Sarah Grey was never going to be as simple as it is for most of us. But with the added impact of her extra sense, giving her the ability to see and hear the dead and the strongly telepathic living, 'normal' has always been a difficult concept. After her husband died, her loneliness was almost overwhelming as she felt surrounded only by the dead, but in the background, there was always Polly, the Grey family housekeeper for many years, to keep her company.

Soldiering on alone, as so many other widows have done, eventually allows her to assume a calm façade and a gradual acceptance of death when it comes so close to home. Selling the old house and moving to a small apartment seems a good idea until her daughter is also widowed but her instincts are to go and live with her to help out. She has long suspected that Clarrie might have latent psychic powers and is concerned about what could happen if Clarrie tries to cope on her own. Once the grief has softened a little, she looks forward to having laughter back in the house...

Clarrie

As an artist's daughter it is, perhaps, not surprising that Clarrie grew up with a love for paint and canvas. Encouraged by her father to accompany him on his painting trips, she learned her trade from a master painter and plies it well. Now an up and coming artist in her own right, everything seems to have come together, until Tom is tragically involved in a crippling accident and she spends the final year of her seven-year marriage nursing her paralysed and dying husband. After his death, devastated by her traumatic loss, Clarrie is grateful for her mother's suggestion so Sarah gives up her original plans to buy an apartment and, instead, moves into Clarrie's home.

Being able to immerse herself in her art proves therapeutic, but the immersion is so complete that Clarrie barely notices the changes in her perception of the world around her, often blurring the reality of the present with the realities of the past and that proves dangerous... Having two psychics in the house is a recipe for trouble, even if one is trying for the "quiet life" and the other is in denial...

Ghostly Echoes by Mai Griffin

The horrific prologue, launches us straight into Mai Griffin's dramatic psychic mystery thriller "Ghostly Echoes". Reflecting the dark side of the mysteries that plague the day to day life of unwilling psychic Sarah Grey and her artist daughter Clarrie Hunter, it also marks the start of the Grey series.

As the plots twist and spiral around the edge of the reader's vision it is possible to see the dilemma of trying to live normally, when everything around you isn't.

Overcoming the temptation to live in denial of their unwanted psychic abilities, Clarrie and Sarah are gradually drawn in to help find a kidnapped woman and a child that has disappeared... and what does Clarrie keep glimpsing, in her picture of an old empty cottage, and why has she been driven to paint it?

No matter where she goes, danger keeps intruding into Clarrie's life and painting is not keeping it at bay...

Reviews for 'Ghostly Echoes' (then Deadly Shades of Grey)

Publisher's Note: We sent out several review copies prior to publication. These are a few of the comments on 'Deadly Shades of Grey' that we received from our first three reviewers:-

1 - I received the book at 5pm and started reading it that evening, I couldn't put it down and I certainly couldn't sleep, until I finished it at three in the morning!

2 - I usually read a book for five or ten minutes, last thing at night, before I go to sleep - I never have time to read in the day, but night after night, until I finished it, I found an hour had gone by, I was so absorbed.

3 - I thoroughly enjoyed this book, it kept me gripped til the end. I cannot wait until Book Two.

As publishers, we feel that this book never loses momentum, every page is a cliff-hanger and everyone who has read it has thoroughly enjoyed it. Available by order from all mainstream UK Book retailers.

"Deadly Shades of Grey" A gripping page-turner writes Barbara Power, (Spain). The creativity of some artists, it seems, just cannot be contained or constrained within the limits of one particular medium, and so it is with the internationally-acclaimed painter, Mai Griffin. In the first of her series which introduces the Grey family, she has turned her artistic talent to the written word and proves as adept with her pen as she is with a paint brush.

For widow Sarah Grey, who only wants to live a quiet life, being psychic is a cause of much anxiety and discomfort. However, she knows that to maintain her peace of mind and sanity she must force herself to respond to the messages that haunt her. Adding to Sarah's anxiety is the fact that her daughter, Clarrie, seems to have inherited the same psychic ability, a situation which could lead her into terrible danger

Deadly Shades of Grey is a well-crafted mystery/murder novel with a gripping and taut plot that has intriguing twists and turns. It is a good and thoroughly satisfying read. Although Book 1 is a stand-alone novel, I cannot wait to get hold of Book 2 to learn more about this interesting family and what happens to them.

Mai Griffin

During her successful career as an artist (www.maigriffin.com), travelling the world and painting portraits of Royalty and other prominent figures, Mai has never stopped writing. The Echoes series may be built around purely fictional characters, but Sarah Grey and her late husband Stephen were inspired by Mai's parents. Mai now lives in Spain. Dividing her time between painting and writing is a challenge, but helps to still her own ghosts...

by Mai Griffin

Renaming an already published book series was a heart-wrenching decision – the contents of the books and the stories has not changed, however, so for your convenience and that of booksellers the new and the old titles are below

~~Deadly Shades of Grey~~ 'Ghostly Echoes'
~~A Poisonous Shade of Grey~~ 'A Poisonous Echo'
~~Grey Masque of Death~~ 'Dangerous Echoes'
~~Haunting Shades of Grey~~ 'Haunting Echoes'
'Restless Echoes'

Stand Alone

'Somebody Came'

Follow Mai on **www.maiwriting.com**

www.ingramcontent.com/pod-product-compliance
Lightning Source LLC
Chambersburg PA
CBHW070847260626
47170CB00007B/2532